Toxic Turkey

Gage Irving

Toxic Turkey
Copyright © 2025 Antoinette Beck
ISBN: 978-1-970153-49-1

Distribution: Ingram Book Company
Cover Image: Shutterstock

Maison
La Maison Publishing
Vero Beach, Florida
The Hibiscus City
lamaisonpublishing@gmail.com

Dedicated to Richard Witt

Prologue

Ricker Basin, Vermont
11:35 AM Tuesday, May 13, 1986

In 1783, pioneers built a town situated between Cotton Brook and Stevenson Brook named Ricker Basin. They also constructed three gristmills over the nearby rivers. A flood destroyed most of Ricker Basin and the gristmills in 1827. The destruction was powerful enough to send the inhabitants away, and that turned out to be a good thing. Nine years later, another storm washed out almost everything left behind. It was hard to find the bones of the settlement hidden deep in the wild woods of Vermont, only a ghost town four miles from the Waterbury Reservoir in Little River State Park. Waterbury had taken ownership of the land around the reservoir, including Ricker Basin, through eminent domain. Workers dismantled what was left of Ricker Basin in 1960 — with one exception. Residents in Waterbury remembered Ricker Basin, and they petitioned the state government to leave Calvin Goodall's house alone. The ancient dwelling was constructed on the highest elevation between the rivers, and it had weathered the floods. Their proposal was accepted, and the state certified Goodall's house a historical monument, even if no one would ever see it. Apparently a pointless endeavor, the government employees in Montpelier realized that leaving the house up would end the project faster and cheaper.

Years yawned into decades. The house creaked and sighed out there, utterly forgotten. Bricks from the gristmills had tumbled into the rivers, lying in the rushing water like shattered bones, while the forest crept into what was left of the town's carcass, remains divided and conquered. The Goodall house guarded over the desolation — until an uncommon action rang an alarm someone could hear. Something hibernating out there woke up.

*****

Spraying paint on the walls of his church heated him up. Billy ripped his shirt off and tossed it on a broken fence post nearby. He was happy to work in a T-shirt. After over three years of hard labor, his town was almost done…the façade of it anyway. Five houses, a general store, and a church now stood on an unpaved track called 'Main Street.'

Dropping the sprayer, he limped to the bed of his truck to grab his cigarettes wedged under the toolbox. Lighting one, he leaned against the side of his F350 to puff out smoke rings. At forty-two, his body still responded valiantly to his current obsession. Brown hair with streaks of grey, he'd grown a goatee.

Billy Leiden had been locked in a federal prison in Danbury, Connecticut, from 1972 to 1978. He was freed right after his thirtieth birthday, returning to the construction trade in New York. Then, he fell twenty-eight feet off a ladder and broke his hip and his skull in 1981. Billy remained in a coma for a month. The insurance company was dismayed when he woke up. The following suit was settled out of court. The developer and the insurance company split the nine-million-dollar reparation a year after the accident. Billy ended up with four million in his account. The Montano Company that had used Light-Brite Ladders at the construction site took them out of circulation, starting their own suit against the company that built them.

Billy's rehabilitation ended in 1983. His balance problems were resolved. He drove off on Interstate 95 in a brand-new truck to see his friend, Butch Dawes, who lived in a ramshackle farmhouse in Waterbury, Vermont.

After he got there, they drank beer and watched sports games on TV. The next day, they went into the woods to hunt for deer. Going off on their own for a while, Billy tracked hoof prints into some dense foliage. The trail opened into a clearing, and the Goodall house stood before him. Whether it was the classic carpentry or an odd aura radiating out of the shadowy dwelling, he was driven to the building like a moth to the light. Hobbling around the site, he quickly found the old foundations of the lost buildings. It was clear to Billy that a town had been there years ago, and a strange connection clicked inside of him. Walking deeper into the woods, he even found the cemetery. He sat on a gravestone, transfixed by a revelation—*he would rebuild the town. The lost souls in this place would finally be able to haunt the world again, and maybe he could direct them and control them...*

He met his friend on the main trail an hour later, not telling him what he'd found. He looked like he'd won the lotto or something, and Butch thought he must have fallen and hit his head on a rock.

The employees in the main office in Montpelier accepted his generous bid to buy Ricker Basin. They installed a clause in the transfer papers releasing them from any liability connected to that land from that point onwards. Billy Leiden returned to Montpelier three weeks later with a bank check for one hundred thousand dollars printed out to the state of Vermont. At the end of the day, Mr. Leiden owned thirty-seven acres of land that included the echo of the Basin. It was difficult to get there, and the place had no electricity or running water, but he was ecstatic. His dreams would come true.

Billy used a chainsaw to cut the overgrowth away from the trail to the town. It took him three days. After that, he hauled in two generators and a John Deere tractor up the bumpy track.

He intended to live in the Goodall house and that meant he needed to install new weight-bearing beams on the floors and the interior walls. He didn't have enough time to get that work done before winter closed in. The trail was not stable enough to plow yet, so Billy stayed in a rooming house in Montpelier, busily pouring over his blueprints for the spring projects. He'd drive over to Butch's house twice a week to hang out. In April, he went back to work, positive he'd be in that house next winter. He intended to set the trail up for plowing by the end of the summer.

Using a wellpoint, he found water near the house, and then he installed a well. Upgrading the conditions in and around the house, Billy quickly made the swaybacked ruin into a livable home — two bathrooms, a full kitchen, electric lights, and reliable heat.

No licensed architect or engineer would accept that his rebirth of Ricker Basin was perfect...but it was certainly magnificent to Billy. And no one was around to tell him if a roof line was tilted or a windowsill was a smidgeon off-true.

He painted one house light blue, another yellow, the rest white. All the roof shingles were grey. Windows had blinds and curtains, and there even was a sign in front of the general store: Millet seed and fertilizer on sale. He installed stained glass windows in the church, and every doorknob in town was brass, sparkling when the sun was out. Billy had screwed numbers on the doors of his houses, starting with twenty-nine. A backpacker hiking into this lost village might assume that things were fine at first.

But Billy was losing control. He couldn't take care of everything alone. A vine had grown under the front door of the first house he'd built, and across a dirt road named Main Street, a sapling had broken through the first floor of the facing building. Its lower branches had shattered a side window from the inside out. Besides Goodall's place, the only other building in Ricker Basin with a real second floor was the first house he'd built, and that was left rough. The rest of the homes, the church and the store had no real interior walls, just beams to support the walls.

The forest was creeping back. Billy's offhanded fight against it was haphazard. The uneasy boundaries of his twilight town were unraveling, but he was almost done. His town would be the outlet for the departed to come back. He would set them all free, and in his mind, few weeds wouldn't matter.

Waterbury, Vermont
3:27 PM Saturday, May 17, 1986

Route 100 crossed the Winooski River in Waterbury. There was a hairpin curve after the bridge, tricky to drive if the road iced up. Half a mile from there, the hardware store's owner had just rung Billy Leiden's latest order up. Billy shouldered through the door, holding his bag of hinges. The owner's son was stocking shelves in the back. When he heard the front door slam, he untied his apron and tossed it over a large cardboard display for windshield washer fluid. Clarence sprinted outside while his father bore holes in his back in a baleful stare.

He trotted up to Billy. "I know you're building something out there. I need to know what it is."

Billy ignored him, walking straight to his truck on the other side of the street. The vehicle was coated in dirt, and he was mulling over buying a new one...but Clarences's irritating voice kept on intruding into his thoughts.

"HELLO! I've seen you at the store before. You don't hang out in town—you're never anywhere. I watched you haul a John Deere around that crazy corner near the river. Don't know how you managed it! I got on my bike to follow you, but you were long gone."

Billy got in his truck and started the engine, snapping back at Clarence, "Go away."

"Yesterday, hunters in the store told my dad they saw construction where Ricker Basin used to be."

Billy's driver's window was closed, and the truck began to roll down the street. That didn't stop Clarence. He jogged along with the truck, talking louder so Billy could hear him...

"You might not know it, but there are ghosts in the Goodall house... and around the Basin. I've heard some stories. Be careful if that's where you're going!"

The word 'ghosts' sparked Billy's annoyance. He stopped the truck and lowered the window. "What are you talking about? You don't know shit about that place. *I* know what's up there!"

Clarence's guess had worked; however, it wasn't time to congratulate himself. Stepping closer to the truck, he brushed his long, dark hair out of his eyes.

"So, you are working in Ricker Basin." Clarence had installed a northern drawl in his words. He thought it would give him more charisma. Billy stared at him from the driver's seat. Usually, Leiden pushes everybody away...but this time, he felt stuck between curiosity and disdain. The kid was almost six feet tall, with fingernails painted black and jeans ripped to shreds. He didn't look like a country boy — more like a young version of Alice Cooper.

"Why do you want to tell me dumb ghost stories about Ricker Basin?" Billy said.

"I know the legends connected to the Basin, and most of them are crap, you're right. I don't really want to tell you anything at all. Listen, man, I'm bored shitless. I know you're doing something interesting up there. It might be a starting point for my own project. I could give you free labor in the process."

Curiosity won the battle in Billy's mind, and he laughed. A wild child with magnetism. Who knows. He could be a kindred spirit and help him find a way to populate his town.

"What's your name?"

"Clarence Hanson. What's yours?"

"Billy." He opened the door and shook Clarence's hand. "There are no ghosts in Ricker Basin. The only thing I see at night are bears going through my garbage. I've lived in the Goodall house for two years, so I know. Oh, by the way, it's my town. I own Ricker Basin. Could have changed the name to Leiden Basin if I wanted to…anyway, I'm almost done with the first part of my plan. If you're interested, I wouldn't mind advice on the next step."

Birds had returned to Ricker Basin, and their songs blended into the boisterous rush of the brooks swelling higher in the spring thaw. Verdant buds popped out on previously dead-looking Oak branches. Everything was sprouting. A patina looking like green fairy dust covered the forest floor.

If Billy Leiden hadn't stumbled into Ricker Basin, if he had not rebuilt the ruins with his manic devotion, the town and anything connected to it would have remained asleep. Shaking the old skeleton back to life, he didn't realize what he'd done — until it was way too late.

Billy invited Clarence to have lunch with him at the Basin, giving him directions to the playground. An hour later, the teenager parked his motorcycle near the swing set. He saw Billy sitting on the low wall of the sandbox.

"Your town wasn't too hard to find."

"Hello, Clarence."

"Hey, before we eat, can I look at those other buildings?"

"Sure. Go ahead. I give you permission to look at anything you want."

Leaving his helmet on the seat, Clarence ran off to check things out.

Waiting for his return, Billy thought over his earlier ideas about the playground. He'd hoped it would attract the children's spirits. Clearing half an acre near the cemetery a year ago, he bought a swing set, a slide, a jungle gym, and extra hardwood to create the sandbox. He installed it all on the empty land. The playground was done, but he got no response. No spirit from any age group arrived to play. There were no supernatural events of any kind—no floating orbs of light, no twig sculptures left under the jungle gym. Nothing.

He never forgot the conversation he'd had with a ghost he'd created himself after a bloody transformation initiated with a switchblade in 1971. The ethereal talk gave him the proof he needed, and Ricker Basin was the clarion call. Lost souls must hear his invitation and come out of their graves and haunt with extravagance. *But. It. Was. Not. Happening.*

Stymied, he had not given up. He still believed there was a way to get them here.

Returning from his exploratory trip through Ricker Basin, Clarence sat down on the swings. They ate the ham and cheese sandwiches Billy had picked up at the luncheonette in Waterbury. They'd both heard the story about the trapper camping near Stevenson Brook in 1940. He'd fallen into the brook and drowned, and a manifestation of one of the first settlers had tossed him into the water. Clarence told Billy another muddled tale about a jealous husband, a dead hound dog, and a drunken hunter. They jawed over those tales. Billy had decided to invite the boy into his own world, explaining his plan and dilemma. He hoped for advice on what might be the best action to get results.

Clarence looked over at him. "You built this ghost town in the woods with no ghosts? Not even a nibble so far?" He laughed. "Do you have any ideas to fix that?"

"I don't know how to bring them here or even wake them up. Not a clue. Well, I do know an easy way, but that's not something I can tell you about right now."

Clarence realized Billy Leiden was crazy as a bedbug. That's okay. He could use that knowledge to manipulate the man for his own devices. Ricker Basin was perfect, a malleable environment. He could create his own devilish plans. Clarence didn't believe in ghosts, but Billy did not need to know that.

"Exasperation is coming out of you like sweat. At least you found the gumption to ask for my guidance." Clarence put an easy rhythm in his words. "You have a problem. We can't leave this town empty! The aura you've created is powerful enough to be haunted by young female spirits."

Billy's eyebrows rose. Did Clarence have the same idea he had? Murder was an easy option. He had to be careful in the way he responded. "That's an easy way to create spirits, but right now, I don't know how to invite anyone over here to enter the ethereal world."

"I'll do some work on that problem tomorrow, Billy. The local stories make this place a magnet. I'll just print out invitations to a haunted weekend. I can select certain candidates. If they're interested, I'll tell them the history of Ricker Basin, revving them up for meeting ghosts out here...don't worry. I'll invite the

11

guests you need. It should only take a few weeks. Oh yeah, the emptiness you have here will be filled. Ricker Basin will soon be haunted."

Hashing out their scheme, Billy thought it would work. In the next few days, he looked at different things on the property or in his house used in the grisly transformation. *Yes, creating the haunting will be done by hook or by crook...or maybe the sharp knife he had in his pocket.*

11:48AM Monday, May 19, 1986
Harwood High School, South Duxbury, Vermont

Kevin Fielding was tall and skinny, but he'd pack on muscle next year. At the moment, one of his unusual abilities was sending him to a difficult and possibly risky place. Padlocking his locker, he was on his way to the cafeteria. He'd overheard Clarence talking to some girls in an empty classroom, and Kevin had gotten a funny feeling in his belly as he walked passed. There was a tinge of menace swirling around that guy, but those feelings didn't fit anymore. Now, he felt smoke coming off a psychic fire. People might get hurt soon. He had to check on that warning sign. If he didn't, his conscience would pick at him like a skin condition.

Putting his lunch on the tray, he sat down to swallow his fish sticks like a robot. Other students around him laughed or gossiped, yet he stayed miles away. Clarence entered the cafeteria with the same girls in tow. They sat four tables away. Kevin stood up and moved passed them. They were whispering, and his concern intensified. Some of his own acquaintances were sitting at a table right next to Clarence, and Kevin sat down with them. He could tune into their murmurings a lot easier…

"A haunted weekend at Ricker Basin will include a real confrontation with a spirit!" Clarence breathed the information to them with hypnotizing power. "You'll know the truth about what was behind the end of the town. I'll escort you through one of the houses. If you don't run away, the International Ghost Tracker Association will give you certificates of courage." The girls remained goggle-eyed, listening to him with fascination.

"And remember," Clarence said, "It's hush-hush. No one else needs to know about this place. If everyone knew about it, the ghost power out there would weaken…no. No one needs to know about the secrets we'll learn next weekend. Whatever you do, don't tell your family or your friends. Make up a feasible excuse to explain where you are going Saturday. We don't want to be interrupted or have them call you to interrupt the investigations or break the tenuous and difficult connection with the dead."

"That won't be a problem," Rebecca said. "We go to Daryl's house on Saturday to work on our science projects in the garage. We'll tell her we aren't coming… and tell everybody else we are. It's worth lying. We've tried to communicate with our Ouija Board, but we got nowhere... and even our seances didn't work."

Nancy and Rebecca both swallowed Clarence's story, hook, line, and sinker, and he reeled them like juicy trout about to flop around on his plate — an illegal dinner ready for the frying pan.

Done with lunch, Kevin was on his way to science class, but he was preoccupied. What he'd listened to in the cafeteria connected to a future event was still murky, and he wanted more information. Obviously, there was no way out of this. He must go to Ricker Basin.

Waitsfield, Vermont
6:55 PM Wednesday, May 21st, 1986

Kevin lay on his bed in his grandparents' house in Waitsfield, with his hands under his head, gazing at the ceiling. He'd asked his grandfather about Ricker Basin and how he could get there. Harold Fielding used to help the fire department and the police with electrical problems, so he could usually answer most of his questions about the area. He told Kevin he'd found an ancient map in a government office years ago, and one of the supervisors had given it to him as a present. It clearly delineated exactly where the town had been. Little River Road would get you there. Harry gave the map to Kevin.

He thanked his grandfather, instantly scouring over the designations. He needed to get to Ricker Basin without announcing himself to anyone. *Harrier's Loop* was printed on the old map right above a dotted line. It looked promising. It petered out on the back side of the Basin. His grandfather said it was a hunting trail, still in use and Kevin could reach it from the Interstate.

Powerwalking into the garage, Kevin started tuning up his quad. The wild woods out there were rough and tumble. His ride had to be in great shape to handle it.

If he intended to go to Ricker Basin and come back before dark, he skipped school the day he decided to go. Loading the ATV into the back of his pick-up truck, he drove on Interstate 89. Reading the mile markers, when he saw the number he wanted, he stopped. And there was even a break in the line of trees at that point. It had to be the start of Harrier's Loop! He parked on the shoulder, dropped the tailgate, and attached the ramps to the back of the bed. Rolling the quad onto the road, he tossed the ramps into the truck and locked them up. He put his helmet on.

After the quad had warmed up, Kevin jolted between two large oak trees, pushing the four-wheeler through a tangle of vines and shrubbery. Smaller branches whipped into the shield of his helmet. It was slow going. After five miles, the track ended, and he hid the vehicle under a pile of brush. From there, he still had a mile to get to the abandoned town. Kevin was careful going through the thick vegetation. He had on leather pants and a corduroy shirt against the thorns. So far, he only has one gouge on the back of his hand. Checking his compass, he kept moving northwest to reach the abandoned town.

Soon, he peered between the trees to see the Goodall house. He moved silently toward the building. His perception of the upcoming tragedy got sharper with every single step he took. Kevin already knew the owner of the house was in Waterbury — and he'd stay there for a few more hours. His intuition was a powerful tool, knowing he could now investigate without interruption.

The front door had been left unlocked, and Kevin stepped into the living room. A large oval table sat on an oriental rug in the center of the room, six high-back chairs tucked around it. Tall lamps stood in the four corners of the room, and there was a fireplace on the opposite wall. Heavy olive drapes with golden tassels attached adorned the windows funereally. The area had been staged for a seance.

Suddenly, internal pictures slammed into Kevin's head connected to the upcoming weekend horror show. He cramped over for a minute or two before shaking his head. He absolutely had to get the visions out of his head and get back to work.

Scouting out the rest of the house, he ended the short tour by climbing the wooden stairs to the basement. He stood on the dirt floor and formed a plan. He looked at his wristwatch…it was already getting late. Taking the stairs back up again, Kevin trotted into the woods. He gathered logs and branches, and hid them under the steps leading to the back door before he retraced his path back to his truck on the interstate.

Right after school, Kevin returned to his grandfather's workshop in the garage on Thursday and Friday. He began to build the devices he needed to save the girls — and he didn't have a lot of time to get it done.

Ricker Basin, Vermont
10:15AM Saturday, May 24, 1986

Billy and Clarence sat in front of Billy's façade of his church. They were excited.

"What time are you meeting them?" Billy asked.

"6:30. Told them the seance would start at eight."

"We have to go to Montpelier to get the incense and the candles and the white wine — and we can't forget the tablecloth. It's important to escort them into their new world with the right atmosphere."

A chuckle erupted out of Clarence, and it sounded like a bean fart. "Escorting them, my ass. We'll amuse ourselves with them just like cats playing with cornered mice." He wasn't using his sugar-sweet platitudes to support Leiden's psychosis with the same frequency lately.

Billy hobbled over to his F350, shoulders wrenched tight. He started the engine, and the truck slowly rolled away. Clarence had to run over to the passenger door and leap in at the last second. Neither of them said a thing on the ride to Montpelier.

17

Waitsfield, Vermont
11:11AM Saturday, May 24, 1986

Kevin's grandparents had stopped asking him about his projects a while ago. They watched him pack his truck that morning, praying he'd make it back in one piece. Bungee-cording a metal suitcase onto the aluminum frame on the rear of the ATV, he then rolled the four-wheeler onto the truck. He finally tossed his backpack into the cab. It was filled with two sandwiches, four bottles of water, a fleece jacket...and a loaded 45.

Having ridden through the gnarly woods one more time. His following walk through the woods was even harder, hauling the cumbersome suitcase behind him. The backpack didn't help. It didn't matter. He had to have those tools to win the day — or the night. Using his inner knowledge, he already knew that Clarence and Billy would not be around until later in the day. He would have enough time to set up his hidden diversions before they got back.

The front door was still unlocked, and he dragged the suitcase into the center of the living room. Then Kevin went back outside to bring his cache of wood left under the back stairs inside. He positioned the pieces on the grate in the fireplace. Taking a minor charge of buffered magnesium out of the suitcase, he inserted it in the middle of the logs, transmitter attached. Drenching the wood with starter fluid he had brought in his backpack, he knew most would evaporate...but a small amount sucked into the deepest part of the kindling would remain. Kevin did not think they'd notice the appearance of the wood, and if they did, he was sure they'd assume the other one would be responsible for its appearance...but he instinctually knew they'd ignore it. He would start the fire at the perfect moment during the chaotic actions that evening.

Another thing he'd done in his grandfather's garage was to pour condensed flash powder into tiny, flattened bulbs. Kevin took them out of the suitcase and placed some of them under the base of the standing lamps. He put one beneath the reading light near the front windows and three more under the brass clock above the fireplace.

Then Kevin dragged the stepladder up from the cellar to install four small speakers with transducers and transmitters attached to the high moldings above the windows. He still had a few more, and he placed one on the mantle behind the clock and two more behind the lamps.

Kevin planned to send his voice through all those speakers towards his finale'. He would distort his words through a synthesizer, intending to blanket the room with eerie screams and terrible pronouncements. It would eclipse their own show...frighten the girls out the door and into their vehicle. The murderers would be baffled and confused without enough time to stop their escape—at least, that was what he was hoping for.

Balancing on the backrest of the antique sofa, he set up a video camera in the carved wooden scroll above a window in the middle of the living room. That camera would transmit an image of the entire room and most of the stairs leading to the second floor to a black and white monitor in the basement, allowing him to watch what was going on the first floor.

Jumping off the sofa, Kevin went over the long list in his mind, and he smiled. Things were copasetic. The backpack hanging off his shoulder, he snatched the suitcase handle to bounce down the stairs to the basement.

Forty-five minutes later, Clarence and Billy arrived. They didn't notice the wood in the fireplace, and the living room looked fine.

Ricker Basin, Vermont
6:43PM Saturday, May 24, 1986

Clarence was waiting at the turnoff onto Little River Road. When the girls saw his motorcycle headlight, they slowed to a stop.

"Is that you, Clarence? Should I follow you?"

"Hello, Becca...yeah, just follow my taillight. I won't go *too* fast."

He rode off on the dirt track, and the girls followed, bumping around in their seats. They didn't want to slow down, excited to get to the ghost town, excited to have a seance. Believing they were spiritualists, they'd wrapped themselves in thin fabric printed with multi-colored flowers, eye makeup, and red lipstick. They believed their getups elevated their psychic presence. In reality, they looked more like actors in a cheap X-rated film. At least they had the wherewithal to wear their blue jeans and sneakers underneath those yards of gauze.

Parking next to Clarence's bike in front of the Goodall house, Nancy and Rebecca looked through the jeep windows to behold Ricker Basin. Lamps glimmered below on Main Street, and battery-driven candles flickered in the windows of the church. The young seekers of spiritual truth were not thinking about the generators running full tilt in a shed one hundred feet away. They didn't realize how far away from civilization they truly were.

Clarence helped them out of the jeep to escort them through the door. An electric candelabra hung above the oval table. Real candles burned on the mantelpiece and on the small tables. The embroidered tablecloth Billy had picked out in a thrift store in Montpelier had turned out to be the perfect choice.

Billy was waiting for them. In a dark blue suit, he'd even trimmed his goatee and mustache. He limped towards them, looking devilish and engaging.

"Good evening, ladies. I'm Mr. Leiden." He shook their hands *softly*. It's not right to squeeze those virgin hands too hard. "I'm the owner of Ricker Basin. It's wonderful to meet you. Clarence tells me you want to learn more about the other side. I can certainly help you open a channel with them to communicate."

"I'm Rebecca Lewis. It's great to meet you, Mr. Leiden."

Nancy chimed in, "We're grateful you've decided to open your house up for a séance. Oh, my name is Nancy Poole." The teenagers smiled at him, but they were getting more nervous by the second.

Billy glanced over at the fireplace. He was impressed that Clarence had filled it with firewood. Thinking about starting a fire, he changed his mind — things were rolling along well enough. He didn't want to interrupt the flow.

Clarence took the girls off to see the rest of the house. As soon as they were out of sight, Billy hobbled over to the bureau in the corner of the room and opened a drawer to reveal a crystal ball nestled on a piece of black velvet. A plastic cradle lay next to it. He placed the cradle in the middle of the table in the middle of the room. He covered it with the velvet and put the globe on the holder.

Girls in tow, Clarence climbed to the second floor, beginning to ramble on about the Goodall family and the calamitous flood that had washed most of the town away. Easily creating stories right out of his head, he was also a gifted conversationalist and deceiver. Rebecca and Nancy listened to his flimflam, happily enthralled. At the end of their tour, they followed him down the back stairs ending up in front of the basement door. Clarence was about to turn the door, but something stopped the movement...and his thoughts got scrambled. He stopped talking and just stood there, frozen. The girls felt stuck, and Rebecca was about to ask Clarence if he was alright, but things straightened out in his head. He had intended to take them down to the cellar, but the motivation was gone—*I am not going to the basement after all.* The new idea had popped into his consciousness...as if it could have been inserted into his mind from an outside source.

"Um...I think...I think it's getting late," Clarence said. "We have to get to the living room and begin the seance."

He passed the basement door and led them through the kitchen, returning to his latest story. Clarence didn't remember anything unusual when he paused at the door. He assumed he'd simply changed his mind, was all, even if Kevin was actually responsible for the decision.

Leaning into his captivated audience, Clarence went on, "Spirits are gathering. I can feel them, and they know we're here. The departed are breathlessly waiting to build the necessary bridge. Forgotten out here for way too long, we will invite them to cross over... I know they'll connect with us."

"Is there anything we can do to open the pathway?" Nancy said.

"Yes. Empty your minds from material thoughts and guide your souls towards your third eye."

Clarence just kept going with his endless nonsense able to make it sound real. The girls followed him as if he were the Pied Piper, not realizing where he was actually leading them.

The velvet-covered holder elevated the orb six inches above the surface of the table. Billy had bought the ball and the holder in a yard sale for fifteen dollars.

It had turned out to be a steal. The polished piece of glass, supposedly a crystal, was now a doorway to the afterlife. It supported their deceit with flashy ostentation.

Billy pulled two chairs away from the table, and the girls sat down. The high schoolers stared over at the crystal ball. The non-existent depths dragged Rebecca and Nancy in.

Billy bowed to them, and then sat at the table as well. "Powerful waves are in the air tonight. We'll have an exceptional link. You ladies are the yin to my yang."

Billy had been alone in his room on the second floor yesterday, endlessly sharpening his knife. When it couldn't get any sharper, he just kept on with a repeating stroke, skimming the edge of the blade up and down the strap. It was a comfortable beat to support his growing anticipation. The bloody solution he and Clarence had been working for would be realized very soon.

Physically a lot closer to their host, Nancy, and Rebecca's concern ramped up. They didn't know he had a knife in his jacket pocket; nevertheless, intuition was ringing a warning bell in their heads. That did not matter. They were too jazzed up over their so-called enlightenment, stuck in the fake commercialization of the unknown—apparently sealing their fate.

"We must hold hands," Billy pronounced. Clarence had found a book in the library in Waterbury loaded with spells and invocations. He'd memorized a plausible gem to make the thing seem real as if they were actually bringing spirits to the seance.

Kevin's use of a mental barricade dissuaded Clarence from taking the stairs to the cellar. It worked like a charm. Sitting on a milk crate, he watched the monitor teetering on a three-legged table he'd found in the corner. He'd left his microphone on a stair tread, easy to get to. As he installed his deceptions, he'd noticed a fishing line tied to the legs of two chairs and a gavel under the main table that Billy and Clarence had set up. It was just slapstick to Kevin; his own displays would overwhelm this silliness. He observed the action upstairs. It was important to time his own show depending on the right forecast happening up there.

There's a chance his plans could derail. That was why he brought a gun. It would be unfortunate for Billy and Clarence to face the other side of him. Be that as it may, Kevin has had to use this last-ditch insurance before — but only when there was no way out.

A week ago, Clarence had given Billy all the names of everyone in the Goodall family, telling him he'd found them in an old registry in an office in Waterbury. Billy thought he needed the information for his séance, not knowing his cohort had made all the names up in his head. To Clarence, what difference would it make in the end?

Billy was impressed by Clarence's sing-song supplication to the lost. After a few more minutes, he really thought it might work…then he remembered his own attempts.

As Clarence's invitation ended, Billy took control, making his voice louder. "Unclasp your hands and fall into the bottomless sphere…that's right…look deep, deep inside. Yes…. Ethan Goodall, are you with us today? Olivia, where are you? Evelyn, Johnny…stop playing, come down here and talk to us." Billy breathed in and sighed. "Put your fingertips on the globe…that's right. Leave them there. It will be our conduit. It's magnetized. The space between their world and ours is shrinking. We're getting closer, and soon, we will become one. Aah! I can feel it! They're joining us. You will appear and speak to us. Tell us what you want. How can we appease you?"

There was nothing but the sound of wind lashing through branches outside. Billy kept on, "We honor your memory and what you lived and died for. We wait for your presence to be revealed."

Billy's eyes closed, swaying back and forth in his chair. Two loud knocks finally answered his question. "One knock will tell us you are Ethan. Two, Olivia, three, Evelyn. And four, Johnny."

Two knocks. A clear response. The girls were anxious, but they wanted the certificates…and the spirits were about to impart secrets to them. They stayed at the table, fingertips shaking on the crystal ball.

"It's the good lady of the house," Billy said. "Get to us if you can."

The empty chair next to Nancy jumped backward and fell over. Another skittered away from the table.

Billy glanced over at the girls. "Don't worry. Olivia will tell us what happened to her children. We wait for the knowledge."

Clarence whispered to Rebecca...but he stopped when he heard an unusual hum. It was low enough to make the cavities in his teeth vibrate. That strange droning was not affecting Billy. Clarence assumed he was responsible for the sound since his eyes were still closed as he communicated with the other world.

With a snap, the wood in the fireplace burst into flames. Rebecca and Nancy looked over at the fire, eyes widening. The low vibration stopped, and Billy opened his eyes. A lamp in the corner of the room fell over with a crash, and the young girls' nervousness transformed into fear.

Billy glared over at Clarence, thinking he was responsible for the additions. A loud howl sailed down from the second floor like an invisible force.

"**AAAAAGH....OOOUUUEE**."

This strange voice bounced against the fireplace to then envelope the living room, sounding like a woman being tortured alive. The heavy brass clock flew off the mantel to land with a thud on the floor. Another standing lamp near the front door fell over, and one of its bulbs burst open like a firecracker. The ongoing painful lament localized in the middle of the room, coalescing into words.

"No…ah…noooooo…aagh.....IT'S TOO LAAATE FOR ME. THEY WON'T p…p…PUUULLLLL MEEE OUT OF THE WELL…AAAAGH!"

With the power of a screech owl, the pathos was her garbled words intertwined with heartbreak, finally fading away in a shivering wheeze—an adieu from a brutalized soul.

Dread settled into the girl's emotions like lead. They jumped to their feet, sneakers giving them traction as adrenaline burst into their blood like racing fuel. Sprinting across the room like an Olympian, Clarence really tried to grab Rebecca's ponytail, but all he got was thin air. Nancy wrenched the front door open, and they ran for the jeep.

Billy was furious. He thought that Clarence was responsible for the over-the-top theatrics.

"Bring them back before they drive away, you lunkhead! Go on! Go right now!"

But Clarence hadn't heard him. He'd gone after them instantly, and he was already at the front door. Then Billy's attention was suddenly diverted when the back door slammed open, and a trespasser trudged up the back stairs. Eyes filled with savagery, Billy needed to confront the intruder, and his hip wasn't bothering him as he limped off to face this troublemaker. Grumbling to himself about what he'd do to anyone interfering with his plans, he moved through the entrance hall. Clarence lay unconscious on the floor near the front door—but Billy had no interest in that. In his mind, his 'partner' will deal with his own problems for the moment.

A minute or two earlier, Nancy reached the front door, opening it with the strength of the damned…and it swung into the wall. The knob punched straight into the sheetrock while the girls sailed off into the night. Nancy hadn't known she'd anchored the door to the wall, leaving it wide open, but an invisible force had fixed that problem. Something invisible lifted the knob out of the wall, and the heavy door slowly closed a second before Clarence got there.

He opened the door easily enough, but the process sped up so fast it knocked him off his feet, leaving him on his back, arms and legs akimbo. Clarence opened his eyes speedily enough. Getting his bearings, he watched the door sedately close on its own with a conclusive click.

Clarence was just as incensed, believing that Billy had frightened the girls off. He didn't know why he had not told him about the extra stuff. And now? His attempt at hunting the bitches down had so far tossed him off his feet! *And that was the last straw!* Billy could deal with the rest of this disaster himself!

He intended to walk out of the house, get on his bike, and ride away…but the door was stuck. Clarence tried to open it with both hands on the knob, putting one of his booted heels on the wall for support. Then he wrenched harder. He didn't seem to think about the idea of escaping through a window or trying the back door. He was obsessed with a puzzle that might not have been one anyway.

Billy climbed the backstairs as fast as he could, trying to stay on the tail of a giant of a man. Reaching the second floor, the intruder entered Billy's bedroom and closed the door behind him. Hobbling and hopping over there, he opened the door. The stranger had on a camouflage jacket and cap, and he held a rifle. He stared down at Billy with no expression. Robotic.

Billy screeched up at him, "Who are you. Why are you in my house?" Ignoring the switchblade in his pocket, he grabbed the handgun in the waistband of his pants and aimed the weapon at the man's left eye. Billy wasn't really interested in an answer to his angry questions.

"I have a housewarming present for you," he snarled. "Guess we'll figure out where you're from after you're gone."

The towering trespasser's face was the color of raw fish, and his empty eyes got blacker. Billy Leiden's threat triggered a reaction in his opponent. Dropping the rifle, he offhandedly slapped Billy's gun out of his hand before sandwiching him against the wall. Using his impressive weight, he'd made him into a human pancake. The pancake could barely breathe. Short wheezes leaked from Billy, and the giant leaned further to him like a ton of bricks. Deciding not to suffocate him to death after all, he moved away. He picked up his rifle and walked out of the bedroom, closing the door behind him.

Billy fell to the floor, heaving for air. He was trying to get his strength back. His gun was inches away and he picked it up. Using the energy he had, he got on his knees and shot through the door—twice. The hulk couldn't have gotten out of range yet. Billy waited to hear the following thump as his dead body fell to the floor...it should have hit the floor by now. Nothing happened. He could not have missed!

Anger gave him more strength. He stood up and opened his bedroom door to see the man halfway down the front stairs. Billy stumbled forwards. If his first bullets had missed, the next ones wouldn't! Standing on the first tread, he aimed at the man's back, exactly where his heart was.

Clarence's war with the front door was forgotten when he heard gunfire from the second floor. He trotted to the coat closet to grab the rifle they'd hidden there. Turning around, a colossal man in hunting clothes was climbing the stairs to the first floor. Clarence raised his weapon. The giant stopped moving, squinting his bottomless eyes at him while he lifted his own gun and aimed. Clarence wasn't worried. The stock of his own rifle nestled into his shoulder as he targeted the man's heart. The fool didn't have a chance.

However, the height and girth of the interloper hid important facts. Clarence had not seen Billy at the top of the stairs, and Billy only saw the guy's back.

After Billy and Clarence fired at the same time, they thought he would tumble down the stairs. What actually happened did not register in their heads at first.

In any other scenario, their attempt would have worked. The trespasser should have died. However, the reality in Ethan Goodall's old home was not quite right. The entity that had just squashed Billy against the wall was solid during that interlude, but it had changed form on the stairs. Their bullets zinged through him, and that friendly crossfire was devasting.

Billy's jubilation ended almost instantly. He died from a headshot. Meanwhile, Clarence collapsed on the living room floor, hanging by a thread. Three bullets from Billy's handgun had pierced his torso.

The apparition on the stairs lowered his rifle and climbed to the first floor. It stepped around the dying boy with contempt. Clarence watched the oversized being float through the front door while his life leaked out into the carpeting.

Kevin had saved the girls with technological panache and his ability to transform his voice. The girls raced for the hills and out of harm's way. His future concerns over Billy and Clarence were resolved. Surprised by the intervention from the other side, he leaned back and stretched. It was time to pack up and skedaddle and he started by unplugging the monitor.

Kevin thought over what had been behind the supernatural appearance. Could it have arrived from Clarence's innocuous incantation out of a library book? More likely, hibernating shades in the forgotten village had gotten riled up by Leiden's construction, and the not-so-restful dead geared up with a reaction of their own.

Theres no explanation, but it was clear enough the spirits were returning to slumber. Kevin walked outside to check things out. The Jeep was gone. Rebecca must have hit the gas hard, leaving deep tracks behind.

Back in the house, he packed everything he'd brought with him. Even the garbage. And he wiped his fingerprints off anything he'd touched. He erased any clue that could possibly connect him to the murder scene. He called the authorities anonymously the next day, directing them out there.

As the years passed, Kevin's new career settled on his shoulders. Advising his customers to avoid destructive motivations, he used tarot cards to bridge the gap between what's accepted and what he can really do for them. 'FIELDING'S FINDINGS' expanded. He got rich. And then he got richer.

He also helped those in law enforcement. The prejudice against the sixth sense was prevalent in the field, but after giving them exceptional results, their intolerance was replaced with acknowledgment. Soon, they'd call him up on their own on difficult cases.

Finding criminals was unsettling to Kevin, reaching out to touch evil. He had to swim to the bottom of a dark barrel. Occasionally, he would find a lawbreaker so demonic his own courage would falter. His stamina was generally weakening.

He got married at twenty-seven, but no children were produced in this short-lived union. He was single again in only two years — and the divorce fortified his plans. No more entanglements with women. He limped off to heal. At thirty-one, he closed his business and ended his relationship with law enforcement. Kevin started a new life.

He became a marine technician and changed his name to Keith Fischer. Stories of his ingenuity burned through the grapevine like quicksilver. The fishermen working on commercial draggers called him MacGyver, a fictional character on TV. He seemed able to fix anything with a Swiss Army Knife...but Keith was careful. He used his abilities with discretion. Be that as it may, he was still considered the best technician on the East Coast.

He bought a house on fourteen acres. His closest neighbor was a graveyard. It could have been a sanctuary, but his phone kept ringing. Everybody wanted him.

But Keith did not realize his reputation expanded beyond the boating world and simply changing his name hadn't erased his earlier fame. Attison Korybant had investigated him. The power he saw within Keith was impressive enough to invite him into the grievous meeting that would happen in the next few months. Besides Attison and Keith, two other individuals shall also be drafted into a team to save the world.

Part I

Interstate 15, Nevada
2:30PM Thursday, September 23, 2004

Samuel Eveland's payment to his creditor was late. That may end his life. Things were getting more dangerous every day. He called his cousin to borrow money to pay off his loan. All he got was his answering machine, and his frantic messages were ignored. Finally, his cousin called him, explaining it would be the last penny he'd ever get out of him for the rest of time. Richard told him he would not wire the money or send it in the mail. He had to stare into his eyes to give him that loan. Samuel agreed to that, telling him he'd pay him back in spades by November. He drove two hundred and seventy-five miles to Los Angeles.

Driving home was not fun. At six-two, he didn't fit into the cheap rental. The only good part of the trip through the badlands on Interstate 15 was the knowledge that the check was in his wallet. Polishing off a box of cream donuts on the passenger seat won't kill him, but his gambling addiction might.

He'd been crunched in the driver's seat too long. Rubbing at his road-weary eyes, Samuel drove into the next rest area. It was important to stand up straight and let his long tendons un-cramp. He couldn't stay out there for long. The heat would soon boil him alive.

Nothing out there but cacti, and the horizon had liquefied into a shimmer. Samuel's gaze hooked on a wavering point in that haze as he leaned against the car...and he slipped into a daze.

He used to work as a real estate agent, but those days were gone. Samuel avoided his memories, but these bad things crept into his mind in this catnap. Sweat covered his body. He thought he was in a cell with a verdant garden on the other side of the bars, and he strained between the bars to touch a flower. Samuel mimicked that movement with his body, and he fell off the edge of the rental and onto the pavement. He got a light burn on the side of his face. He woke up and got back in the car. He'd left the engine running to hold the AC on, and he put the transmission in drive. Cheap tires hissed up the ramp back to the interstate.

Arriving in Las Vegas, he dropped the car at the rental office. He lived four blocks away. Vendome Apartments on 11th Street. The distance was long in that heat, and he scaled the stairs to the second floor like a zombie, deader than the rest. He breathed in the cool relief of his apartment. His answering machine was blinking. Samuel knew what the messages were. He hit a button and erased them. He will deal with the problem tomorrow. Tearing his clothes off, he left them on the floor, and he had a shower — and then he went to bed.

His bladder woke him up. When he was done peeing, his exhausted body told him to go back to sleep, but his need overpowered that. Samuel got dressed and left his studio.

Taxiing to the casino, he knew things were going to be fine. More than fine. His exhaustion lifted as he walked into the building, pupils now dilated. Samuel's pulse sped with excitement as he passed the slot machines, card tables, and roulette wheels.

A cocktail waitress wearing a small strip of white cloth, management called a toga, bumped into him. A pleasant bump. He got to Minerva Cove, his favorite cocktail lounge. Samuel sat at the bar, lit a cigarette, ordered a gin and tonic, and sighed with satisfaction. His impossible mission had been possible after all.

The futility gnawing at him during the trip had been a chimera. Rick's money was now his, and that would straighten his problems out right as rain. He'd pay off his loan and change the remaining eight thousand into eighty.

Samuel ordered another drink. He thought over which game would ignite his stalled life. Flying out of the fire of monetary disaster, Lady Luck would be in his arms.

Bridgewater, Massachusetts
8:45AM Friday, December 19, 1975

Robert Donnelly's birth dismayed his father. Born with pyloric stenosis, it clamped the pyloric valve at the end of the esophagus tube, and food could not reach his stomach. Robert vomited everything up. He'd die from starvation unless they cut the pyloric valve in surgery. Using full anesthesia on newborns was a dangerous process, but Robert got through the operation okay. However, he got a staph infection, and it raged through him like a forest fire. The surgeon told Latham and April that the baby was dying. April felt devastated. The couple would walk along the embankment above the Taunton River every day. They paid a nanny to take care of their other son as they waited for the outcome. Their vigil went on for nine days. It seemed endless to April.

A counselor advised them that full anesthesia on Robert may have diminished his acuity — if he lived. April did not accept any forecasts. Latham did.

Latham was doing well in the Heinem Pharmaceutical Corporation, dealing with high-speed wrangling over shipping and taxing costs to distribute drugs in Canada. Robert's health problems were diverting his attention from the negotiations. That seemed wrong to him.

Robert fought the infection off. He appeared normal enough. Be that as it may, Latham did not want the same thing to happen again. He would tell April that he would have a vasectomy to forego any future repeats. No more deformities could come out of her. But he realized she would not like his idea. He decided to leave her in the dark about the operation. Two years after Robert's precarious birth, April was ready for another child, and it should be a girl to balance the scales. Telling Latham about her wishes, he insisted they shouldn't have any more children since the next child may have the same disability. His concerns fell on deaf ears. Her feelings stayed the same. She would cajole him into her way of thinking with an extravagant breakfast, flapjacks, eggs, and bacon.

And he enjoyed the meal. Latham leaned back from the table and opened the paper. April stood against the large dining room window, sunlight touching the reddish gold in her hair. Hazel-green eyes half-closed, the domestic temptress's clothes clung to her curves. Her concentration did not waver. She'd filled him with a tasty meal, and she would be dessert. He continued holding his newspaper up like a force field.

"Latham, put the paper down and listen to me. I can't wait any longer. I stopped using birth pills last night. We must agree to create another life."

Paper left of the table; he frowned. He'd been gambling that the problems in her last delivery had unsettled her enough to avoid this. Latham had lost the bet.

"Oh honey, come on. Remember what happened when Robert was born? We decided on this. We're fine as we are. You know he almost died. We don't want that to happen again, do we? No fun to live through the same thing, and it might get worse." Latham got up and began to walk into the hallway in a quick escape. April threw her coffee cup to the floor, and it exploded. Pieces of crockery flew everywhere.

"I won't wait—and I won't listen to you. What happened, happened! Robert's alive and fine, and so is Jay. *I'm not*! We're going to have another baby, and it's going to be a healthy baby girl. You will give me what I want!"

"Whoa, slow down, girl." Latham had no way out, so held her hand and agreed. "You're upsetting my

41

heavenly breakfast. Okay...alright, you win. We'll make a sister for the boys. Just calm down. Everything will come out fine."

They had sex that night and again over the next few weeks. Holly got pregnant, beaming with joy. Since he never told her about his vasectomy, he thought she'd turned him into a cuckold. She had to have cheated on him. He even returned to the doctor to make sure the procedure had been done correctly. He was furious over her two-timing, and he stopped having sex with her after she began pregnant. Any affection he had for her was gone.

But April had not cheated on Latham. She had been loyal to him, and she remained baffled by his sudden antagonism.

His secret vasectomy and the following impossibility of her pregnancy lay between them like a turbulent ocean, uncharted or understood.

Bass River, Massachusetts
2:43PM Monday, November 9, 1992

Hammers pounded, and saws buzzed in a loud chorus of expansion. Prosperity revved up in the residential construction going on in the previously sleepy towns in Cape Cod. People bought shorefront property as if it were gold. Developers picked up large parcels to slice them into smaller lots.

The Donnelly's owned land off Bass River on Cape Cod for a hundred years. William Donnelly, Latham's father, was a hard nut, holding onto the fifteen acres like a lodestar. His land's value skyrocketed. William was in his seventies when land investors approached him. He did not accept their first offer of a million dollars in 1978, but he did sell ten of the fifteen acres for the same amount two years later. He would not sell the last five acres. It was security for his son and a remembrance of him after his death.

Latham inherited a million dollars after his father died in 1990, but he also got something no one else on Bass River had. Those five acres. Between his own income from Heinem, the sudden inheritance made him rich. Builders still hounded him to sell his acres, but he was like his father. He would not budge. He didn't need to.

Taking the Bass River Bridge, the black pines that followed the road dropped away, and Donnelly's new house shone like a beacon on the top of the hill. Latham and April had told his father they loved his farmhouse; however, their real feelings emerged after his funeral. The old building was too countrified--they couldn't invite guests to that! Going into overdrive, they razed the farmhouse to the ground as trucks dragged the pieces off to the dump. An architect, a contractor, a landscaper, and an interior designer created their modern palace.

The driveway swept into an expansive parking area for a seven-thousand-foot house. Three arches adorned the front of the mansion with gothic accents working well with minimalism throughout the interior.

A tributary forked off from the main river and that followed the property. It curved gracefully behind the house, defining the edge of the property with natural charm. The large backyard ended at the water's edge. On the survey, land on the other side of the brook can't be developed. It was stamped as wetlands.

The stream remained serene unless a storm with a full moon behind it deformed the glittering surface. The owners of 1900 Bass River Road sipped espresso and meditated on the tranquil scene outside. They imagined Tom Sawyer fishing off the small dock they'd built on the turn of the rivulet. The property looked like a diamond. No one knew they were living in a Pandora's box, and someone would open the top soon enough.

Bass River, Massachusetts
1:45PM Thursday, November 11, 2004

Latham Donnelly was checking his guest list for a catered cocktail party set up for his well-heeled friends flying in from Boston. He didn't think about his family much—wasn't even sure where his children were… and he didn't care.

44

He knew enough. Justin, a lawyer, was thirty-two, the oldest of the crew. Latham thought he was working out of state somewhere. Robert, a year younger, was a drug addict in rehab—he could stay there forever for all the difference it would make. At twenty-nine, Holly worked in the local hospital. That was what he needed to know about his children at the moment.

The whole family had not met in over five years, and April has arranged a reunion this Thanksgiving. Justin moved back to Cambridge five weeks ago, and Robert was out of the Langhorne Rehabilitation Center. Holly's problems with her husband, David Russell, had been settled. Finally! Everyone could attend. April sent out formal invitations, but she was calling them all up anyway. She needed to tell him about the reunion...yet again, walking into his office on the second floor to do just that. He was busy on the phone, and he didn't have time to waste on this silliness.

She stood in front of his desk. "Honey..."

No response.

"Latham!"

He stared past her as if she wasn't there.

"I'm setting up a reunion this year," April said loudly. "I've told Vince about it, and Mirabelle will serve. Put the phone down and talk to me...this is important."

Latham smiled at her, nodding, not listening to a single word she'd said. April tapped her long fingernails on his desk. She was not leaving until this was resolved…that was clear enough. He ended his call.

"Hold on, George, I've got another call coming in…yeah. We'll wrap this up soon…ah, huh, that's right. Iron this all out on Monday…alright…alright, later."

Taking his headset off, he looked at her hovering on the other side of his desk. "What are you babbling about?"

April rolled her eyes. "Thanksgiving dinner, remember? This time, we won't accept last-minute excuses, hmm? Nothing is going to stop you from being here. No flights to the city or anything like that!"

"Yeah, yeah, okay…so everyone is coming? Even Robert?"

"I've told you this three times. He's out of Langhorne, and he's fine. Looking forward to having the holiday with his family."

Latham stretched in the chair. "Okay, okay. You have me. I'll be at your reunion with bells on…just like in the old days." Then he put the headset back on, returning to his laptop with even more concentration. April was boring holes in his forehead with her eyes.

"Thank you, Latham…oh, by the way, what did you mean by the 'old days?'" She knew he wasn't listening to her anymore, but she kept going, "The reunion is going to be a solid connection we all need. We'll come together again."

April left the office, wanting to slam the door so hard it would fall off its hinges. But closed it softly and walked away.

Bass River, Massachusetts
2:30PM Thursday, November 25, 2004

Justin parked his BMW and hung his sunglasses off the visor. His success showed in an expensive haircut, an Armani suit, a Rolex watch, and diamond cufflinks. He strode across the auto court, hoping that the clouds lining up on the horizon were not a harbinger of trouble. Gluing the necessary grin on his lips, Justin rang the bell.

April had been pacing. When the doorbell rang, she almost ran to the entrance before Mirabelle had reached it, tapping along in her high heels. She had put on a green silk dress, an emotional defense against any red flare-ups showing up at the party. She opened the door and stepped toward Justin. He raised his hand, stopping her affectionate advance.

"Excuse me! Excuse me, miss, I'm here to see my mother. Who are you?"

April knocked his hand away and hugged him. "This is a dream come true! Finally seeing you in the flesh, Jay! You've been gone way too long. Now that you're living in Massachusetts again, you can stop by any time you like."

"Of course, I will…between cases anyway."

"I hope you're hungry! Latham's in the library, starting in on the appetizers. You don't have a coat? It's cold out there…we have to catch up on everything!

Have you found the right girl yet?" April was chattering like a wind-up doll until she noticed the time on the grandfather clock standing against the back wall. "Oh no, I must check on the dinner, make sure everything is perfect. Please say hello to your father, okay? I'll meet you in the library."

"Mom, calm down. You're worrying about nothing." And then he laughed. "Of course, that sounds like the pot calling the kettle black."

"I know you're right, Justin, but I can't stop. Everything has to be right. I must deal with these last-minute details. I'll meet you in the library in a flash."

April hurried off. Justin's eyes closed in the following silence, but it didn't hold on for long. A motorcycle rumbled up the driveway and parked next to the main door. Robert took his helmet off and left it on the seat, walking into the house without even knocking. He was delighted to see his brother standing there.

Justin looked over at Robert. Any fraternal sympathy he'd for him was long gone. He watched him take his leather jacket off. Robert's outfit was brand-new and his eyes were clear, yet these indications had not been enough to affect his prejudice. His brother's hair was still long and shaggy. Justin thought Robert had been born damaged.

"Jay! It's a gas to see you after all these years. Mr. Fantasy will play us a tune! I guess you don't know what happened to me. I'm free, forever free. It'll never snow around me again."

"Good to see you, bro."

"I'm working at Home Depot these days and I'm picking up side jobs around my neighborhood. Trying to get a real estate license, and I've been studying. Bet you're still doing the same slimy stuff you learned in school. I'm not sure if you're going to heaven or hell." He grinned.

"I've been working in Connecticut on a trademark case for quite a while. Thank God it ended. I'm living in Boston again."

Justin motioned to Robert, who followed him through the front door.

"Looks like a mean-looking ride, Rob."

"Thanks. I cleaned it up well and fine-tuned the engine yesterday."

"You did a good job. Looks brand new...but maybe you should park with the other cars and away from the front door?"

"Okay."

Robert rode off, and Justin went back inside, waiting for his immediate return. Irritated that genetics had fused him to his brother and sister, he had nothing to do with that.

The Donnellys had hired a world-renowned designer named Rol Manon, having seen him in an article in the *Architectural Digest*. He was drawn to the concepts of fire and water, a foundation for many of his motifs. The living room floor was done in white marble. A large fishpond sat in the center of the room, with a fireplace on the north wall. Velvet chairs huddled around a coffee table near the main door, and more chairs circled the fishpond. A couch, two more stone tables, and four wing chairs faced the fireplace. Hidden in the north corner of the room sat a grand piano. The entire east wall was mirrored, and cathedral-sized windows in the facing wall allowed sunlight to energize the room during the afternoon hours.

The Donnellys called the living room their great room. Any traveler hiking through it would reach a hallway leading them to the dining room and the library.

Latham had been adamant to the designer that he wanted the dining room and the library to have an air of conviviality. He envisioned himself cajoling his business connections and acquaintances over a meal and then having a cigar in the library. Manon had bowed to his demands. Olive-colored curtains hung in the dining room, and a painting of a gondola by Jane Peterson graced the wall, and thick carpeting had been installed in both rooms.

April created table centerpieces for the holidays. This year, she'd set up candelabras on either side of the table with a wicker horn-of-plenty filled with fruit in the middle.

Daylight faded, and thunderheads swelled on the horizon. April turned the electric chandelier hanging above the table on. Long fingernail flicking through the place cards one last time, she carefully arranged them next to their water glasses.

Driving over the bridge, David Russell glanced over at Holly. A malpractice suit hung over his head.

He'd already paid a quarter of a million dollars in legal bills in the past six months. His attorney wanted more, but David was tapped out. He intended to borrow five hundred thousand dollars from his father-in-law that evening....he'd be fine after that. Even if he lost his license, what's left of the loan would help him start another career. Holly would inherit a third of the estate after her parents died, but that couldn't save him now. She already knew about his idea about the loan, but he wasn't sure how she felt about it. He gulped. He ignored his nervousness. It was time to iron out the plan.

"I should invite Latham to the library right after dinner and explain my problem to him.... then I'd ask him for a loan. Is that an okay plan? It should work, shouldn't it?"

Holly looked troubled. "You're not that close to Dad, honey. Your timing is good, but he'd be more agreeable to hear the request from me. He's giving me more respect lately. I'll ask him if you like...we might have a higher chance." Holly rested her hand on his thigh. "I'll take care of this for you, okay? I'll invite him to the library right after dinner, just as you mentioned."

"Okay. I'm not sure what's going to happen to me in court. That's why I'll ask for five hundred thousand. Do the best you can. It will help us both in the end."

Holly didn't really have a relationship with her father, good or bad. She had told David a lie, but he lapped up her flimsy words because his financial and medical stability was crumbling. He'd broached the subject only a mile from the estate, so he didn't have time to reconsider or re-think Holly's real history with her father.

Financial salvation in his heart, David parked next to Justin's BMW, rushing to the front door, too excited to remember his partner. In brown corduroy pants, a pink shirt, and a suede vest, he looked like a college professor, not a neurosurgeon. His extra fifteen pounds were not noticeable on his six-foot-tall frame. He was an exceedingly handsome man with a symmetrical face and full lips. Thick brown hair fell over his blue eyes as he held his jacket over his shoulder, looking picturesque without even trying. He rang the bell, and Mirabelle opened the door.

"Good evening, Mr. Russell… I thought the Mrs. was coming along?"

David was surprised, and he turned around. "Holly! Where are you…Holly!"

He jogged back to the car. His wife was not around. He had not been looking when she raced off to the hedge maze behind the house, grey dress fluttering behind her. Something had summoned her. Holly quickly reached the large fountain in the center of the maze. She stared through the branches of a fifty-foot-tall silver birch to make out a winged creature perched up there. And it was sizeable. Her connection with the entity deepened--but she knew the bond had to end. They were waiting for her at the house, and she had to return to the party.

Mirabelle stood in the driveway, looking around. It was almost dark, and David was looking into the passenger window of the car again when Holly crept up behind him and tapped his shoulder. He jumped and twisted around and grabbed her shoulders way too tight.

"Where the hell did you go!"

"Sorry, sweetie. I followed an orange warbler. The bird is supposed to be extinct, and I wanted to see if it really was the warbler. But it got too dark out there. I couldn't see a thing."

"It sounds ridiculous running around like a lunatic. You have to get back to earth and realize why we're here. Use some of that energy to help me to avoid bankruptcy."

David was still holding her shoulders harder enough to leave bruises. Holly cajoled him, "What's important is to let me go…. calm down and enjoy the holiday."

He let go — somehow not leaving any marks on her skin. He found his composure. Holly grinned, and they walked to the house. Mirabelle held the door open for them. Holly and David strode across the living room and into the library.

The winged creature flew through the storm clouds and burst into clean air. Feathers gleaming, it turned away from the mansion. The foundational connection to Holly was over.

Stepping into the library, David put his arm around Holly's waist. They were the final link of the familial chain. The reunion began. David noticed goosebumps on Holly's arm from a chill she'd gotten when the winged entity swooped closer to the roof of the house before flying off.

The library was a refuge, an escape from the hurly-burly of a maddening world. The grey-green carpet lowered decibels and the filters on the ceiling lights made the haggard look hale and hearty. The family had not gotten together in five years. Tentativeness stayed in the air for the beginning of this gathering. Cocktail glasses and half-eaten canapés began to crowd the coffee table. Mirabelle could barely keep up.

Latham and April settled on the divan, David and Justin on the couch. Holly and Robert stared out to watch trees lashing in the wind outside. As they watched, a branch cracked off a poplar tree and flew across the lawn.

Alcohol lifted their tension, and camaraderie continued as Mirabelle opened the double doors of the library to announce, "Dinner is served."

April used candlelight, thinking it was better than the electric chandelier. The table could hold eight, but only six places were set. Everyone read their place cards. Latham and April sat across the table, with Justin on his father's right and Robert on his left. David and Holly bracketed April. Latham asked April to put as much space between himself and his daughter as possible. He'd been insistent about that, and he wanted Justin on his right. April had followed his directions.

Mirabelle pushed a rolling cart through the kitchen doors, holding a steel pot of lobster bisque. She served everyone but Justin, who was allergic to shellfish. She gave him the bowl of cheese and broccoli soup resting on the lower shelf of the cart, and then she returned to the kitchen.

"Good soup, mom!" Robert slurped another spoonful into his mouth. "Can't eat the rest of my dinner if this fills me up!"

"Thank you, Bertie. Don't worry. You can bring anything you want home. How's work going?"

"Boring. I'm stocking shelves. I guess you have to go through a lot of crap to get anywhere. I'm taking a real estate course now. It would be exciting to sell houses."

Justin questioned his father. "So when will the tennis court be finished? You know I'll beat you this time, sir. My upcoming triumph will not be linked to love. Your long list of victories is almost over. I've learned some dangerous tricks and the problems in earlier my attacks are gone."

"The court is done, Jay, but I don't think we should play out there right now. Whenever you find the time, stop by. I'll throw your so-called tricks right back at you, play with you like a mouse until I decide to swallow you and end the game." Orange-tinted half-glasses perched on his nose had sharpened his stare.

Mirabelle took their soup bowls away, and returned with roasted turkey. Latham carved. Yams, oyster stuffing, baked potatoes, gravy, fresh homemade cranberry sauce, and creamed spinach were lined up at the steam table against the wall.

Everyone filled their plates, but David. He was too worried about Holly's meeting with his father-in-law, and his appetite had soured. And he wasn't saying much either, holding his glass out for Mirabelle's attention.

"Can you bring me another brandy from the bar, Mirabelle? Thank you."

She took his glass and walked off. Hearing stress in his words, she returned with a larger glass of brandy. David smiled at her with appreciation.

After dinner, the housekeeper used a butler to brush the crumbs off the table. Latham would soon ring the bell on the sideboard to bring in their coffee and dessert. Robert burped, excused himself, and returned to staring into space. April and David were chatting about vacation spots, and Latham and Justin argued over a convoluting point in business law about a small company distributing medicine in Ecuador.

And Holly was bored, deciding to create some excitement. She pulled the sleeve of her dress above her elbow, and then she skewered a plum out of the display with the fingernail of her first finger. Her elbow rested on the table. The ripe fruit skewered on her long nail began to leak quite a lot of juice across her palm to follow the inside of her forearm. This cherry-colored stain spread onto the white tablecloth. Her childlike ploy worked. Latham and Justin stopped talking, and everyone else at the table stared over at her hand. Then, the dark blue plum dropped off her fingernail with a gentle plop. Holly filled the following silence with a holiday story…

"The horn of plenty you created in the middle of the table is stunning. It's transitory art."

"Thank you, my dear."

"Did you know the Cornucopia symbolizes a plentiful harvest? That meaning comes from a mythological story, and the most prevalent is the best, I think. As an infant, Zeus's mother Rhea gave him to Amalthea, a nymph, to hide him from his father... who wanted to eat him." Holly stopped and sipped her wine. No one interrupted.

"The nymph gave Zeus magical goat milk, and that made him even stronger. Reaching adulthood, he found the goat that had given him that milk and broke one of the animal's horns off, endowing it with more power of his own. Whoever owned that horn would get anything they wanted. Zeus was grateful to Amalthea and what she'd done for him. He gave her the horn. The Greeks named it the Horn of Amalthea, and the Romans renamed it Cornucopia... or the Horn of Plenty. We pray our own Cornucopia will bear fruit, and we will not starve--of course, if anyone at this table was giving that powerful gift, they'd simply explode." Holly picked up the plum and took a bite.

"It's too late, sis, way too late. I'm about to pop, everyone...duck." Robert laughed.

"When you're done expexploring'll get the gold flowing out of the Horn since I'm a saint," Justin said.

"You wish," Robert said. "You're popping buttons off your shirt. After eating dessert, you'll explode, too. Follow me into the boneyard...hey! I can tell you the joke I heard at work last week. It's about Thanksgiving, sort of."

"Yes, Bertie, tell us!" April insisted.

"Okay...um...a minister died and found himself standing on a line of people going into the pearly gates. The minister asked the guy in front of him what he used to do in his life. He told him he'd been a taxi driver. When an angel at the gate called out 'Next,' the taxi driver stepped up. Saint Peter was at the gate too. He gave the guy a golden key and...ah...a *cornucopia* filled with stuff." Robert winked over at his mother. "The gates opened, and he entered heaven with his items."

The minister was next. St. Pete gave him a wooden staff and a crust of bread--and that got him angry and he yelled up at St. Pete, "You gave that guy better stuff than me! I worshipped God and spread his word my whole life. All you gave me was a twig and a dried-out cracker!"

Peter looked down. "Up here, we only pay by actual results. Your parishioners slept through most of your sermons, but anyone in the back seat of his taxi prayed that God would come down and save their lives." Everybody laughed.

Latham glanced over at Holly. He wanted to ask her a question. She picked up her wine glass and looked back at him, and he instantly avoided her eyes. He rang the bell, bringing Mirabelle out of the kitchen with the dessert tray and coffee. Yet, Latham's curiosity dragged him in...

"How do you know about the mythology surrounding the horn-of-plenty?"

"In school, I minored in folklore."

"I thought you were there to learn medicine. Folklore doesn't have anything to do with that."

"Understanding the human body is also facing our mortality. I wanted more understanding to deal with the difficulties of a possible afterlife. Folklore encompasses customs, beliefs, and religion. Those subjects helped me to accept death as the final culmination of our lives." She paused. Everyone else was listening to her as well.

"Our cultures are ego-driven. Historically, the power-hungry used religion to get power over their population. I have not found an easy explanation for that since we have not evolved much on that motivation--besides new technology that gives us even more control. I'm still trying to learn as much as I can to make the unknown known and familiar."

Holly's answer was nothing but dribble to Latham. He had stopped listening to her almost from the beginning of her answer. "I can't remember anything I learned in school, and I have no interest in the workings behind anything--besides who's in control in a business meeting. Superstition is hot air farted out by claptrap and bunk."

Latham didn't know why he'd even started this ridiculous conversation! He respected her for the managerial position she'd just been promoted to at St. Luke's Hospital in New Bedford. But she will always be an intruder.

Mirabelle served coffee and pumpkin pie. On her way back to the kitchen, she stopped for a moment and whispered into April's ear.

As soon as the housekeeper returned to the kitchen, April stood up. "I'm sorry, something has come up. I'll be right back."

Latham watched her leave. It didn't seem to faze him in the least. He kept on eating his pie.

April ran down a corridor at the rear of the house to get to an inconspicuous door, allowing her to reach the servant's quarters. She took the phone off the wall and hit two numbers to link her to the service line. Peter had been on hold there, waiting to talk to her.

"Peter, why would you call me in the middle of dinner? That puts me in danger. Latham might be riled up."

"Calm down, sweetheart! I don't want to be responsible for new worry lines on your face, but I have important news. More good than bad. And I'm sorry about interrupting, but my flight to Japan is leaving in half an hour. I have to tell you what I overheard at the airport lounge. It's linked to your divorce."

"Don't worry about that, I can…"

Peter interrupted her, "We have no time to talk. You have to know about this *right now*. I was having a drink before the flight, and I overheard a conversation that would curl your hair. Had to be lawyers or maybe real estate agents, but they were talking about *your* estate. They didn't use your name, but you're the only person on Bass River Road that has five acres. I got very interested. They said your property will be on the market next year. I didn't get any more information at that point, but you need to know. The profits from the sale can be divided between you and Latham. If I were you, I wouldn't start the divorce proceedings yet. Latham is a weasel. He'd slice you up in court and bicker over the estate for months, and he'd lock you out of any Heinem stock. Don't you see? If you hold on, we can count on that income! We'll be on easy street! I don't think it was happenstance giving me this tidbit. The three sisters of fate have just given us this power! Anyway, I have to get on that plane."

"Okay, Peter, I won't do anything, and I need to go, too. Call me when you get back. We'll have champagne in the cottage." She tried to sound positive, not frightened and confused. Whatever those people in the lounge had said, may not have anything to do with what Latham will actually do.

"I love you. Don't worry. It'll be a fine flight, and we will get our freedom soon."

Her affair with her plastic surgeon was the only skeleton rattling in her closet. Peter told her he'd help her get through the divorce in one piece. She should feel better, knowing what Latham had up his sleeve, but April felt worse. She knew enough about the man to realize what Peter had told her could be nothing at all. Returning to the table, everyone had already eaten their dessert. Staring down at her plate, she didn't even pick up her fork.

"What was the emergency, Mom?" Justin asked. "What dragged you away from our feast?"

"No emergency, just a woman I met in the hospital when Bertie was born. She'd called with holiday cheer, using my old cell phone left in a drawer in the kitchen. Mirabell answered it. We became friends. Her baby was sick, too. She'd moved to California a few years ago."

April pushed her pie away. Latham remained indifferent to her latest actions, busy talking to Robert, but appearances can be deceiving. Talking to his son didn't use up a lot of his attention. He was able to absorb the info April was telling Justin, pigeonholing it in the back of his mind. After that, he raised his voice.

"Kids, it's almost nine. I can't stay awake much longer. We shall adjourn to the great room and enjoy the fire and try the cognac I picked out."

He walked out of the dining room. David nudged Holly. It was time, and she nodded and sidled up to Latham. David remained close behind.

"I've heard something unsettling at work, and I think you should know about it." Latham stared over at her as she went on. "It's too unpleasant for general consumption. I need a moment of your time in the library." He nodded.

The rest of the family had convened around the fire. Mirabelle had been waiting for them, holding two bottles of cognac on a small tray. Louis XIV and Remy Martin. She filled their snifters already lined up on the table. The liquor worked coincidently as a distraction.

No one noticed Holly and Latham's absence. David sat on the edge of the couch and tried to look relaxed.

Holly and Latham were both intent on their upcoming talk to brighten the library lights.

"So what's this about?" Latham said.

"I didn't want to interrupt the party, but I can't get it out of my head. An overdose rolled into the emergency room last week. The nurse told me the man on the stretcher had used our name in his ranting. She told me he said, 'Donnelly took off and left me alone!' Everything else he said was gibberish. It's likely nothing, but I wanted you to know about it anyway. Maybe you should watch Robert more carefully. He might not be one hundred percent stable yet."

But Robert was truly drug-free, and no one had used the name Donnelly in the emergency room ever. Holly made the entire thing up. Not wanting to hurt Robert intentionally, he had still become a pawn in a critical game she did not understand. As if another force within her had directed Holly to use these denigrating tales to control future actions.

She relaxed on the couch. Her laissez-faire expression fueled her magnetism, and her violet eyes shone. Dress tight on her lithe body, she invited the beholder to look deeper if they dared. Latham knew she was not his own child. However, the rest of the family had gotten used to her beauty. He looked at her, frowned, and redirected his gaze out to the windswept yard. A small escape from her.

"I really thought the treatment had worked this." Latham frowned. "He was loopy at dinner, but he seemed optimistic, a new trait I'd never seen before.

I'm surprised you went out of your way to help. I didn't know you cared about him that much."

"Actually, I'm more concerned about our own reputation. You might have to corral him before he runs off the rails and tarnishes us all. And his inheritance could be another obstacle. He may squander all your money for no good reason. He shouldn't hurt himself and those around him with that kind of power."

"Don't worry. Your brother isn't going to do anything. I'll check what you've told me. I thank you; you've done the right thing." Latham stood up. "We've been gone long enough. I don't want them to worry."

Walking to the door, Latham looked back. There was blue light glowing in her eyes. He shook his head and looked back again. The odd radiance faded. It had to have been just a trick of the light.

"About to send a search party out to find you two," Justin said. Prodding at the fire, he leaned the poker back in the stand and smiled at them, slapping ash off his pants.

"Forgive our disappearance. Holly had some questions about hospital politics. We didn't want to bore you." Latham shook his head. "I can't remember the last time we've been here together. Has it been five years since our last powwow?" He poured Remy Martin into a brandy glass and handed it to Holly. "This will take the chill out of your bones, my dear."

He sat on the couch, crossed his legs, and sipped at his own cognac. Everyone had quickly been lulled by the crackling flames. Completely relaxed. Robert had fallen asleep.

"We should have another Thanksgiving feast next year...another reunion," Holly said.

"I concur," Justin replied. "Underline it on our calendar. Avoid any last-minute jaunts to drag you away." Those words were clearly directed at his father. Latham grinned at him.

"You've been out of state for years, so you're not in a position to preach to anyone on the subject...but you're both right. We need to do it again. I'll be careful that my business obligations won't interfere with our reunion next year. Let's have a toast! We have to support our resolve!"

Robert had helpfully woken up. The entire group stood up and raised their glasses. Latham rang out the challenge: "Another Thanksgiving Reunion next year!" Glasses clinked. The tipsy chorus echoed his toast.

"**Another Thanksgiving Reunion!**"

Robert staggered backward. April grabbed his shoulder, guiding him to his chair.

After they all sat down, Justin came up with another idea. "I couldn't eat the lobster bisque, and there are oysters in the stuffing, but I love ham. I know a distributor in Boston that could ship out a gourmet ham for our next meal. We could have turkey and ham. What do you think?"

"A good idea, Jay," April said. "I'll tell Vince about it."

Robert was hunting for his jacket and motorcycle keys, but April touched the back of his hand. "Bertie, you should spend the night in your old room instead of riding home. You're tired, and it's too windy out there."

"I agree," Holly said. "You don't need to get to work tomorrow, Robert. And you're too sloshed to ride anywhere anyway."

Robert shrugged and sat down. "You have me then. My old waterbed will feel great. You didn't throw it out, did you?" He wore a sheepish smile. "I put my bike in the garage a few hours ago. Even wiping it down. I was hoping you'd invite me."

The family gathered at the front door for necessary goodbye hugs. David shook Latham's hand, and he winked. Latham winked back at him, amiably enough, clueless over his son-in-law's gesture.

Justin opened the front door. The wind rushed across the granite tiles as Holly, David, and Justin ran into the storm. Looking through the small windows in the front door, April watched them race across the auto court. Latham was on his way to the library to watch the football game. Turning away from the door, April saw Robert standing motionless, apparently staring at the wall. She stepped over to him.

"Robert, you must be exhausted. Go upstairs and rest! There are pajamas in the lower left drawer of the bureau. If you're still hungry, I can bring you more to eat." She was talking to him as if he was a young child.

"It's okay, mom. I'm fine, but I am tired. I'm going to bed."

He hugged her and kissed her cheek. Holding the banister, he swayed up the stairs to the second floor. Along the hallway, his old room was the third door. The waterbed wasn't there. He wouldn't sit on the new bed, instead perching on the cushioned seat under the window. Raising his legs onto the bench, he stabilized himself. Pressing his forehead against the cool glass, he watched Holly's Mercedes turn on Bass River Road. Rain pattered at the windowpane, a natural lullaby. His head slid towards the sill, paint-peeling snores shaking the room.

Holly had pickpocketed the car keys out of David's pocket like a pro. She sprinted over to the driver's door and locked herself in. He ran up behind her and rapped at the window, holding his jacket over his head against the downpour.

"Get out now, Holly! I can drive us home. I'm okay, really. I drank coffee after dinner. I only drank two cognacs. My blood alcohol is low… *I'm getting wet out here, damn it!*"

She ignored him.

"You drank more than I did! I should drive, damn it!"

Rain hit his head like pellets through the jacket. There really weren't any options, and he stepped over to the passenger side and got in.

David Russell knew his wife had a high tolerance to alcohol. That was a gracious way of saying it. A three-hundred-pound linebacker would lose a drinking contest with her. During a party they'd attended a month ago, she'd imbibed nine martinis. Her makeup remained flawless, her clothes unwrinkled, and her diction perfect. Nothing in David's medical knowledge could explain it. Accepting her impossible tolerance, he chalked it up to her metabolism…and he tried not to think about it too much.

Getting in the car, he sat there dripping. Holly looked at him and giggled.

"Go on…shake your head like dogs do. It would get the water off your eyelashes. They're too heavy now, drooping into your line of sight."

David did have long lashes. She was right. He wiped his palm across his eyes, glowering over at her while she drove the Mercedes onto the main road. David really wanted to know what his father-in-law had told her.

"Dad winked at me when we left, so I guess we'll get the money! I told you, Wilson won't defend me until I have more money!"

"How much celebrating did you do tonight, sweetheart?" Words soft as velvet, she went on. "Have you forgotten? Your malpractice insurance won't run out for another four months. Destruction is not coming for you quite yet. You wanted five hundred thousand dollars to hold the fort, but…" Her attention suddenly shifted back to the road, leaving David hanging there.

"For God's sake, tell me! Is he giving us a hand or not!"

"Maybe you should go to Las Vegas and solve your financial troubles by winning big."

David straightened up. He pivoted towards her, fists clenched. "Gee, that's a great idea! Why haven't I thought of that? Go there and gamble! Holly, my position right now is not a joke. Stop screwing around and tell me what happened, just answer me!"

"Alright, alright. I can see your knickers are in a twist. A CD will mature in a few months. You can borrow from that, okay?"

David's tension grew. He rocked back and forth, and his words came out as a sibilant hiss. "How much money is in the CD...honey? Could you consider telling me that? What is the amount?"

"Five hundred thousand, okay. Calm down. Have a nap. I'll drive us home."

David reached over, kissed her, and melted into a comfortable position. "Always darkest before the dawn. You came through for me after all."

He passed out. The beat of his snoring matched the rhythm of the music Holly had picked for the ride.

Bass River, Massachusetts
11:58PM Thursday, November 25th, 2004

Robert woke up with a cramp in his neck. Half-asleep, he still wanted more pumpkin pie...might take his mind off that nagging pain. And returning to the window seat won't be an option. He'll sleep on the damned bed after he comes back from his trip to the kitchen.

Hadn't been at the house in years. He forgot the seamlessness of the elevator. Hitting the button, at first he thought it was broken. No sound came out of anything, but the doors quickly whisked open. He blinked, yawned, and got in.

Getting out, he entered the service corridor leading to the back entrance to the kitchen. In a bright symphony, the lights went on when he walked in. Robert squinted, wishing he had on sunglasses. Glittering pots and pans were hung above two commercial ovens. Everything else in the room, including the center island, the counters, and the floor tiles, twinkled.

He walked into the cooler and tried to find the pie. Pawing through some of the containers, he couldn't find it. The metal door whooshed behind him as he left. There were pastries on the counter, and he grabbed a croissant. The sound was faint, but he could hear his parents talking in the library. Curiosity drew him toward the conversation. He stepped into the dining room. Easier to make out what they were saying…

Latham had relaxed on the divan, finally free from holiday cheer. He dropped the screen out of its hiding place in the ceiling to watch the football game. It turned out to be an exciting game. The score was close. Yet he began to think about other things---what Holly had told him about Robert was bothering him. What on earth would Robert do with his inheritance after he dies? That might be a serious problem. While he mulled this over, April entered the library. He had just lifted his glass to his lips while she bent down to kiss his cheek. Sherry dribbled down his chin.

"Is it a good game? It's certainly running late. It's almost twelve-thirty."

"You made me drool on myself, woman! Watch what you do in the future…and yes, it's a good game, but I'm concerned over what that passed-out idiot upstairs will do when I die."

"Do what? And why are you calling him bad names? Robert looks great. He's starting a new life after the rehabilitation. Thinking about a career in real estate. I haven't seen him so…" She paused for a second, "relaxed, happy, and drug-free in years."

Latham stood up and refilled his glass at the small bar. "Yeah, yeah, okay, but you saw how much he drank tonight!"

"It was a party, for God's sake, and a reunion on top of that! He wasn't anymore tipsier than anyone else…and he doesn't have a lot of tolerance after years of teetotaling."

April refreshed her own glass of wine and sat on the couch.

"You may have a point, but Holly told me about a rumor running through the workers in the hospital that Robert might be back on drugs. Even she was worried about it, and decided that it was important I should know about it as a dangerous possibility."

Leaning against the bar and smiled. Usually, Latham didn't believe anything his daughter had said in the past. This time, his own ingrained disparaging opinion about Robert had been supported by unverified gossip he had learned about from another gossiper. But Latham really wanted that rumor to be true.

"My God, Latham! I don't believe this! It could be nothing. Or a bad misunderstanding. Maybe--"

Latham cut in on her, "I've had it with Robert's screw-ups. I won't pay for any more clinics or rehabilitation centers---or his rent, for that matter. If he makes it, he makes it. If he doesn't, well, that's the way the cookie crumbles. I won't let him destroy his own heritage...and what would he do with the money anyway? Buy drugs and alcohol, that's what! I'll put a stop to that for his own good to hold up the family's reputation."

"Wait a minute," April said, raising her voice. "You have to check on the main source of that story before you do anything. There is a good chance you're about to devastate him for no reason."

He stared at her as if she was speaking gibberish. "I'm going to Boston the day after tomorrow. I don't need to corroborate anything. I don't need to. Robert is a lost cause. I don't want our public association with his filthy habits to tarnish our reputation...and I don't care what you think. I'm calling Attison to revise my will. Robert's money will be in a trust with Justin in control. If Justin dies, Attison will take his place. Someone must have discretionary control over his capital."

April instinctually knew the story about the drugged-out patient was preposterous---and Latham's reaction absurd. Yet she could not dissuade him from his decision. Her own future has precedence. She was already worried that Latham was checking on everything she did financially, even afraid he was paying someone to follow her around. Thank God for Holly! She'd call her and ask her about the nonsense about Robert.

Living with Latham was tough and getting tougher. April's 'joie de vivre' was gone. He'd thrown fake facts at her like diarrhea, and this ongoing deceit could not be avoided. The invisible stain on the shoulder of her beautiful dress would never go away, and her own worries burned it through the cloth and into her skin.

Robert crept closer to the library door to make out exactly what they were saying. *So, he'd never get his inheritance? Justin will dole it out if he thinks he needs it?* A very bitter pill to swallow, he dropped the croissant and ran back to the kitchen. He slammed the door behind him hard, not worried about the sound, but it didn't matter. April and Latham assumed it was part of the commercial on TV.

Robert ran across the great room in emotional trauma as the last of the embers in the fireplace crackled. His father was about to cut him out of the life he was born to... and the disdain in Latham's voice burrowed into him. He picked up the cognac bottles left on the table next to the fireplace to bring them to his room.

The fragile ropes he'd woven were unraveling as Robert sailed off on deep and rough water. The cognac bottles in his arms were the only treasure he had left. He climbed the stairs, now believing he had nowhere to go.

New Bedford, Massachusetts
10:55PM Thursday, November 25, 2004

Blue pines accented one edge of David and Holly's elegant property, a three-bedroom ranch on Merchant Drive. Their garage door opener broke a week ago. Holly parked outside in the pouring rain, and they sprinted to the front door.

David was on his way to the kitchen. "Want anything?"

"Water. Thanks."

He left the bottle on the table next to her, making his way to the oversized lounge chair in the far corner of the large room. Turning the TV on, he flicked through the channels while Holly was instantly engrossed in a magazine article written by Keith Fischer. He was a world-renowned marine technician currently working on a custom yacht for a shipping magnate. The American Yachting Magazine asked Fischer to write a short article about the project. Having asked the owner for permission to use his yacht in the article, he then agreed. He'd created a new communication structure in the vessel, installing that system for the first time. The design integrates different systems throughout the ship, mimicking our own nervous system in a way. The ship will have a kind of central intelligence, allowing one person to monitor all the different levels in real time. Controlling a complex craft of that size with a much smaller crew would be an impressive accomplishment.

Holly was lost in the article---meanwhile, David was getting bored. Nothing to watch, he returned to the kitchen to get another beer. And then he thought about his wife...well, not 'thinking' exactly. Visions of her body bloomed on his own internal screen--- she was not wearing a bra or any panties. Maybe her help with his father-in-law had been a sign. Maybe she was warming up to him by now. They could both heat up together until the sun came up.

A few months ago, David had a foray with a young intern in a supply closet on the third floor of the hospital. Should have ended that dalliance quickly. Holly found out about his affair, and the imbroglio ripped their marriage to shreds. It was surprising she hadn't divorced him, but she'd put out rules. No sex until she gets over her irritation. As time passed, he prayed she'd soon relent with vehemence. He needed to relieve this pressure. Self-release was not enough. David was a good-looking man, but he couldn't touch anyone else if he wanted his marriage to survive. Waiting for Holly to accept him back in bed was making him crazy. Flipping through the channels, he was dazed with drink and desire, deciding to seduce his wife. Talking to Holly first would have been a safer choice.

She sat on the couch in front of the picture window. David crept out of his lonely corner to stand behind the back of the couch and massage her shoulders.

"I'll take the tension out of you, honey, untangle any painful knots."

Holly moved away from his kneading fingers and turned a page in the magazine. Her negative reaction did not stop him. Instead, he reached forward and cupped her breasts in his hands.

"I'm busy, David," Holly said quietly. "Go away."

He nibbled her ear. The softness in her voice tricked him. What she'd actually said was forgotten by the throbbing between his legs---self-preservation overwhelmed. He got up to flick on the stereo. An instrumental from Pink Floyd. Then he lowered the lights...and Holly turned the desk lamp on and kept on reading. David was lost in his hormone-driven dream, switching her light off.

"You were my savior with Dad today, and I think we need to restart a new chapter in our relationship. Remember those nights we used to have?"

Gulping down a few more ounces of beer for inspiration, he slid his hand along the curve of her neck. Holly wasn't reading anymore, so she redirected her attention to David. He squatted behind the couch, blind to the blue light growing in her eyes.

As he described a Tantric position they'd used in the past, he intended to jump over the back of the couch and snuggle up to her. Holly remained silent. David thought she was mesmerized by his seduction.

Half a second before his prepared leap, she slapped his face. His beer bottle crashed into the front door and shattered as he soared over the loveseat behind him in a flight ending when he reached the side of the fireplace installed in the opposite wall.

Holly looked over her shoulder. He was unconscious on the floor. Possibly using too much of her gifts, she psychically assessed the damage she'd created. He'd be out for a few hours, but he'd be able to move well enough after that, healing up completely in a few weeks.

She turned the lamp on. She felt regret--- shouldn't have slapped him quite that hard. In the future, she'd be more precise on whatever she does. Finetune her actions. Holly was learning, after all.

Whistling along with an obscure melody, she returned to Fischer's article. His name had driven her to the article. She knew there was a connection between them, soon to be forged together to fight a battle of some kind. Holly was truly frightened about that. Keith would be part of a close-knit group. Himself, Attison, and her...and one more person. She hadn't quite pinpointed that last one person yet. She knew it would be a detective anyway. This prediction weighed on her, and Holly tried to ignore the real means in this ominous forecast.

Bass River, Massachusetts
6:25AM Friday, November 26, 2004

Throughout her professional life, every family paid her well. Mirabelle's disinterest in the lives of the people who employed her was highlighted in her resume. The Donnellys liked that quality, and it landed her the job. During the time she'd been working for them, she had not seen a lot of secrets---just a depressing bleakness in Latham and April's relationship.

Not too long along, a news article described a man bludgeoned to death on the kitchen floor of his multimillion-dollar house in Easthampton, Long Island. Apparently, the family's electrician, who was installing a security system in the house, was responsible for the murder. He'd been having an affair with the man's wife. She had implored her lover to kill her husband. He would be in jail for the rest of his life, and she died from cancer a year later. Mirabelle saw a moral in that story: always maintain distance from those you work for.

Mirabelle knew Mrs. Donnelly was having an affair. She assumed everyone else knew about it, too. Adultery appeared to be normal in most American marriages. The housekeeper thought it was there to infuse the contract with excitement and pizzaz. Be that as it may, she still would not tell anyone about it.

She drove the last miles up the hill to the mansion, leaves swirling into pirouettes in her wake. It was a beautiful day. Mirabelle parked on the side of the house, reserved for help. It was 6:30 in the morning as she unlocked the service door and hurried inside.

The family has had charitable events at the house before, bringing in workers at that point. She moved passed a utilitarian-looking dining room used when those extra employees were here. Farther along the corridor, she entered the large closet to take out the cleaning cart. Mirabelle pushed it into the kitchen.

Vince had cleaned up most of the kitchen the night before. She rolled the cart into the dining room and left it there. Pulling the vacuum hose out of the wall, she sucked up the pastry crumbs she'd seen on the floor in the hallway door.

Robert's motorcycle was starting up outside. That was odd. *Why would he leave so early?* She shrugged as the engine rumble faded away. She vacuumed the rest of the room before kicking a button in the wall. The hose was then sucked back into its hole.

April's suite had a dining alcove, a kitchenette, and a sitting room. Latham had the same arrangement farther along the hall. Robert's early departure hadn't bothered them since their rooms were on the other side of the house.

The scientists working for Hienem Pharmacological Company to create new drugs sometimes come up with concoctions that work too well. Not sold to the public, some of them make it to Latham's bathroom cabinet. After the previous evening of merriment, he got out of bed and staggered into his bathroom to grab an unmarked bottle. He twisted the top off and popped two pills in his mouth.

79

Fifteen minutes later, a burst of energy erased his hangover. Showering, he dressed and got Mirabelle on the intercom to order fresh coffee brought to his room.

Then he called the family lawyer, explaining the revisions he wanted in his will. Attison told him those changes could be done within a week. All he'd need was his signature to legally support the updates. Then, the phone call was over. Latham felt relieved. Robert won't be able to throw his money up his nose... or any other illegal things he might do. His previous concerns over the bugbear Holly had described the night before were gone. He was ready to move to Russia.

His feelings towards April had shifted like sand. Affection for her vanished in her third pregnancy, even though he accepted her adultery. After dealing with her disloyalty for years, things were now changing. The parentage of his sons and his public reputation had stayed his hand thus far, but now he no longer cares. Their upcoming divorce could burn across the pages of the tabloids. However, the Hienem Company and Lathem's place within it can't be affected by lowbrow soap opera drama anymore.

Attison told him the company should encroach into Russia's financial fabric during the next few months, and he'd invited him to oversee the corporate invasion. He had described their economic invasion as an adventure, and that had prodded Latham into calling a realtor to put the estate on the market. Secretly beginning divorce proceedings against April, he imagined himself flying off to Russia and leaving her divorced, dumbstruck, broke. He stepped over to the window. Cumulus clouds raced along, and the green grass was painted in a moving tapestry of light and dark. But he was blind to this natural splendor, calculating his next move.

Meanwhile, April walked into the dining room, looking forwards to having breakfast with Robert. The dining room was empty. She walked into the kitchen. Mirabelle was arranging fruits on a platter.

"Good morning, Mirabelle. Have you seen Robert?"

"Good morning, Mrs. Donnelly. Would you like something to eat? Vince isn't here yet, but I could cook for you...oh, I'm sorry. Robert left around seven this morning. I heard his motorbike start up."

"Did you talk to him before he left?"

"I didn't see him, just heard the engine start up outside."

"Okay...alright, I'll go check on that."

She was suddenly on a mission, breathing hard, when she reached his room. April knocked. No answer. She tried the door. It was unlocked, and she entered to see the bed still made... and shattered glass on the floor. A decanter sat on the very edge of the windowsill across the room. Her entrance had affected that iffy balance. Glass hissed under her heel as she leaped towards the bottle. Too late. The second bottle of brandy crashed to the floor. April moaned.

Her son had left her alone and forgotten. He didn't care about her---there was no one out there to love her anymore.

Her 'oh woe is me' went on for a minute or two before she remembered Peter and the romantic tryst planned with him. Her worries over her son's selfishness vanished. Lifting her head, April gazed through the window... *It's beautiful out there! I'll go to the garden and see if there's any wind damage from the storm last night. I'll just tell Mirabelle to clean this mess up.* Shaking her head, she left Robert's bedroom... of course, it wasn't his anymore, just a comfortable place for the guests to stay.

Latham watched from the second floor as April disappeared into the hedge maze. He wanted to check out his wife's story. He will call Carmen to figure out what is true and what is not. He wanted to know if her latest actions were still unconscionable. She was out of the house. Time to get the info. He entered April's bedroom. Her pink phonebook was on the nightstand. She had this paper version as a backup if something went wrong with the phone.

He'd winced when he first stepped into her room. Creeping around behind her back made him feel like a louse---but he couldn't stop himself. He looked up Carmen's number, entering it into his own phone. Then he glanced through the window... April wasn't on her way back yet. Putting her phone book where he'd found it, the duplicitous snake he was slithered off.

Back in his suite, he refilled his coffee cup and relaxed in his massage chair. Not knowing Carmen's schedule, he had nothing to lose by calling her in the middle of the day. He'd come up with a fragile excuse for his call while he punched in the stolen numbers.

"Hello."

"Hello, Carmen?"

"Yes. Who am I speaking to?" The woman had strained ferocity in her voice.

"Forgive me, I'm Mr. Donnelly. I'm April's husband. April called you last night, but she's tied up today and she asked me to call and give you the information you requested."

"I was at a benefit last night. I didn't talk to anyone on the phone."

"Oh dear…. I guess we got so happy with the cocktails I got the wrong information. I'm sorry to bother you over our silly mistake." He chuckled. "I give you a belated Happy Thanksgiving and to say a polite goodbye."

"Yeah, okay…I guess. It sounds weird… I'll call April. I haven't talked to her in years." She sped up, "I have to get off the phone now."

"Okay, my dear, no worries."

Latham didn't care how she felt or whether she'd call April or not. He broke their connection with a gentle tap. So, it was clear. April was having another affair--maybe with the same guy!

Donnelly had been galvanized. Whatever cruelty he'd planned for her had ratcheted up. Pulling the rug out from under her feet would not be enough. He'd take the floor under the rug away too, so she could fall into the basement and break her neck!

Las Vegas, Nevada
10:15PM Monday, November 29, 2004

Fred's Fast Draw Grill and a pawn shop next door were on Lamb Boulevard. The throbbing radiance of the main strip was blocks away. The alleyway between the businesses was dark, and the piles of black garbage bags left against the walls accentuated that. Fredrick owned the gambling den, and he ignored the citations the city sent out to him to clean up the outside of his property. Every few months, they would fine him for unsanitary conditions. He'd pay the fine and clean it up and forget about it again. Currently, the cycle has reached its upper limit. The alley looked dreadful.

Someone driving down Lamb Boulevard had thrown the last of their lunch out of the window of their car, and it landed in the middle of that filthy alley. A rat, fat on Fred's laziness, dove inside that open bag, beginning to devour the last of the hamburger and fries. It was enjoying these tasty morsels... until something else grabbed its attention. Peering through the bag's opening, it watched a drama taking place just a few feet away. And the rat smelled a wonderful perfume in the air. Fresh, warm blood.

Human conversation was indecipherable to the small animal. It did understand the violence in their barking noises. That was a clear signal. More food would soon arrive, and its filbert-sized heart swelled with excitement. Luscious red syrup filled a crack in the asphalt...and that tiny river was getting close.

"Cindy told you. Your bill had to be paid on the twenty-eighth, Jake. I spelled that out for you last month."

Lazzo threw an uppercut into the man's thorax, even as he continued with his scolding. "We saw you in the strip club on Randall Street yesterday. You told us you'd meet us at seven-thirty at the coffee shop on 3rd. You didn't get there!"

Lazzo emphasized his repeating statement with punches. "No...you...were...not...there!"

Lazzo had been holding Jake against the outside wall of the pawnshop. He finally let go, and the man slumped to the asphalt. Edgar, Lazzo's partner, stepped over. He kicked the fallen man in the head and smiled.

"Laz, are you sure Sinderella wants this guy offed?"

"You know we aren't supposed to use her stripper name, Eddie." He whispered that to him. Then he picked Jake up and pushed him against the wall again. "Cindy doesn't wanna remember her dancing days. If she hears you talk like that, you could be sorry." Lazzo's voice got louder. "As to your question... yeah, she wants to end her relationship with this guy." He stared straight at Jake. "Sorry, dude."

He was barely conscious, but he tried to beg for his life. "Ple...plea...aagh...magh."

Lazzo let go. He slid on a pile of open garbage bags. Edgar looked up and down the alley, even checking the few grimy windows above them. He had to make sure no one was looking. He took his gun out of the shoulder holster. Lazzo had put his boot on the man's throat as if this recalcitrant gambler could somehow run off. While Edgar screwed a silencer on his gun, Lazzo stepped away. He pressed the muzzle to Jake's forehead, and Ed pulled the trigger. A muted pop. The bullet's short flight ended in brain matter.

Ms. Cindy Grayson had arrived in Las Vegas in 1990. She was twenty-one, with strawberry blonde hair, big green eyes, and oversized breasts. She used her gifts to sinuously climb the ladder of exotic dancing easily enough. She was also double-jointed. Cindy twisted around the poles and wriggled across the floor like a human snake. The audience loved those contortions. Many hadn't seen poses quite like hers before. Displaying her personal flowers to an expanding fan base, she thrived on their adoration. Her stage name was Sinderella.

A rich bookmaker fell for her. They lived together for a few months, and then they got married. Three weeks after the ceremony, he got a fatal aneurysm, leaving all of his holdings to Cindy. The young widow instantly got rich.

She had hidden her intellect behind her mesmerizing eyes. Now, it was time to peel her baby-doll disguise off to take control of his business. Any greedy scavengers at the gravesite were left behind in her dust.

She stopped stripping and leased offices in a private dinner club on Freemont Way. At thirty-five, she appeared civilized with a twinkle in her eye. Ms. Grayson's inherited business prospered under her control. In her sultry voice, she'd tell her customers-to-be that the interest on her loans was the lowest in town. She usually seduced most into a contract, not telling them that delinquent payments were always collected, sometimes with deadly support.

Looking like wet laundry sinking into the pile of plastic bags. Jake's loan was now null and void. Cindy's henchmen relaxed and strolled back to the street.

"Should we go to Ventura or Caesar's?" Edgar asked.

"Did you see that?"

"See what?"

"It was the size of a small dog!" Lazzo waved his hand in the air. "It ran out of a paper bag right over there, almost tripped on it."

"I wasn't looking...come on, where will we go?"

Impressed, Lazzo wanted to see the rat again, and he scrutinized the rubbish. The alleyway seemed to have gotten a lot darker after the murder, and the shadows looked pitch black. Lazzo couldn't see a thing in this iniquitous ink. He gave up and answered his partner's question.

"Ventura, I guess."

When Samuel came back from his trip, his first action was to pay Cindy off. Having done so, he then changed from living in his squalid flat on 11th Street to a presidential suite on the thirty-third floor of The Ventura. It was Samuel's favorite casino. Whether a dark angel was now on his side or he was born with the luck of the damned, his remaining capital grew. He defied the odds. The house was not winning. He was. Floor managers watched him like hawks, but he hadn't done anything out of the ordinary---besides winning. Management decided to pamper him a bit longer. They knew his luck would change soon enough. His winnings would soon return to their coffers like metal filings to a magnet.

Samuel enjoyed his time living in Ventura. One afternoon, he held a glass of champagne in one hand and Willow McCabe in the other. He was sitting in an overstuffed chair, and Willow was on his lap wearing an echo of a dress. Housekeeping would leave chocolate mints on his satin pillow in the morning, and she was another tasty candy he freely enjoyed.

"Is it time for dinner?" Samuel asked. "Are you hungry? Let's go out on a stroll and find a restaurant." She got off his lap. He stepped over to the closet and picked out a suit.

Next to a potted palm tree next to a manmade waterfall on the main floor of the Ventura, Edgar and Lazzo sipped their Long Island Iced Teas. Looking out at the boring parade of tourists going by, they perked up when they saw Samuel Eveland strode past.

Lazzo was a mountain of muscle, three inches over six feet. He maintained his physique by going to the gym. Edgar, his partner in crime, was under six feet, but he had his own gifts, good reaction speed, and competence. Their individual strengths worked well together. They were a solid team.

Tilting his stool against the wall, Lazzo watched the thin column of smoke from his burning cigar float to the ceiling. Wearing a tan suit, he wore a tight t-shirt and a snakeskin belt. Three golden crosses hung around his neck.

Edgar wiggled his toes in his sockless loafers. It made him feel free. He wore a black silk shirt tucked into khaki pants. A few spots of Jake's blood stained one of his pant legs, but no one noticed it.

As Samuel went by, with a female escort under his arm, he looked like royalty. Noticing the men looking over at him, he gracefully nodded in their direction. He had no idea who they were.

Edgar took out his own cigarette from a platinum case, and he lit it, puffing out a line of smoke rings. "There goes our winner." He wore a small smirk, but his eyes were blank. "I can't believe he hasn't borrowed any money yet."

The cutthroats were riveted to Willow's sequined behind, sashaying out onto the strip.

"No one knows how he's doing it," Lazzo said. "I hope he makes it...since things are tougher when you're older."

Edgar snickered. "You're imagining a fairytale. You know he can't stop gambling, you numb nuts. He'll start losing soon enough, and we'll see him back at Cindy's door."

He whistled, and a cocktail waitress came over. They ordered another set of Long Island Ice Teas. A wolf in sheep's clothing, it tasted non-alcoholic. Margarita Mix collaborated with Coca-Cola to build a placid mix, but sharp-toothed spirits swam below the surface. Vodka, gin, rum, and tequila whirled lazily in their glass topped with triple sec.

The uninitiated enjoyed the taste. After drinking the first one, they remained sober enough to order another, even as the hidden posse in their blood stole their concentration and self-awareness. After drinking the second heavier-loaded drink, a smile bloomed on their faces while unconsciousness began to creep up on them.

Lazzo and Edgar were veterans. They needed that heavy level of alcohol to calm the devils thriving in their dispositions.

Finalhaven, Maine
8:00PM Friday, December 3, 2004

Attison Korybante was a corporate lawyer. He was also the Chairman of the Board of the Hienem Pharmaceutical Corporation---and a trustee of the same company. His driver's license indicates he was forty-nine. However, his real age remained a mystery. Attison's unusual strength clearly negates the document's date...and his actual ancestry was also unknown. Never answering any questions in that regard, his swarthy complexion seemed to connect him to Greece or possibly Italy. Again, there was no documentation to support a thing.

He owned most of an island called Finalhaven off the coast of Maine. Its coastline is mostly rock-ridden. However, there was a thousand feet of sandy beach on the southwest side of the island. The entire place was picturesque. There were two islets just five hundred feet off the tiny beach. You could skip a stone and hit one. Attison owned the beach, the islets, and the entire southwest coast of the island. Glaciers had gouged out a natural inlet in their northern retreat, and he docked his yacht there during the summer.

Building his manor on an elevation, it overlooked the western horizon. Concrete over steel, he painted the building beige and the shingles reddish-brown and the colors meshed perfectly. The walls met the roof and connected like warm brown butter. Yet his home was heavily reinforced, weathering through the storms unscathed.

Inside, the residence was graced with every nuance. A steam room, a whirlpool, a sauna, and an Olympic-sized pool. The vastness of his home seemed overblown. Why would anyone want eight thousand square feet as the only inhabitant besides the help?

Attison had no explanation for this. He also owned a residence in Belize and another in England. Finalhaven was the most remote and bitingly cold for at least six months---yet it was his favorite. It reminded him of the Fortress of Solitude he'd seen in a Superman movie.

Attison had flown to Finalhaven a few days ago, knowing he could get most of his work done online or on the phone. Done with dinner, he floated in the whirlpool, mobile phone and a glass of absinthe on the nearby tiles. Jets pounded water into his back muscles and an expression of relaxation across his face.

Latham punched the Attison's personal number into his phone. Spearheading the intrusion into Russia would be interesting and a perfect escape from his entire family. Yet Attison hadn't told him whether the project had been accepted...or not. His uneasiness was growing, and he needed more information to make his next decision.

Attison dried his hands off on a towel and answered his phone.

"Hello?"

"Hello, Attison. Sorry to interrupt you. I hope this isn't a bad time?"

"Your calls will never interrupt me, Latham. What can I do for you this evening?"

"I'm getting worried. I don't know what Heinem's future in Russia is really going to be. Last week, you weren't one hundred percent sure if the company was actually going to start up over there. Are things getting close to a final decision? It still looks like a good opportunity for me right now."

Attison lifted himself out of the whirlpool and sat on edge. "Relax. I went through a conference call yesterday, and the primary movers all agreed. It's a go, Latham. It will be a real exploration for you. Listening to your excitement right now, it sounds like you've been bitten by the bug of adventure. We're all happy that you'll lead the operation."

"Great! My plans have been in neutral, but now I can get things rolling."

"We have to have another meeting to hash out the last of the outlines for the plan. Your input is important. Besides, we have to talk over some other concepts."

Attison grabbed a towel off the hook behind him and tossed it over his shoulders.

"Okay. Let's decide on a time," Latham said.

"My Jaguar is parked in a garage in Boston. I could drive from there to your estate, an excuse to put my car through its paces. Does that sound feasible?"

"Fine idea."

"What about the day after tomorrow. That would be on the fifth?"

"I'm supposed to be in the city tonight night, but I'd been done with those licensing problems the next day. I can get back to Bass River by Sunday."

"See you there."

Finalhaven, Maine
1:30PM Sunday, December 5, 2004

Attison's coat blew sideways in his short jog on the landing pad on the roof of his house. Getting into the helicopter, the pilot dropped him off an hour and a half later at the Logan International Airport. A limousine transported him to a parking garage in downtown Boston. He walked up the ramp to the second level, footsteps loud in the empty garage. The Jag was sitting in a corner lot. He'd ordered a new paint job on the vehicle. Rolling the dust cover off, he looked at the hue he'd picked. A metallic aquamarine, and it shimmered. It was haunting. Attison was pleased as he tossed his briefcase on the front seat and started the engine. It was important to let it warm up for a while. He got out of the car. Taking his long coat off, he tossed it on the briefcase on the back seat. Raising his arms, he intertwined his fingers and stretched, looking forwards to the drive.

Passing most cars with a seasoned touch, he took I-93 to exit on MA-3 South to hug the coast to Cape Cod. But he was frustrated. Traffic was slowing him down; he couldn't get enough space to move. Daylight was waning, and time was getting short. He got off the crowded highway to find a less-used route outside of Plymouth. Turning on a road going through St. Andish State Forest, it turned out to be exactly what he was looking for. Well-paved without a lot of tight curves, and nothing surrounded it but woods. He quickly reached a hundred and ten miles an hour.

The bloated moon hung on the eastern horizon as the sun sank in the west. Twilight fingers couldn't reach the Jaguar whistling across the asphalt. Attison Korybante reached one hundred and thirty-five miles an hour, and he finally felt serene.

Officer Sellman tried to end a long day with some kind of relaxation. It was the last hour of his shift, and he stopped at Carla's Coffee Bean and bought some donuts and a regular coffee. He had decided to stop at the rest area in St. Andish State Forest. It was usually quiet there. Local kids sometimes race their cars around that road, so Sellman would turn his radar on. One more speeding ticket would finally raise his monthly count to the astronomical level the main office was asking for. Parking there was a feasible excuse. He tossed his sunglasses on the dashboard and rubbed his temples. Then he took the cinnamon bear claw out of the bag.

A deep thump shook the patrol car, and a half-second later, a car raced by. Tomb-like silence followed. Birdsong resumed as he looked over at his blinking radar. *137...137?* He dropped the pastry, put the old cruiser in drive, and peeled out of the rest area.

Attison slowed to ninety-five, negotiating the curve, and when the road straightened out again, he returned to triple digits. *Was that a siren?* He checked his rear-view mirror. A police car was attempting to overtake him. He could have easily left him behind, but it would be more fun to hang out and play. Attison stopped the Jaguar on the side of the country road. Officer Sellman parked behind him, and Attison watched as he walked towards him, frustrated. Lowering his window, he greeted the uniformed man with politeness.

"Good evening, officer. What can I do to relieve your worried mind?"

Sellman had just pushed the cruiser way too hard. This Jag wasn't like any beefed-up muscle car a local teenager owned. He'd barely kept the sports car in sight. The frame of his old workhorse had been creaking, and the engine screamed out of key.

The Jaguar clicked with heat as he strode up to the driver's window. Things around Sellman began to have a tinge of oddness somehow…but he had a job to do. He kept on with his duties. When he was tailing the car, he didn't think he would actually reach it. He was relieved when he saw brake lights go on in the distance.

"May I see your license and registration, sir?"

The automobile seemed to be radiating light. Officer Sellman got a funny feeling in his belly; something was dragging on him.

Attison reached into his jacket for his wallet while Sellman gauged the dilation of the driver's pupils. He was ignoring the numbness in his toes and fingers and the sweat on his body. He knew he must stare into the driver's dark eyes…but Sellman drifted away. He forgot where or even who he was---before shaking his head and looking down at the pavement. The strange individual in his sports car had gotten to him. Sellman had to avoid any more staring contests.

"Guess you know why I stopped you. You doubled the legal speed limit. The state law could suspend your license."

Attison did not respond, giving the officer his license and insurance card. Sellman walked back to his cruiser. The farther he got away from the Jaguar, the better he felt.

"Hold on, Officer." Attison's voice burrowed into his mind like a worm. "Would you mind coming back?

Christopher Sellman thought he was about to hear the usual whining about their innocence: 'I really couldn't have been driving that fast....'"

"I really couldn't have been driving that fast. It must have seemed like that, I mean, my car can go fast..."

Officer Sellman interrupted him. "The speed limit on this road is forty-five. I clocked you at one-hundred and thirty-seven miles per hour...*sir.*"

Sellman was at the end of his shift, and he was already exhausted. Having just pushed the old cruiser as far as he could, he'd lost his patience.

"I'd like to see the radar gun," Attison said.

"You don't need to see anything. It'll work out in court."

"I know my rights. I have the right to see the number on the instrument. What's your name?"

Sellman wasn't positive the real legal parameters really were...and what difference could it make anyway? He can look at the number. It won't go away, and it won't change.

"My name is Officer Sellman. I'll bring the radar gun over so you can see the screen."

Back inside the patrol car, Sellman punched Attison's license number and car plates into the system. Waiting for the info, he took the radar gun off the brackets. Tapping his fingers on the dashboard, he stared down at the man's license. Mr. Attison Korybante. Hadn't been easy talking to Korybante about anything and he suddenly felt worse. Nothing came up on the screen. How could anyone with a car like that have no record? He shook his head...well, he had thrown his impossible virginity into a double X mudpuddle!

With the incriminating evidence in his hand, he slammed the patrol car door. For the first time, he had a smirk on his face. He held the gun at waist level. Mr. Perfect could see the evidence of his evil ways.

Attison looked up at him and frowned. "It's blinking at forty-five---isn't that the legal speed limit of this road? Maybe you are over-tired, seeing things that aren't there?"

"You're the one that can't see!"

Sellman lifted the gun and looked at the display and then he slapped the device hard. That should fix the problem, but it didn't work. *Damn it!* Obviously the blasted thing had broken at the worst possible moment. The number had actually changed to forty-five...wasn't it nice that it kept on blinking perfectly.

The officer sagged against the Jaguar, momentarily obviously that his belt and handcuffs could scratch the paint of this expensive vehicle. Oddly enough, Attison was not worried about that possibility in the slightest.

"It seems there will be no problem for me in court after all. My registered speed is legal…do you feel okay, sir?" Attison seems sympathetic to Sellman's frustration while a strange kind of magnetism oozed into his words. "You're at the end of your shift. Go back to your car, close your eyes, and sleep. I need to go now. It's time for us to go our respective ways."

Sellman, badly rallied, used his own exasperation to fuel his response. He stopped leaning against Attison's car and stood straight as an arrow. His following words had power. "You were speeding. I know it, and you know it. The radar broke, so I guess you're lucky. Racing around like this will wreck your life; you'll crash and burn, and I pray to God you won't take anyone else with you!"

Sellman had been hard-driven and overheated like the engine block in his cruiser. He walked away, but he was not free yet. Attison's next words wheedled into his head.

"You will wind down and have a nap before you enjoy the rest of the evening, Christopher."

Sellman stopped in his tracks. *How did he know his first name? Only his last name was printed on a tag on his shirt.* Curiosity tried to turn him around, to ask this strange man why he had this impossible knowledge. He kept on walking.

No more turning back. The riddle will remain unsolved. He'd rather forget the entire incident, praying he'd never see Attison Korybante again. And he'll park somewhere else to drink his coffee in the future!

Closing the car door, he stared at the number on the gun one more time. It had registered one hundred and thirty-seven miles an hour a few minutes ago. Looking at the pastry crumbled in pieces on the passenger floor, his head began to lower, and he fell asleep. It seemed that Attison's suggestion had been a lot more like a command.

Looking through his sideview mirror, Attison watched Officer Sellman stumble slightly on his trip to the cruiser. He started the engine and checked his watch to make sure the officer had passed out before dropping the Jaguar into gear. As if he was riddled with hormones, he spun the back tires hard enough to burn heavy strips of rubber on the pavement. It was a flippant 'adios' to Sellman.

Attison pushed the Jag to sixty in under four seconds, and the forest around him faded into a blur.

Sellman woke up. Looking at the dashboard clock, he'd been out for half an hour. He got out...there was nothing around him, just the gentle susurrus of leaves moving in a gentle wind. The speeder had left skid marks easy to see in the moonlight. He'd slept right through it. Christopher returned to the cruiser and straightened things up and radioed in. While he replaced the gun in its holder, the previous speed, 137, suddenly reappeared on the screen as if nothing had gone wrong.

And he never told anyone what had happened besides his wife. Other officers would have ribbed him about it forever. He ordered a new gun with an explanation that had little to do with the preposterous truth. Waiting for its replacement, the 'broken' one worked perfectly.

Memories of this uncanny story faded, but Officer Christopher Sellman would never be completely free. Attison would occasionally drive his Jaguar into his dreams like a virus no antibiotic could heal.

Bass River, Massachusetts
6:15PM Sunday, December 5, 2004

Latham glanced over at the grandfather clock against the wall. Whatever his role in the expansion would be had not been ironed out yet, but between himself and the Chairman of the Board, they'd shake out those last kinks over dinner. Attison should arrive by six.

Twenty years ago, Latham had lifted the company to greatness. Lately, he hadn't been doing anything exciting. Just a shepherd walking along next to a slow-moving goliath. His expertise is no longer needed. The venture in Russia would unleash the old trickster he used to be--and he can also leave his family behind. Forget them all completely.

6:25. He stared at the clock and kept pacing.

6:35. April was not there, and he didn't care where she was…probably having sex with her back-door man. Latham hoped her boyfriend didn't have much money since he was about to take the silver spoon out of her mouth. He imagined them both living on garbage and dying from botulism.

6:40. He heard the Jaguar's sweet growl. Latham polished off his martini and checked his appearance in the mirror…and then he opened the door.

"Good evening, Latham! Forgive my tardiness. I'm looking forwards to a happy evening of collaboration." Attison gave him a firm handshake and a manly hug.

"Late isn't a problem, sir. I was running late myself. I knew you'd get here eventually. What happened on your trip?" Latham smiled and shook his head. "Was it fire or flood?"

"A disagreement over how fast I was driving."

"I still don't know how you get out any ticket. The last time I was riding with you, we were going to Long Island City. It was unforgettable…and that's a nice way to describe it. I'll never go back in your car again!"

"You made it to your flight after the meeting, didn't you?"

"By the skin of my teeth! I am still happy I didn't have a heart attack. You must have already gone through more than nine lives. I guess getting older hasn't slowed you down." Latham stepped over the intercom. "What would you like?"

"Irish Coffee."

Mirabelle answered. "Please, bring out two Irish coffees."

"Certainly, sir." She clicked off.

"Where's April?" Attison looked around. "She should be excited about moving to Russia."

"Currently, April has previous commitments, and right now, she doesn't even know about the move."

Attison walked over to the koi pond and looked into the water as if he were reading the future in those shallow depths--there was a very good chance he could.

A striking man, he wore a black silk suit with an open white shirt, looking more like a Mediterranean Lothario than a middle-aged corporate lawyer.

Mirabelle came out of the kitchen had left their hot drinks on the table near the fire. Attison sipped at his coffee, busy fine-tuning what he was going to tell Latham. He knew what was at stake at this juncture in his life, and if Donnelly took this road, it would change his life forever...

"What you've done for Heinem has elevated the company," Attison said. "You've given us forecasts resulting in financial blessings. When we first started to work on the project, your previous decisions and insights jumped into the spotlight."

Latham bowed in deference. "I'm honored by this praise."

Attison went on, "I've checked the trends in Russia during the past twenty years, and there's a shift towards—"

Latham interrupted him, "Wait, Attison, please. Vince cooked dinner for us. If you're hungry, we can eat now."

"No, no, I'm fine for the moment, but thank you. A drop of cognac should tide me over for a few more minutes." Attison went over the bar and filled a snifter.

"Heinem doesn't want to lose you in this expansion, but you need to think this decision over. Moving to Russia will take you away from your family for a long time. April could meet you over there, yet not in the start-up. You won't see your children for at least a few months…and it will be a lot of work. I know you've always put Hienem in front of your own personal needs, but I counsel you to weigh your old motivations. You won't be able to slow down for quite a while--no vacation on your yacht, no flight to a Polynesian island with your family, and no Broadway show." Attison sighed. "You don't have to accept the offer, Latham. You've already won the prize. You can't climb any higher, and we really don't have a lot of time on this planet. Maybe you should do something different, let go and enjoy yourself and dive into the natural world. There are endless places you could go. Hell, buy a fast car and race me. *Why not?*"

Latham had been sitting in one of the chairs sipping his drink. He got up, grabbed the poker, and stirred the embers. The flames crackled up. He put the implement down and picked up a log to toss it on the fire.

"You don't know about the personal problems in my family. It hasn't been peaceful over the past few years. What's wrong with my marriage can't be fixed."

Attison looked over as Latham went on.

"Russia will be a perfect escape. I love solving equations, and this one is huge and it's a different location. Heinem has been a powerful force in my life, and my commitment to the company is my own reward. A separation from my family will be a blessing, not a curse."

"I congratulate you then." However, Attison put gravity behind his next words. "Accepting the metamorphosis, you have what we need to get the corporation anchored into the bedrock of one of the biggest countries on earth."

Latham had not seen the rebuke on his lawyer's face, nor did he hear the soft sigh of regret as he pressed the intercom to order their dinner. Mirabelle arrived quickly with a pot of Fondue, arranging the container on a heater already set up on the table.

The philosophical section of their conversation was over. Attison explained what would be needed during the first year there. They had to be swiftly entrenched into Russia's pharmaceutical programs. They discussed the complexity of some of these actions as they relaxed and enjoyed their dinner.

After the meal, Latham knew it was time. Attison, as the Chairman of the Board of the Hienem Pharmaceutical Corporation, had the power he needed to financially excise his entire family from getting any of his wealth. Without Attison's help, it would not work. Latham truly hoped he'd accept his plan. He wanted to take away their future riches forever.

"I'm not sure what April will do when I leave--and I don't care." Latham lit a cigar while tension tightened his face. "I'd like to erase my ownership of my holdings before the divorce decree gets filed. I want to create an open-ended agreement with the company. Heinem could buy this property and put it into an escrow account with a hidden clause. The ownership would revert back to me in thirty-six months. If I don't sign the contract at that time, any funds and real estate would just roll over for another three-year cycle. If I die, the contract dissolves. Hienem would then have full ownership." Latham slowly breathed in and kept on going. "The new command center is supposed to be in St. Petersburg. The company could build an estate there for me to live in, camouflaging my future ownership in an LLC account hidden in Heinem's assets."

Attison laughed. "Seems like you've thought this whole thing out. You don't want April or anyone else in your family to live on your laurels."

"That's not completely true…if Justin can remain in my good graces and settle down, I still might include him. Of course, he hasn't given me any grandchildren yet, and I'm getting worried there's something wrong with him. But that mystery has nothing to do with what I'm trying to set up with you. I'm still worried you might not want to help me."

"I'm here to support you, Latham. I'll slide the whole thing past the board. They won't have enough time to read it. I can even refine your plan. You've done so much for the company; I can certainly shoulder this… *transition* without a hitch. What do you want to do with the rest of your assets?"

"Siphon off most to an offshore account in Belize."

"I can accelerate that modification as well if you like. These transfers could take place seamlessly with my help. The company can hold your capital as if it's in a vault. Yes, things happen in a complex international move to Russia. These small hiccups won't attract any attention at all." Attison shrugged.

"Thank you for helping me with this. Let's call it a conversion," Latham said. "Can we go through my files tomorrow, maybe wave a bureaucratic wand over them, and send most to the next dimension."

"Certainly," Attison said.

Latham felt relieved. Another puff of cigar smoke floated out of his mouth. "With your support, my churlish family will never get rich."

Latham got back on the intercom, asking Mirabelle to bring out the espresso.

"I hope that these things won't use too much of your time. It doesn't have to be done that fast..." Latham sounded concerned.

"The entire thing should be tied up quickly enough. And it won't slow me down... no worries."

And it was good that Latham could not make out Attison's eyes in the soft illumination of the great room.

Robert Donnelly huddled in his pickup truck parked across the street from the state offices in North Dartmouth. He'd just gone through another real estate examination he'd failed a month ago in the same building. Positive he'd screw it up again, his results would reach his mailbox next week. White snakes of snow slithered across the road, pushed by a north wind that moved fast and hard. It even rattled his truck. He closed his eyes, imagining himself riding his motorcycle on a highway inside his mind.

He'd whittled his hours at the Depot down to twenty per week, but he was scheduled to work that afternoon. Staring out at the cold and colorless street, he groaned. He started the truck. Robert should not have used any drugs the night before the test, and the upcoming hours in the warehouse were moving towards him like a load of bricks.

He showed up late. Lately, he'd been hiding out in odd places in the building and not doing anything for a few hours in his work detail. The floor manager hadn't noticed his disappearances yet, but lately, Robert didn't care if he did. Be that as it may, he was not going to get away with that this afternoon.

Fluorescent lights buzzed thirty-five feet above his head while he lined up cans of paint on a shelf in aisle twelve. Tossing empty cardboard boxes on the cart behind him, no one could hear him whine like a small child.

There was a birthday party that night at *Heavy Turns*, a biker bar in Dartmouth, and he needed to be there. When his shift ended, he clocked out. He ran out to his truck and stuck his fingers behind the rotted fabric on the driving seat to snag out a vial he'd hidden there. Coke could not lift him up anymore. It just stabilized him. He needed to feel normal on his drive to his rental in Fall River to have a shower and get ready to go to the party…

And the place was packed. Robert squeezed up to the bar and ordered a shot and a glass of beer. A woman across the room waved at him, weaving through the crowd to reach him.

"Where've you been?" She had to yell the question. The music was loud.

Robert shouted back, "Good to see you, Jennie!" He gave her a hug. "Have you seen Mark?"

"He's next to the dance floor, near the stage."

The Almost Brothers was a tribute band, and they were pounding hard and shaking the floor. Robert tossed the shot down his throat and inched his way to the dance floor…it wasn't easy to make the beer stay in the glass. Mark was there to help him sell the product. Four girls were gyrating right next to where Mark was sitting. Robert squeezed between them and sat down.

"How are things, Mark? A lot of orders?"

"Hey, Rob! 'Bout time you got here! They're going nuts. You have it with you?"

Robert drank the rest of his beer and wiped foam off his lips. "You're an idiot." He had to scream that out.

They wove to a locked door in the rear wall. Robert had the key. It was a storage room, giving them the privacy they needed. The cocaine was already divided into plastic bags. He gave half of the bags to Mark. Their meeting in the small room was short and sweet. They were ready to go out there and give a rush to anyone who wanted it. Many partyers will soon be beyond happy-- and certainly much poorer.

Done with another of his profitable sales in the parking lot, Robert returned to the bar. He'd go to the bathroom once in a while to use his own product. He really should have felt good about making a lot of cash--but he didn't. Robert felt nothing. Alcohol and cocaine had polluted his psyche in a biochemical battle he had created but not controlled.

The band stopped playing at 2:00 AM. Most customers leave *Heavy Turns* at that point. Mark and Robert were playing pool in the back room. The music from the jukebox seemed tinny after hours of thunder from the stage, and their sinuses were dead and gone. No smells of the bouquet of spilled beer, half-eaten chicken wings, or anything else coming out in the garbage pail in the corner of the room, and the perfume of sweat molecules floating around them was just mist. Not many people left, the waitstaff was cleaning up as fast as they could.

"Damn it, Mark, you did *not* call that shot! It's my turn!"

"I did call it. You just didn't hear me, that's all. You were staring at Sallie's ass when she walked into the kitchen. You even whistled at her when she bent over to pick up the mess in the corner. Nope. You didn't listen to a damned thing I said."

Sallie sailed past yet again, tired out and wanting to go home. She rushed into the kitchen. The double doors slammed open and closed behind her.

Robert looked over at Mark. "Okay. Damn it, go. You're gonna screw up that bank shot, anyway."

Mark did not screw it up, and he won the game, yet Robert believed he would win the next one…he just knew it. As their next game progressed, Mark missed a shot. Robert went into attack mode, sinking all his balls and ending up with the cue ball set up perfectly in front of the eight ball. It was a straight shot into the pocket.

"I'm impressed, Rob. Looks like you're gonna get your fifty dollars back out of my pocket."

Robert Donnelly grinned. He ran the blue chalk on the end of his cue knowing he would tap that ball with the perfect force to end his day in a win. "Eleanor Rigby" came out of the jukebox. He picked up the beat of the song to center himself and he bent over the table and shot the ball into the pocket. The cue ball followed it down, a stupid mistake from a seasoned player. Robert slapped his stick on the table with a bang. Mark cringed.

"That's it. I'm going to the bar to have one more drink," Robert said. "If you're coming, you're buying." A thorny invitation, but Mark nodded. Robert walked off, singing along with the song:

"….Father Mackenzie, writing the words for a sermon that no one will hear, no one comes neeaaar.

Aaall the lonely people, where do they all come from…"

The bartender was rotund with pale skin and reddish hair. The management of *Heavy Turns* believed Nicholas was the best mixologist they'd ever had.

"What can I rustle up for you, gents?"

"Bored of beer," Robert mumbled. "Wanna end the night with something different…don't know what."

"I'd like something else, too," Mark said.

"How about trying a concoction I invented last week. I call it 'Broken Glass.' Summer is hiding in the glass. Besides the vodka, the rest will remain a mystery."

Robert and Mark nodded. As Nick began to mix up their surprise, Mark told Robert about his latest family soap opera.

"My sister was a serious bitch last week! I went to John's apartment in Boston, and Glenda flipped out. I didn't invite her. I told Linda not to tell her about it, but the backstabber told her anyway!"

His confusing story had enough darkness in it to light a fuse in Robert's head.

"Well, your sister and Linda weren't very nice, but my family can leave them both behind on that score. I've been born into a pit of rattlesnakes. I shouldn't tell you what my father is about to do, but I'll do it anyway. He is about to stop my inheritance when he dies."

Nick sailed over and placed oversized electric blue drinks in front of them.

"Thanks, Nick." Mark put the straw in his mouth and sucked. "It tastes great...and it looks like a swimming pool!"

But Robert kept going, too deep in to stop his whining. "I'm crap to Dad, nothing but a piece of crap." He didn't even taste his drink. "He's going to give my percentage to my brother even after I got straight...and he didn't acknowledge that either! Shit. I should have stayed home—shouldn't have gone to the Thanksgiving dinner. Maybe he would have treated me better if I'd stayed away!" Robert was staring at himself in the mirror behind the bar as if he was the only one in the room.

"You gotta calm down, Rob, get a handle on things." Nick put his hands flat on the bar. "It's never as bad as you think it is. Really, it's not...hey, he could still change his mind." Nick went back to cleaning things up, but he still looked concerned.

"He'll never change his mind or change his will. I'm over. He'll give my share to Justin...or maybe to the damned family lawyer. I'm just a sack of shit to him." After a moment of silence, he started up again, like a broken record--or maybe a broken man.

"I should stop him in his tracks. Hit him on his head or push him off a cliff or something. That would even the score...that would change his mind alright, forever. Yeah, I might--"

Nicholas interrupted him, "Stop talking like that, Robert! You can't say things like that. You're doing great right now, aren't you? You made a bundle tonight. Why don't you just fly away? Have a vacation south of here, where it's *warm*. Do that, okay?"

Nick tried, but what had found purchase in Robert's head could not be unrooted.

"You're right, Nick, you're completely right. Escaping into a vacation is a great ticket to ride. Thanks...all I need is a goodbye party to my father before I go. I'll have no more troubles after that. Yup. I'm looking forwards to it."

Robert leaned back on his barstool, finally sipping his cocktail.

A few days later, he ripped open the envelope holding his real estate test results. Reading the information, he threw it into the fire. He grabbed another beer out of the fridge and relaxed. Then thought over his future plans. It had nothing to do with real estate.

Boston, Massachusetts
3:30PM Friday, February 11, 2005

David needed an excuse to get the hell out of his house. His lawyer wanted a consultation with him since the hospital was asking for more information about the case. Okay. That was an excuse to fly to Boston.

And he had to give his lawyer more money. His pleas to Latham had been ignored. Calling Holly, he asked if he could dip into the half a million dollars her father had said he could use in another thirty days. He just needed something right now to hold the legal contract with his lawyer. She hadn't given him an answer, instead inviting him to meet her at The Swan's Nest over the upcoming weekend. It was a cocktail lounge on the first floor of the Park Plaza Hotel in downtown Boston. She had a surprise for him.

High-rises needled into the clouds, squatting over the city while the barometer plunged. The forecast predicted snow later on that day. The lowering pressure increased the ache in David Russell's neck. He had a dark blue three-piece suit on, with a silk shirt and a sapphire tie to accentuate his eyes. But the white neck brace screwed up the connection. Yet without that support, his bedroom eyes would be closed tight in pain, and he wouldn't be able to entice a damned thing.

Two and half years ago, Holly purchased a cottage on Nantucket, an island thirty miles south of Cape Cod. She'd taken out a loan on the property in January for one hundred thousand dollars to pay some of her husband's legal bills. When she got off the phone with David, she wrote out a check to Parker Law. She could have wired the money over to the company, but she thought going to Boston and playing with David would be more fun. She loved him in her unusual and unique way.

Parking on the third tier of the garage from the Park Plaza Hotel on the day of their meeting, Holly got out of the car in her five-inch purple boots from Prada. Lifting the car keys over her shoulder, she locked the doors behind her and took the elevator to the street.

Most women intending to spend a night in a motel usually bring more than they need, but not Holly. All she had was a small bag with a long strap, and it didn't hold much. Makeup, a hairbrush, lingerie, and a small PC, plus a sequined clutch. A paperback written by Keith Fischer was in the side pocket of the bag. Blowing through the access door of the garage, she swept onto the streets of Boston.

The hotel's understated entrance faced Arlington Road at the corner of Stuart Street. David had been staying in his friend's apartment on Blackstone Street, five blocks away from the Plaza. He just walked there. It was almost dark when he entered the lobby. Walls were papered in light gold, and the floor was tiled in pink and gray granite. The center of the concourse had a large fountain adorned with white marble nymphs. A chandelier sparkled forty-five feet above his head, and for a second, he thought he might have slipped back in time. A white-wigged courtier dressed in emerald studded robes could suddenly rush passed him…but the vision vanished when he saw the Swan's Nest's sign. It was done in fluorescent letters at the far east corner of the lobby. Entering the establishment, he was drawn to the tables facing the windows, looking out at the street. David picked one and sat down, quickly ordering a double martini. He hadn't seen Holly in three weeks. He was nervous…besides the unstable future of his license, his wife was responsible for the injury to his neck, even if his actions had triggered her response. His blood pressure was rising as the waitress returned with his drink. He didn't drink it. He swallowed it. Even as she began to leave, he ordered a second drink. Glancing at his watch, he knew she should be in the lounge…now.

Snow was beginning to cover the grass on the other side of the road. David watched his wife stride along the sidewalk… and his eyes widened. A gust of wind opened her cape, revealing a minidress and shapely legs wrapped in cashmere legwarmers. Wearing fingerless purple cashmere gloves, David thought her palms and knuckles had to be warm. Inches away from him on the other side of the glass, snowflakes melted in her black hair. She looked like a model in a fashion shoot. Surprised by her effortless walk on a sidewalk getting slick, his curiosity kicked in. He tried to figure out how much money was on her back. Her outfit looked like Yves St. Laurent or maybe Ralph Lauren. That was likely three thousand dollars. He ordered another drink.

Holly arrived at the Swan's Nest entrance, waiting for the coat check lady to give her the plastic token. The bartender, the wait staff, and most of the customers gawked at her. David could not turn his head. He twisted around in his chair to see what was attracting so much attention… ah, his dark angel. He was surprised he hadn't figured that out. He shouldn't have turned around with the resulting pain.

Taking the three stairs down to the window tables, Holly stood behind his chair. He felt a feathery kiss on his cheek, and he stood up and embraced her. Since he'd come up behind her when he had tried to seduce her, his paranoia was in full bloom. She might be mimicking his pointless attempt.

Hanging her bag on the back of her chair, she sat across the table from him. David waved to the waitress. He oozed obsequiousness as a gentle weapon in his arsenal to get out of the hole he'd dug for himself with his wife.

"Holly! You're on time. Was it an easy drive?"

"Hello, dear, and yes, it was fine."

Holy ordered a Cosmo and David another martini. She looked over at his neck brace, frowning.

"I thought you'd be healed by now. Why is that brace still on?"

"I'm sorry, honey. The air pressure is low and I get stuck with the brace. Meet me again on a clear spring day, and I'll be a well-dressed neurosurgeon on the prowl. You'd fall for me then. Right now, I'm just a woebegone hack, unable to hypnotize a weasel, forget about a classic like you." To David's utter relief, Holly began to laugh.

"You look fine, sweetheart, but I really thought you'd be healed by now. Hold on…I might have an answer. Last week, I was talking to a physical therapist at the hospital. She told me about a new massage that can rehabilitate cervical sprains. She tried it on me so I could learn it. Could I try it on you? Maybe I can free you from that pain once and for all. Get that brace off your neck."

"I'll go for anything."

David bowed his head and removed the brace, and Holly got up, and stood behind him and started to massage his neck.

"Your touch is amazing. I think it's already working."

In reality, her massage was not fixing anything. David was lying. Nevertheless, the gentle interaction between them was about to change. Their waitress was done cleaning off the nearby tabletops, and she disappeared into the kitchen. No other customers were sitting close enough to matter. Holly didn't want anyone to see what she was about to do.

Obviously, she'd lied about the hospital therapist, just an excuse for her own kind of healing. Light grew in her eyes, and blue radiance pulsed out of her fingers. She touched her husband's neck above the injury. David's face relaxed as Holly healed all the damage she'd unintentionally inflicted when she'd tossed him into the wall. What was wrong in his cervical vertebra was gone. She truly felt regret for that level of damage. Curing him was the correct thing to do.

"No...Holly, I'm serious. Your massage worked. Nothing hurts now. I'm fine!"

"That's wonderful. I guess what she told me was true."

The blue in her eyes and fingers quickly left. She didn't want David to see her own ability and she kept massaging his neck for another two minutes. David stared at the neck brace on the table, knowing he wouldn't need it anymore. That was wonderful, but that simple freedom was not enough. The future of his medical license was still circling him like a hungry shark. He couldn't stop himself. She may have good news about the financial position he was in. He blurted out a question like intestinal gas.

"I can't stand it. What's the surprise!"

"The bartender is very good; this drink tastes perfect."

"Holly, stop this. Answer me."

With a come-hither intention in her gaze, she took the sequined clutch out of her shoulder bag. And out of that smaller purse, she removed an envelope, resting it on the table between them.

"Is that the surprise? Can I open it?"

"Yes."

He ripped the envelope open.

"A hundred thousand dollars! But that check comes out of your own bank. You don't have money like that lying around. What did you do? How did you do it? Why didn't you just ask Latham to help us out? I mean, we could…"

She interrupted, "Whoa, slow down. Thought you'd be happy. I know, I know, it's not enough, but it might hold the fort until the CD matures in March. Getting the money wasn't hard. You forgot about the cottage I bought on Nantucket. I just borrowed on the equity. You can reimburse me when you get money from the next loan."

David flushed, reaching across the table to hug her and snuffle his next words into her neck, "Thank you, thank you, and thank you again! You're a Godsend.

What a surprise! I didn't know what I was going to do."

"It's not a big deal...calm down!"

He sat back, now revved up, telling her the twists and turns of the case--suddenly thinking he might actually get his medical license back. Holly appeared attentive in his monologue, but she really wasn't listening, instead musing over her backhanded blow responsible for his injury. She remained irritated with her own over-the-top action...but it was time to interrupt him.

"David...David, please...shush and listen to me."

"Yeah, sure. I've been talking too much."

"I booked a suite on the top floor of the Plaza. Would you like to spend the night with me?"

David grinned, quickly changing that smile into puzzlement. "I'm not sure. Eating cold soup in Steve's drafty apartment has been so much fun...and the taste of metal in the soup has become a delicacy for me. Hmmm? Staying in a penthouse with you or wrapping myself up in a blanket in a brownstone by myself? It's a tough decision."

The couple left the bar and went to the restaurant. After eating a lavish dinner and having Tiramisu and coffee with Frangelico for dessert, they walked over to the elevators. David felt like a kid about to unwrap his presents on Christmas morning...

Naked, he enjoyed the deepest bond he would ever have with his wife in suite 2499 on the highest floor of the Park Plaza Hotel. Holly had pushed him past any normal sexual threshold. She always does. He gives her full dominance in this part of their relationship. At that moment, his hands held her torso tight, and her back muscles contracted under his fingers. Her tendons slipped across her rib cage like they were in hot oil. Holly had the agility of a double-jointed acrobat from Cirque du Soleil, arching back and twisting above him. She writhed in abandon as he lay below her, pumping upwards inside her body. The public shall never see her carnal dance nor her upcoming rapture arriving in petite mort. She tossed David over the cliff with her, exploding together in ecstasy.

The sexual tug-of-war between them was over. David fell asleep. Holly stepped over to a window. The city sparkled in white, windows burning like jewels of gold scattered across satin pillars.

She looked at David. He looked peaceful, but he had fallen into a nightmare, believing he was walking along a hotel corridor that had no end. He began to feel uncomfortable...some of the doors on this endless corridor were half-open, too dark to see anything inside those rooms. And there was no sound coming out of any of them. He walked faster, and he was more upset. The hotel was empty. It had to be.

Reaching the end of the hall, he turned the corner facing another endless carpeted length of corridor. His uneasiness turned to fear, and he began to run. The place reminded him of the Overlook, the fictional hotel from a book called The Shining... and suddenly, he knew he was inside that building.

'No! It can't be! There's nothing in those rooms, nothing to worried about… I just…I just need to get the hell out of here as fast as I can!'

Racing around a corner, he stopped in his tracks at the foyer at the top of a staircase on the second floor leading down to the lobby. Red carpeting covered the staircase--and the lobby below. He saw a fire blazing in the fireplace on the far wall below. Any uncertainties he might have had were gone. He was in the Overlook. His screaming woke him up, and he sat up ramrod straight, bed sheets wet with sweat. The tendrils of his dream clung to him — the armoire in the corner of the room looked like a troll, and the chair, a crouched animal of some kind. These waking hallucinations quickly faded. Finally, he saw just furnishings, no more subconscious overlays. And he wasn't alone anymore. Holly was gazing through a window. Yet looking over at his wife did not have a calming effect. Her naked body was glowing in the darkness of the room, and he turned the lamp next to the bed on to stop the latest weirdness.

"Holly...HOLLY!"

As if she couldn't hear him, she just stood there motionless.

"Please…. talk to me."

Finally, Holly turned around with an expression so enigmatic he was momentarily afraid he'd fallen into another nightmare.

Cambridge, Massachusetts
12:35PM Sunday, March 27, 2005

The Trattoria De Capua was in Western Cambridge, but it was off the beaten path. Because of their chef's reputation, Justin had picked it. He checked his watch and placed the files in his briefcase on his way to a business lunch with Arthur Baxter. The man owned a cable channel with call letters that came out PYNCH. Seemed silly to Justin.

He'd reserved a table at the restaurant, but he still arrived early to check the room out. Rustic tables and chairs looked perfect in the room done in a light-colored wood. The place was trying to look like a café in a town in Italy.

Justin's table was in the corner of the room, a peaceful place for the meeting. As soon as he sat down, the waiter stepped over. He ordered a glass of merlot. Sliding the briefcase under the chair, he hoped the food would offset the boredom of his conference. Opening the menu, he disappeared behind it. Someone quietly sat down on the other side of the table, and Justin didn't know anyone was there. Putting the menu down to have a sip of wine, he suddenly looked into Alan Costa's eyes, a food critic for a city paper. The young man was Italian and Indonesian. When Justin had met him years ago, he had fallen for his buttery dark skin and his hypnotic voice.

"Hello, Jay. I didn't know you knew I was reviewing this place today! We can have lunch together! It'd be a blast!"

"Great to see you, Alan, it really is, but I'm waiting for a client. I'd rather have lunch with you, but right now, work is work. He's coming through that door any minute." Justin looked regretful, worry lines pinching his brow...and he also didn't want his client to see his lover sitting where.

One of Alan's shoulders lifted. "Alright, alright, but the coincidence is telling you something important, I think. I haven't gone out with you since the beginning of our relationship. You aren't even trying to balance your love life against this fake persona, and your problem is going to get bigger. The list of places we *can't* go to is getting longer, and our schedules aren't helping. Being pulled apart one more again is the final straw. It's breaking my back. Figure out your priorities, honey. I won't be a prisoner in a gulag your family erected around you anymore!"

Justin flinched, even though his attention was directed to the entrance of the restaurant. Alan had just burned a painful truth into him.

"He just walked in, Alan. We'll iron this whole thing out on the phone tonight. I'll call you around eight, I promise. You're right. I am going to figure out a way out of this and open up some doors for us." His words were rushing out like an auctioneer.

"Dear, dear. Are your colors showing? We can't have that happen, can we!"

Alan got up and turned on his heel, intentionally bumping into the mousey-looking man heading toward the chair he'd just vacated. Sashaying to the other side of the room, he picked out a table as far as he could get away from Justin. Having lost his patience, he was about to end their relationship.

After dinner with his client was over, Justin opened the briefcase so they could go through the contract. The work was easy, however, Alan's unforeseen arrival had torpedoed Justin's appetite. Nervous over their upcoming conversation, he watched a server set up Alan's table for the next customer to use. The love of his life had left the building. There seemed to be a finality in his latest departure. Stepping out on Huron Avenue, he said goodbye to Mr. Baxter and waved a cab down. Reaching his building, he rode the elevator up, emotions swiftly diving down. Opening the office door, he tossed his briefcase towards the couch. He wanted to lie on the floor and pound his fists, but he sat behind his desk instead. *Hiding himself away isn't going to work anymore.* Justin lowered his head to his forearms and started to cry.

His father wanted to pass the torch on to him. He wanted him to continue the Donnelly legacy, and he felt stuck. A rainbow flag wrapped around his crotch; he had been living in two worlds, and it seemed those painful days were about to end one way or another. His brother and sister can't help him. Robert was an addict, and Holly...well, she'd been a mystery from the beginning. He didn't know what to tell her.

Justin got up and reached the opposite wall in the office. He pressed a panel. The bookshelves that were there swiveled inward, and a wet bar took its place. Pouring himself a shot of Chivas Regal, he instantly drank it. The liquid burned the back of his throat, searing its way down. He hoped it would burn his soul, too. The phone call with Alan seemed impossible. He could not tell him anything, pacing the office like a caged animal. His business phone rang. He wouldn't pick up; the caller could just leave him a message.

"Hello...Justin. I know you're there. You have to hear new information I have for you... Jay, damn it, pick up!"

An honorable brother, he decided to answer. "Hello, Holly. What's got you so fired up? I am in the middle of a workday, and I have no time." He thought he sounded calm enough.

"You're upset, and you shouldn't be. Dad's hard to pin down, but I got my hands on him last week, right before he flew to one of his endless meetings in Boston. We drank espresso in the solarium next to the pool." She took a very deep breath. Holly was about to tell him an unbelievable story; better off explaining the moon was made out of blue cheese instead. Beginning with the fact that Holly had never been close to Latham, she was afraid her brother would dismiss whatever she told him as hokum. She decided to try it anyway. There's a chance it might work.

"We haven't heard his opinion about homosexuality in quite a while, so I tested the water.

Things have changed in his outlook. Since society has accepted it, and some of us idolize it…"

Justin interrupted her, "Holly, stop. You're out in space, talking about nothing. I have no interest in what *you* think the world thinks about sexuality. My father remains a relic from the Middle Ages. I guess you forgot; he has rejected you too. He is already on the warpath against Robert. I'm the only one left to continue the family line. His future plans for me have gotten more intense after I got back from Massachusetts. He wants to play tennis with me, and I'm antsy about it. If he ever realizes I'm gay, he'd disinherit me, for sure. You're telling me you found a way to get me out of his own mess, oh, *sis* of mine?"

At that point, Justin was desperate. His relationship with Alan was about to end, and if he told his father about his relationship, he'd toss him out of the family. His ingrown prejudice that Holly could fix things wasn't powerful enough to win against her father's prejudice against her. He didn't think her sweet tales could find any root in Latham's mind.

"A martyr on the cross bleeding, I see," Holly said. She hadn't given up yet. "I'm telling you something important. I raised the subject to Dad. You have to listen to me, *bro*."

"I had a terrible afternoon trying to answer an unanswerable question--but for you, grasshopper, I'll meditate on what you are about to impart." Justin threw back another shot of scotch.

"I asked Dad about the current shows and movies about gay lifestyles, and he told me some of them were funny."

Justin stayed quiet.

"I swear, he said that. His limo driver is gay, and Dad told me he saw you and Alan in that bistro in Guardian Cross...the place you guys hide out in sometimes. Of course, the driver was a blabbermouth. He assumed Latham knew about your personal life."

"Oh my God! He'll kill me, I think--"

"Stop! Stop the hysterics! Dad told him he'd suspected you were gay. You've shown up with girlfriends, leaving your love life a mystery. Now he knows the truth. He's okay with it. Knowing it's still hearsay, he hopes you're straight--but he's not stupid. The unwanted update from his driver, assuming it was true, left him resigned. This possible truth has not yet gotten a royal decree of banishment out of him."

"What else did he say?"

"He's not in the mood to meet Alan, but you can come out of the closet. Go where you want."

"He said that?" Justin looked like he was staring at a ghost, not his desk in the office. "'I accept my son's homosexuality.' You heard him say those words?"

"Yes, he did; he really did. At least, that's what I remember."

Justin kept asking her questions, slowly and reluctantly accepting most of Holly's story. Maybe talking to Alan wouldn't be so bad... invite him to that hot dance club downtown. He would like that! The whole world could see them together now. Dad has seen the light. And why would Holly fabricate a convoluted story like that? Besides...she was on his side. No reason for her to make it all up! Dad must have changed. Of course, he wasn't going to call him about any of this. That would be weird. He'll broach the subject after their tennis game.

Miles above Plymouth, Massachusetts
11:45AM Sunday, April 17, 2005

Flying on a thermal updraft, Slethim stabilized a mile up as the sun warmed its feathered shoulders. Golden eyes scanning the countryside below, it watched worshippers leaving a church. That amused the entity...from that distance, humans were like ants walking in treacle, not enough intelligence in their tiny doll heads bobbing along in the parking lot.

Raising a wing, it swept southeast and dropped two hundred feet lower just an hour before reaching Bass River.

Bass River, Massachusetts
11:55AM Sunday, April 17, 2005

Parking in front of the mansion, Justin stayed in the driver's seat for a few minutes. He was worried for a lot of reasons. The wind was powerful, lashing tree limbs around. That could ruin his game. He had on beige chinos, a T-shirt, and a white sweater--he was also wearing his *perfect* sneakers. Not the most comfortable, they would give him more traction. They were worth the trade. Reaching over the seat, he grabbed the racket. He'd gotten better, and his father must have slower reflexes by now. Today will be the tipping point. And he'll win more than a tennis game! He jogged around the house and met Latham on the patio.

"Justin, great to see you! We'll have fun breaking the new acrylic layer in on the court." He shook his son's hand enthusiastically, accompanied by a manly hug. The streaks of green in Justin's eyes made Latham think of April's hazel ones. He still wasn't sure if he wanted Jay to be part of his Russian adventure anymore. Cutting his entire family off was gaining hold. Just cut the cancerous growth off, and he'd be cured. Flying solo after his divorce might be the correct answer.

"Hello, Dad. We'll have a great time because I know you'll lose. Do your damnedest. I'm about to bounce you right out of the winner's circle." Justin's grin was wide, and he looked happy.

"Go ahead and believe. You probably think water runs uphill, too. I'm not worried. Nothing will save you from my backhand...oh, by the way, Mom arranged our lunch next to the pool today. It's windy, but those plastic barriers around the table should make things comfortable enough."

"We'll be hungry, for sure. Are we going to play two sets as usual?"

"Sure."

Latham walked onto the court while Justin sat down on a bench to retie his sneakers, adjusting the tension in his laces. Looking out at the court, he could see that his father had held onto his agility since the last time he'd played with him. He was bouncing the ball on his racket and getting impatient.

The game began. Justin was working just as hard as he ever did in the past. His confidence faltered, the easy triumph drifting away in the irritating wind. Latham's long legs transported him to almost all of Justin's far-flung balls without a hitch. After going through their exhausting volleys, Latham's endurance held. It seemed that Justin's five-year absence had not affected much, even as he fired Latham's aggressively aimed balls back at him with tiring vengeance.

Latham won six games, Justin five. A pivotal juncture in their contest. If Latham wins the next game, he'll win the match. If Justin wins, they will play another game to break the tie. Latham had expertly sent his ball to the far-right corner of the court, just an inch inside the boundary line. It was a dangerous maneuver, but it appeared to have worked. Latham thought the game was done. His son would never reach the ball in time. Yet Justin's longing had ramped him up as he raced to that far corner, actually returning the ball. He watched it sail over the net, enjoying the feeling of accomplishment, before it bounced out of bounds. He lost the match.

April told Vince that morning that their lunch would be outside. Cutlery, plates, crystal goblets, and a linen tablecloth were now defying the wind's impudence with heavy plastic barriers set up around the table. Having explained to Vince and Mirabelle that the meal would be at the Gazebo at twelve-thirty, she had already ordered chicken salad, ham and spinach quiche, corn chowder, and a bowl of fresh fruit the day before. Now, it will be sent out there. After a few hours, she stopped at the kitchen for a cursory visit. Everything was moving along, and she returned to her suite to freshen up.

Married to a wealthy man has it's perks. She hadn't broken into a sweat as she set up this sumptuous lunch for her family. Relaxing in her suite, she knew her loneliness would soon recede when Justin got there. Straightening her hair and makeup out, she went to the pool to stretch out on a lounge chair…out of the wind. She imagined living on a tropical island with Peter next winter. Hearing Latham and Justin talking on the other side of the hedge wall, she got up and glanced over at the table. Everything was fine. As they came around the corner, she waved.

"Hello, Jay!" April hugged him and pecked his cheek. "How did the game go? You trounced him right."

"Hi, Mom. Yeah…not so much. Going for the gold, I felt sorry for him at the last minute. I allowed him to win one more time. Couldn't let his world crumble and watch him cry like a baby."

Latham stood behind him, laughing. "It's your world I crushed, Justin. I didn't have to work too hard to do it either. You just need a few more lessons…well, maybe more than a few."

Father and son sat at the table and reached for the pitcher of iced tea at the same time. Justin demurred. April came over. Latham stood up and pulled a chair out for her. The meal began. Their conversation included Justin's law business and people they both knew. Justin was nervous. He felt weird bringing up his own social life--but it was important. It had to be done. Courageously, he dove in. *Maybe he'll win something after all...*

"A bird whispered to me that you'd heard about my hideaway in Worcester. The place my lover and I go once in a while."

April's eyes widened and froze as her fork hung between the plate and her mouth until she happily declared, "Well, it's about time! What's her name? Why didn't you bring her with you? How long have you been seeing her? We were so afraid you were homosexual! Thank God, that confusion is finally done."

Justin stared at his father. "You didn't tell Mom about this?"

"I don't have anything to tell her, Jay, but who cares! This is wonderful. Tell us all about your hideaway. I don't know why you've been hiding your love life away from us for so long."

April jumped back in. "After you got your degree, you never brought any of your dates over to the house. Three weeks ago, we thought something was badly wrong. I was crying, Jay! I really was. I was afraid I wouldn't be able to see you again. Dad was going to change his will and everything. What a relief! Why were you so mysterious about her? Is there something wrong? Tell us!"

Justin turned pale. Sweat beaded on his forehead as the truth burned into his head. *I'm not winning a damned thing today and maybe lose the entire enchilada too. Gotta fix this faux pa real fast...*

Whatever redemption he'd hoped for wasn't there, and Justin felt like he was in free fall. The reaction he'd gotten from his parents had confused him. It was harder to answer their question with new lies to save his hide. He drank some iced tea as an excuse to get his thoughts together, and he swallowed a lot of it before he put his glass down.

"Slow down." Justin patted the air in front of him. "Her name is Lena, and I broke up with her last week. I was afraid to tell you about our fight. Right now, I'm heartbroken over the entire thing. I can't tell you the details right now...excuse me...my calf muscle is cramping. I need to walk it out, be back in a few." He hobbled off on a fake limp.

"I'll put fruit salad in your bowl, okay," April called out. "You can have that when you get back. We'll talk things over and come up with new beginnings."

Justin didn't turn around as he disappeared behind the wall of hedges. Latham's interest in his love life was gone like yesterday's weather. He put more chicken salad on his plate and thought over his future in Russia.

Soon out of sight, he stopped limping and moved deeper into the maze. His upper body actually did cramp in anger over Holly's ridiculous story. He didn't really have that full freedom to be with Alan, and he couldn't hang out at the estate with him. Justin's sudden exasperation was profound. It triggered an emotional catalyst as frustration savaged his conscience into threads. Criminal solutions slowly filtered into his head, and he began to sing...

"Living a lie until they die, oh my, oh my, bye, bye, bye!"

The dreadful ditty ended with a giggle. Justin sauntered along, still humming, hands clenched into fists. His back muscles let go when he reached the center of the maze, and he looked up. A shadow had passed above him. Shielding his eyes from the glare, he assumed it had been a hawk, but whatever it was flew out of sight.

Part II

*"It's wrong to hear melody in dissonance,
and dancing to it is even worse."*
                                        Keith Fischer

New Bedford, Massachusetts
11:30AM Monday, May 2, 2005

David stumbled to the kitchen half-asleep. The belt of the robe he'd put over his PJs had hooked the knob of the closet in the hallway pulling the robe off his shoulders. He left it behind. Getting back from Boston hadn't made him feel any better. His case was stalled, and Holly ignored him—liquor was his only solace. Believing that his father-in-law would give him a loan should have given him hope and a new direction. Perhaps restraining his drinking. It had not. He just waited for the money. Holly told him Latham would wire two hundred thousand dollars to his lawyer's account in a week or so. And that did not raise his spirits either.

Taking coffee and filters out of the cabinet, David set the machine up and flipped it on. He sat down at the table to get lost in the silver reflections on the coffee urn. He dozed off and almost slipped off the chair. The house phone on the counter rang. He answered with sleep, blurring his response.

"Hello."

"David, is that you? It's Wilson. Something came up. The judge is impatient. There was a sudden cancellation, and he wants your case off his desk faster than a summer storm. Your hearing was supposed to happen on June 10th, but it's been rescheduled to May 10th. The hundred thousand you were supposed to send us next week, we need now…by the end of today. Got it?"

"Well, good morning, Wilson."

"I can't sugarcoat this."

"Yeah, yeah. The poison pill will never taste sweet, no matter what you coat it with. I'll get you the money by Wednesday. It's the best I can do."

"I guess it'll have to do. Add twenty-five thousand on top of the extra overtime I need to go through to get your case set up for the hearing that fast. Listen, David, I can't use any more credit on your bill. If we go in there unprepared, you'll lose your license. Get those funds over here by Wednesday morning, and don't forget the extra twenty-five thousand. If it's all there, you have a chance for dismissal."

"So, get me off the phone. I have to get this in gear."

"You're right. The judge has put you in a squeeze play. I'll sign right off." Wilson sounded amused, not concerned. "Life is a chess game, and you have to get out of this checkmate. Call me when you avoid the evil queen's approach." He laughed at his metaphors and then hung up.

David was worried. Calling his father-in-law to tell him to speed up the transfer won't be easy. '*Hi, 'Lath,' old buddy. Just wire me all the money to my law firm right now instead of next week.*' He'd likely bite his head off and swallow it.

But David needed a positive attitude, imagining Latham relaxing at home in a great mood, accepting anything. He poured more coffee into his cup and decided to put good clothes on. Wearing acceptable attire for the call would be like offering a gift to the gods. If Latham doesn't help him, his medical career is over.

Latham was home from his trip. He had just gone to New York, Connecticut, New Jersey, and Washington to find the right employees for his team in Russia. They'd meet him there in the next few weeks. At that moment, he was tired, looking forwards to a short hiatus at his estate. The house phone rang. He ignored it, seeing himself floating in the pool. Mirabelle's voice came up on the intercom. His son-in-law wanted to talk to him. Normally, Latham would ignore him, but the fact that David had actually called him tweaked his curiosity. He told Mirabelle to patch him through.

"Hello, David. Is the house on fire? What's up?"

"Hello, Latham. I didn't want to bother you, but Wilson told me the court schedule has changed. My case jumped forward by a month...so it's important to wire the money now. I thought it wouldn't be too much of an imposition to do that today or tomorrow?"

Latham grinned, and his smile widened like the cat who'd eaten the canary. "Not sure I understand your situation."

David gulped. His response was not good...but it wasn't over yet. "Holly tells me you'll wire five hundred thousand dollars to my account next week. Again, I'm sorry to bother you, sir, but Wilson tells me about the rescheduling. My firm needs the money to iron out the details asap."

"Sorry to burst your bubble, but I haven't talked to Holly about any of this. You're married to her, for God's sake. You should know that."

"You don't remember the conversation you had with her in the library at the reunion to open one of your CDs--and let me use the money for my defense team. I'm sure she explained that to you. And, of course, I'll reimburse you as soon as I get back to work." David got a funny feeling in his belly.

"Yeah, I talked to her at the reunion, that's true, but she didn't mention anything about your financial problems or your court case."

David was now in panic mode. "I guess this is a last-minute plea for help. I can borrow one hundred and twenty-five thousand dollars just for a couple of weeks anyway. You know I'm good for it." He heard laughter on the other side of the line. "This isn't funny, Latham. I'm about to lose my license, and I really--"

Latham off-handedly ended the call and walked over into his closet to get his swimming shorts.

David heard the click, and he dropped the phone. It bounced off the carpet and landed three feet away. Standing against the wall, he sank to the floor while new ways to fix his problem popped into his head. A burglar could walk in and knock him out with a sap and leave him in a coma, or maybe a rabid dog could run down the hall and sink its teeth into his throat for a final bloody ending.

He stopped the ridiculous visions and went to the bathroom to get the small bottle of Lexotan out of the cabinet. Fingers shaking, he opened the bottle and

142

popped two pills into his mouth. Twenty minutes before, the tranquilizing drug kicked in. He tossed the bottle in the sink and checked his watch. David burst outside, leaving the front door wide open, quickly reaching the first intersection before sprinting around the corner of Cowlip Lane. He was going nowhere fast. At Route 22, the chemical, more powerful than Ativan or Valium, began to work, and he slowly down...to a stop. The paranoid terror was gone. His trip home had become a crawl. Reaching Merchant Drive, he staggered until he stumbled into the house, slamming the door behind him with a drunken bang.

Holly had been stringing him along! He wanted to punch her, but he knew that would have been disastrous since she had previously slapped him twelve feet through the air and into the fireplace. Fisticuffs with Holly was not an option, and it's wrong to hit a woman anyway. Currently, he was a drunken neurosurgeon out of work and living on her money. He must accept being a househusband with a smile and look unruffled — for now. He'd turn the tables on her down the road.

Zombified, he poured himself into the chair in the corner of the living room, hands resting on the armrests. He stared down at his cufflinks to fall into a dreamless sleep.

David and Holly's neighbors usually get home at around five or so, windows lighting up and the sound of pots and pans clattering and televisions blaring out. That day, their home remained dark, a break in the lively chain. Since David was out cold, he hadn't turned anything on.

Holly wheeled into the driveway at 8:15 PM, garage door rising and yard lights flickering on with the remote she was holding in her hand. Getting out of the car, she paused at the panel near the inside door. She switched the lights in the house on with one stroke of her forearm and stepped into the living room, dropping her office satchel on the couch.

"Hello, David. Are you napping?" She stepped over and patted his leg. "I'll microwave an Italian dinner from Scotto's and toss a salad together. Do you want something to eat?"

No answer. Holly walked away. She took her computer out of the bag and plugged it into the nearest outlet. Pushing her palms to the ceiling in a relaxed stretch, she took the barrette out of her hair. A glossy river cascaded down her back as she went into the kitchen. David's voice finally came to life, and she turned around.

"Revive my membership in the Bourdon Club, and I need an allowance. I'll brush up on my golf game this summer."

"Just tell me how much you want per month…oh, I called Bourdon yesterday. We're both signed up for the season. Not sure how much time I'll have to play, but at least it's set up…so do you want some eggplant rollatini?"

David would still not answer that question. After hours of sitting, his joints popped like he was an old man when he stood up. He limped over to the bar, still not straightened out. Holly had raised the living room lights to the brightest level when she got here. He dimmed them almost off and poured himself a shot of brandy. Holly was busy tossing a salad on a plate, utterly unfazed by his oncoming silence. Inserting her dinner into the microwave, she returned to the dining room and turned her PC on. The microwave would beep when dinner was done.

The living room and the dining room were included in one large space. David just hung out in the darkened living room and stared over at Holly like a dangerous shadow. She glanced over at him with an off-handed smile, not at all concerned over the treacherous glint in his eyes. Holly's frustration over her brothers and her own husband's penchant for living in deceit had finally driven her into fabrications of her own with the idea of pushing them into accepting the truth to make them live their lives honestly. She was young. Holly didn't realize what she'd done. She didn't understand that you can't exorcise a demon using the same doublespeak to get them out. And her own unusual genealogy may have also tilted her viewpoint.

Be that as it may, the dire consequences for the family would have happened whether she'd said anything or not...and she certainly had not yet left a boat sinking under the dearth of morality. The rest of the Donnellys had just raised the pirate flag, skull, and crossbones, flapping in their own wind of greed even as the water reached the deck.

New Bedford, Massachusetts
1:17PM Wednesday, June 15, 2005

The Bourdon Golf Club's dining room and outside café opened at 6:30 AM, and the entire business closed at 7:00 PM. David picked at his congealed Eggs Florentine under an umbrella on the outside patio while Mr. Duncan Hartley, a local congressman, sat with him, busy pontificating. This discourse didn't bother David, occasionally nodding and agreeing. They'd just played eighteen holes together on a picturesque day. Hartley's score remained two under par, and he won the game.

David had gone through the court case in May, and his medical license was revoked. Seemed losing was his middle name.

The congressman was leaving, and he shook David's hand while they set up another game next week. Holly dashed over in tennis whites and holding a racket.

"Hello, Mr. Hartley, nice to see you. What a day!" Shaking the older man's hand, Holly went on, "It's great to be outside. Breathing in the smell of lilacs with a blue sky over my head is enough to make me a winner."

Duncan appreciated her, glowing in her short white skirt and tank top. He pecked her on her cheek. "My, my Holly, you are a delight. Now I want to stay and chat, but I have a meeting with my cousin at three, and I'm already running late. I must skedaddle."

"Thank you for your compliment, sir. I pray your day goes well."

He walked away, tossing a royal wave over his shoulder. Holly turned her attention to David. "Why didn't you eat your eggs, dear. I thought you liked the cooking here."

"Hello, Holly." He did not answer her question. "How did tennis become part of your work week?"

"Not a scheduled event, mind you, but the game was necessary to bring the prize home." She grinned. "I wheedled a donation out of Raytheon. One of the board members told me he loved tennis, and I told him I felt the same way."

David looked up at her. "You don't like tennis. It must be a huge donation if you were running around like a maniac out there on the court."

"It was a great game, and I loved it! He's meeting me in my office to draw up some paperwork. Raytheon is donating three million dollars to the hospital. Of course, the east section of our building will soon bear their name--I've got to run, get ready for the meeting."

"What does the company make?"

"Marine electronics for government ships and independent owners. The main factory is in Braintree. They were interested in our own research projects, so I decided to shake their tree. It worked. See you later."

David watched her gracefully move towards the parking lot. Then he returned to his dilemma. A helpless, hapless drunk shriveling in his wife's shadow, he felt too young to be forgotten... like a rotten log in the woods.

147

Taking his cell phone out of his jacket, he decided to set up a meeting with Justin, who lived in Cambridge. He could ask him if there might still be a chance to get his license back on an appeal. A week ago, Holly had told him Justin was angry at Latham. If that's true, they could both commiserate over the irritating power he had over their lives. He hit auto-dial.

"Hi, Justin."

"Hello, David. What's up?"

"I have an appointment on Friday morning in the city. Can you meet me for a drink? I have a few questions for you."

"Sure. Is late afternoon okay?"

"Fine. Would six at the Swan's Nest at the Boston Plaza Hotel work?"

"I'll see you there."

Boston, Massachusetts
5:45PM Friday, June 17, 2005

Staring into the mirror behind the bar, David changed his expression. He was trying to erase the furrowed lines on his forehead. David knew the chances of reinstating his license were bleak, and he felt like a puckered raisin—no sweetness left.

Justin's last appointment ended at six, and he didn't go back to his condo to change. He was already wearing the right uniform of the upwardly mobile professional with the necessary moral instability stitched into the seams. A taxi dropped him outside the Plaza, and he trotted to the main door, hugging his raincoat tight to his body. He didn't want to drive home after having a few drinks, and he'd left his BMW in Cambridge.

Entering the bar, he saw David at the bar. His fashion sense was still flawless, fusing nut-brown corduroy pants to a sports jacket---but he looked forlorn. Justin shook his head. Most women would take him home, give him cookies and milk, and then offer themselves up as the last morsel to swallow. He checked his raincoat, liking the swans in the mirror above the bar. David walked over to his brother-in-law and shook his hand.

"I guess the secret order of solicitors gave you a pass to kick your heels up with a civilian today."

"Hello, David." Justin ignored his hand and gave him a short hug. "Come on, I wouldn't miss a meeting with you, considering what's been going on. We both need to laugh and cry and commiserate over the keelhauling." He slapped him on his shoulder, and they both sat down on the barstools. "How's your case going? Heard it wrapped up."

"Wrapped up? No, it imploded, and I sank. I can't practice medicine anymore. Your sister told me a whopper, and I believed her. Isn't pyrite as good as gold?"

The bartender came over. Justin ordered a White Russian and David another martini.

"Not surprised you got duped," Justin said. "Holly should have been a lawyer, born with a knack to make anyone believe anything, fairytales into scientific truths. Have you noticed her interest in the family lately? She told me a story so ridiculous my head began to spin like a top." He used falsetto to mimic her voice, "Dad knows you're gay, and it's fine with him!" He then returned to his normal range. "This nugget of hers was given to me during a phone call. Playing tennis with Dad a few days later, I almost cut my own throat by saying something I stopped myself from saying at the last second….no, you're not alone in the lake of stupid. And you're right. Fool's gold shines, waving it in her hands!"

David sighed. "At least you didn't fall into boiling oil. Remember when she disappeared and talked to Dad after dinner? When we drove home that night, Holly told me Latham would pay my legal bills. And I believed her. Didn't know that truth was a jump for months. I wonder what she really did talk to him about. It had nothing to do with my loan. I never got a hot cent from Latham."

Justin swallowed the rest of his drink. "Personally, I don't care what happened at the reunion, and I'm not looking forwards to the next one. I'd bow out if I could. Dad acts like a preacher from the eighteen-hundreds, not the power-hungry capitalist he really is."

A large screen above the bar was on a sports game, and soft rock came out of the speakers. "Message in a Bottle" ended, and "Sultans of Swing" started up.

Justin and David quickly got well-oiled, and the level of their conversation dropped a notch.

"I should put poison in the ham I'm sending." Justin smiled. "Yup, I'm supposed to send one over. I can create a toxic Thanksgiving, and I can stay home. All my problems end up dead on the dining room floor."

"Fine idea, Jay, but will you give me a heads-up? I'll stay with the turkey."

"It's just a joke." Justin sighed with regret. "I'll go and be polite. The perfect son living the righteous life. I have no other options. When I watch my father slice the damned bird, I know I'll want to take that blade away from him... and carve something else instead!"

Two middle-aged women sipping sherry a stool away heard him, powdered faces constricted in distaste. Justin grinned at them, trying to look evil. They began whispering to each other.

"You've frightened them," David said.

"The plan worked!" Justin waved over at them, and they cringed.

"Look, I need your advice on the revocation of my license," David said. "Is there still a chance an appeal might work? Could I get back to work or forget the whole thing?"

"I'm in commercial law, I don't know much about malpractice cases...I do know appeals are expensive."

"That doesn't sound good."

"I have an acquaintance in that field. I can ring him up right now. I have enough to flesh it out for him. Who knows--maybe there's something you can do."

Justin stood up. "I'll get over to the corner of the room. It's quieter over there."

"Thanks. A miracle would be nice."

David turned around and talked to the bartender about the Super Bowl for a few minutes. Justin came back quickly enough.

"My friend will accept your case, but it doesn't look good. Usually, appeals leave him richer, and most doctors don't get their licenses back. This guy's good, David. I'm sorry." Justin shook his head.

"Thanks for checking it out for me. Even if your friend might be giving me better odds, it wouldn't matter. I'm tapped, drained, and busted financially. The only income I have now is an allowance from my wife." David smiled and drank the rest of his martini.

They grumbled to each other for another hour until Justin asked for the bar menu. Ordering sirloin burgers, they wolfed them down and paid the exorbitant bill without a murmur, leaving a nice tip for the bartender.

David followed his brother-in-law out on the rain-swept street. "The showers aren't stopping."

Justin looked over at him and shrugged, buttoning his coat. "Are you staying with your friend? I'm taking a cab so I can drop you off."

"Sounds great, thanks. You haven't changed your mind about the dinner idea, have you? You aren't really going to send a poisoned ham? I need to know for sure."

Waving down a cab, Justin chuckled. "As much as I want to do it, I can't. I just can't. It's reprehensible."

A taxi stopped, and they got in. The car tires hisses off on the wet streets of Boston. Dropping David off six blocks away, the driver then took Longfellow Bridge over the Charles River, reaching the Regatta Riverview Residences on Museum Way. Justin paid his fare and got out.

The burger had stabilized his belly, but it hadn't sobered him up. Wobbling, he crossed the lobby and got in the elevator. He leaned against the wall and closed his eyes. What would it be like to actually poison the ham? That got stuck in his head.

Entering his apartment, it was fairly large. The only light was coming from the main windows, but it was enough to find the fridge. Taking out a bottle of water, he flopped in a chair. He usually didn't turn the lights on when he got home. He liked to look out at the city and the bridges crossing the river in a panoramic view. It helped him to zone out after a stressful day--- like a seagull flying above it all. Gazing out at the cityscape this time, he couldn't get the new idea out of his head...*what if his whole family was gone? What if his joke became reality?*

He sipped his water with concentration. The previous absurdity of it transformed into plausibility. A heavenly picture of Alan and himself sitting in the hot tub near the pool on his parent's property came into his head. Alan wore a bikini bottom, and he could see his buttery skin... It was late spring, and the sweet aroma of lilacs hung in the air. They held hands. Justin pushed the button on the intercom next to the tub, and Mirabelle answered.

"Yes sir, what do you require of me?"

"Black caviar, truffles, and two hurricanes. Please call Maurice to schedule our massages at five under the gazebo---and don't forget the multi-colored umbrellas on those drinks!"

New Bedford, Massachusetts
11:13AM Sunday, June 19, 2005

According to the bedside clock, it was eleven fifteen. Holly was gone. She disappears on Sunday morning. Justin had no idea where she was going. Getting out of bed, he put his robe on, forgetting to tie the belt, dragging it behind on the floor. On his trip to the kitchen, the belt hooked the closet corner in the hallway, wrenching the robe off his shoulders. He left it there. Setting the coffee machine up, he remembered the exact same thing happening a few months ago. Was he living in a loop, like the Groundhog Day movie?

Justin's answers were clear. There was no cure for his condition, and the dead couldn't come back to life. Pouring himself a cup of fresh coffee, he sat at the kitchen table, hung over and morose. Holly had left the paper on the table, and he flipped through the pages. A memorial for someone named Arthur Mercer captivated him for no logical reason. Mercer's family owned the largest shipyard in New Bedford, and he had been a cornerstone of the community. David stared at the picture of Mercer's friends and relatives gathered around his mausoleum. He put the paper down and closed his eyes. The memory of the dream he'd had the night before took over...*he was standing in a cemetery, the only mourner at the burying of five coffins. There was no one around besides the priest and himself. A silhouette of a female flittered between the tombs, quickly vanishing. The clergyman read an obscure passage out of the Bible--and then he stepped over to David. "You've been blessed, son! You are free."*

The holy man gave him a key. Chains hidden in the priest's robes were revealed, and he raised them over his head and threw them into the open grave.

Justin's joke about poisoning the ham ignited this dream. Opening his eyes, he knew he had found the answer.

Cambridge, Massachusetts
11:25AM Sunday, June 19, 2005

He was on his way to the exercise room on the third floor. Justin would sweat the bad out of his body. Powerwalking out of the elevator and into the fitness center, he reached the treadmills lined up near the windows. Putting his vitamin-enriched water and the Sunday paper in the holdings on one of the machines, he started in.

The screen in front of him lit up an hour later. He'd reached the four-mile marker, hair plastered to his forehead. He was not done yet, and he continued reading an article about oyster stuffing. It made him think about the reunion.

After meeting David, something bad happened. An evil force began to grow like a black pearl in his subconscious mind, and the article dragged a slimy, wicked thing out into the light.

Four years ago, he'd dealt with a case connected to a poisoning in a Japanese restaurant in Connecticut. The victim insisted he had eaten puffer fish flesh, and that was responsible for his sickness. The restaurant owner insisted that the item was not on his menu on the date he was there.

The puffer fish naturally secretes a neurotoxin called tetrodotoxin. Justin had done a lot of research on it. The fish is now banned in the United States but still served in Japan. Customers at a Fugu Palace can order the puffer fish, and occasionally, a customer dies from eating it. Normally, the poison was removed before it was cooked, however, the cleaning process was not always perfect. A bit of tetrodotoxin sometimes gets missed. A warning on the menu takes away any legal action the customer's family might have against that possibility.

Other animals also exude the same poison. A rough-skinned newt has enough tetrodotoxin in its small body to end thirty people, and a festive-looking octopus is just as deadly. Tetrodotoxin is one of the fastest toxins in the natural world, fifty times more lethal than cyanide.

Jusin won his case. Anyone ingesting tetrodotoxin would not be talking about it. It was coincidental that he'd learned about that toxin, enough information to allow him to set up a plan with pretty good precision. Shellfish toxin effects were similar to tetrodotoxin. In the beginning, anyway. He wanted to associate the similarity with the oysters in the stuffing.

He guzzled down the rest of his water and got off the treadmill, hanging his towel around his neck, paper under his arm. He almost ran to the elevators. Time to get to work.

Injecting tetrodotoxin into oyster stuffing should trick the investigators...at first, assuming it was paralytic shellfish toxin. Of course, the lab tests wouldn't match anything an oyster could produce. Their attention would probably turn to his father's competitors in the upcoming investigation. Allergic to shellfish himself, Justin would survive simply by happenstance, unable to eat the turkey---or the stuffing.

While he had an invigorating show. He began to think of ways to get the poison without leaving a trail coming back to him.

New Bedford, Massachusetts
1:22PM Tuesday, June 21, 2005

In white chinos and a cotton T-shirt, David relaxed on a lounge chair on the covered porch in his backyard. He gazed down at the sand garden on the table in front of him. A neon green straw disappeared into his mouth, allowing him to suck vodka-infused iced tea out of the large tumbler. He was off-handedly pushing a tiny rake through the fine sand of the garden.

Holly had left a gift-wrapped box next to their front door. She'd left a note on the box: 'The secretary left this in my office—enjoy!' David ignored it until Sunday afternoon. After a late lunch at the golf club, curiosity finally drove him into unwrapping it. A sand garden. He left it on the kitchen counter. The next day, it would not stop raining. David wandered through the house, stuck. He couldn't figure out what the golden key in his dream had really meant. As the heavy raindrops pounded the roof, his head remained blank.

The next morning was dry and brisk. Going through the breakfast ritual, David was frustrated. His logic circuits were still offline. It was a difficult juncture. Anything could get him back on track--- maybe he should move some sand in the silly garden. Maybe it might help.

He sucked at the straw until there was nothing left in the cup. David stepped over to the outside bar. Opening the small refrigerator, he grabbed the vodka bottle. The cold glass on the skin of his hand prompted the link he'd been looking for; a puzzle piece found in a remembrance.

He'd been having a conversation with another neurosurgeon named John Armata at a cocktail party a few years ago. They'd been standing next to the swimming pool...the smell of chlorine floating up to his.

Pouring more vodka into his cup, he pinpointed the pertinent part of their talk, and David sat back in the lounge chair. He'd found it, word for word:

"You didn't see the insert in last week's Sunday paper, did you?" John said. "How did you avoid the front page! *Four Found Killed by Yew*." The bodies were found near a burned-out cooking fire in the woods. The closest town to where they were was Dunstable on Route 113. I live on Rockville Road. I'm the only neighbor the Lyman family had. They owned the acres the kids got lost in." Doctor Armata sipped his daiquiri.

"I was in a clinical study, John."

David's precise recall went on...

"It was a test for non-responsive coma patients. If Holly hadn't dragged me out, I would have stayed in that lab forever...so no, I didn't see the news. Sounds like a strange story." He was leaning against a pillar supporting a high trellis thick with vines. "You were the only neighbor, John? You must know more about the story than most."

"You're right! Last year, Melissa and Phillip were happy when I bought the adjoining property. It's desolate out there...anyway, they called me as soon as it started. Their daughter was home for the summer, riding out on those back trails. She was following a track along the creek when she found the bodies. Three law students and another had been learning archeology. They'd watched the Blair Witch Project movie. The weird mysteries in the movie had sent them out there. The budding archeologist really thought the lost farmhouse was on Lyman's land. In 1965, a different group tramped into those same woods to find the farmhouse. No one ever saw them again. The locals aren't sure if there's anything out there, and flying over the land didn't help. Too overgrown.

The students were trying to find the building, but they got lost. Reaching a stream, they thought it would lead them out of the woods, but they ran out of food. Seeing a yew tree, they thought it was a holly. They made a cooking fire and boiled the berries and wild grass in a metal pot. The poison inside the berries killed them."

"I'll look it up. The media usually bombards us about the dangers in our own backyards as if the end of the world as we know it is growing in our gardens."

"They are over the top... I still can't believe you haven't heard about it!"

"I'll read up on it now. A plant in the forest stopped four lives! Did you ever ask your neighbors about the lost farmhouse? They might have a hint on where it might be?"

David broke away from this recollection, and he picked up the tiny rake, gently pulling it across the length of the garden. He'd lied to John. He'd never read anything about the case, but now he'd change his fabrication into fact. A sudden devotee' of the Yew Tree, he'd dig up everything he could find about that plant.

Las Vegas, Nevada
9:35PM Friday, August 26, 2005

Good luck had blessed his gambling for over a year---but it had suddenly vanished. Walking past the slot machines, he could hear them jabbering and jangling with a more somber dirge hiding in the background.

Samuel stopped in a rest area on Interstate 15, sixty miles from Sin City. He'd closed his account in San Diego, wiring the fifty thousand to his bank in Las Vegas. The last of his money.

Resting his palms on the guardrail, he stared out at the city, pulsing out there on the horizon, a neon heart replacing his own. The last time he crossed the desert, his cousin's check was burning a hole in his pocket, and the AC in the rental was barely holding on. This time, he crossed the badlands after sunset in a sports car. It was more comfortable, but that would not save him in the end. He stood alone in the rest area. Clarity slammed into his head, washing his addiction away in a touch of preservation.

He'd run a long way on Rick's loan, but he was running out of time. Living in his own chaos, he was sinking into quicksand. Annihilation waited for him in Las Vegas. Late on his payments to Cindy, he parked somewhere different every night to avoid her goons.

Standing in the cool isolation off the interstate, he finally realized he had another option...just drive over the Canadian border and deposit his check in a bank in some small town on the coast of Hudson Bay and start

161

a new life. Forget gambling. Forget the tantalizing seconds he gets when he feels immortal. Forget the unforgettable. Samuel got back in the car and started the engine.

The Ferrari engine rumbled as he leaned against the seat cushions, poised between two opposite directions. North to freedom, or should he return to the illusion? Eyes half-closed, he felt drawn to the shadowy shrubbery on the edge of the southern exit. *Luck runs in waves, doesn't it? And there might be a treasure chest hidden in the gloom over there...right behind the shrub?* The pressure on him suddenly let go. He knew the booty would rise to the surface very soon. Sam dropped the clutch, leaving streaks on the pavement to celebrate his final decision.

He drove off the highway to get to the Purple Tumble Weed, a small casino on the outskirts of Las Vegas. He wanted to test the water before he went any farther and planted himself at the bar. The casino was not up to par — not like the snazzy ones out on the strip. At least the AC worked. The long bar was gouged and burned, and the orange and purple stripes on the back walls had faded. The purple paint near the rear exit had peeled off, white streaks in its place.

"Hey, hey, ho, ho! I have anything you find what?"

The bartender wore a pink leather jacket, jeans crazy tight, and Megan pinned on her chest. Pink eye shadow and lip gloss still left her innocence intact. She looked about fourteen.

Samuel ordered a gin and tonic and stared down at the poker machine installed in the bar in front of him. *A dollar-a-game. Okay. He'd start with that.* Inserting a bill, he ended up even on the first game. Megan returned with his drink. He took a sip and kept on playing. He had a good hand. If he changed one card, he could get a straight flush or fold or bet on the second deal if he threw out the clubs. Samuel needed uncommon luck. It needed to come back! He tossed one card out and bet the limit. He got the straight! He won 1,500 dollars from this old machine in a beat-up dump, a forecast he was praying for. The heavily veiled Lady of Luck seemed to be sitting next to him again. Of course, Samuel didn't know that his imaginary creature whose pulse he lived by was not really a lady at all.

Las Vegas, Nevada
6:57PM Saturday, August 27, 2005

The eight-ton sculpture of a lion in front of the MGM Grand Arena was a fiery orange in the rays of the setting sun. Bernard Hopkins, aka "The Executioner," would soon defend his middleweight crown against Jermaine Taylor in the ring that night.

Nevada usually has dry heat, but it was muggy out there that day... and there was no breeze. Traffic snarled around the complex, and the surrounding streets were torrid with the extra heat of those stopped cars. Exhaust fumes hung only four feet above the pavement, a poisonous fog getting thicker by the moment.

Patrons walking to the arena to see the fight were trying to get off those streets fast. Anyone with breathing problems struggled to get inside.

Lazzo and Edgar stared up at the large screen against the wall in the main concourse as they checked the odds in their racing forms. Cindy owned a suite that overlooked the ring. She'd ordered them to meet her there after the match---and they were nervous, afraid she'd reprimand them over something they might have done wrong.

Lazzo stood up and waved his wristwatch in front of Edgar's face. "It's getting late. Mike and Cindy gave us good tickets...we gotta go."

Edgar scowled up at him, putting his racing form down. "It's ten after seven, numb nuts." But he stood up too, and they both walked off towards the arena.

All the lights went out. Suddenly, the blinded audience heard the announcer's voice boom out to them..."The Executioner is about to tangle with Bad Intention."

A spotlight pierced the black and pinpointed Hopkins on his walk to the ring, hands in the air. The next spotlight zeroed in on Taylor. Seventeen thousand fans clapped, whistled, and howled. That wall of sound shook the arena floor. The prizefighters met in the ring and touched gloves while the crowd slowly quieted. The bell rang. The fight began.

Cindy sat in the front row, wanting to be close to the action. It was good to smell their sweaty bodies and radiate in their physical power. Hopkins pounded into his opponent's face as they careened off the ropes. A drop of Taylor's blood landed on Cindy's thigh, and it spread through her nylon stocking. She looked down at this widening red spot, and she purred. The bell rang again, and the fighters shuffled off to their corners for a momentary respite.

Tall and pale, Miles Barker sat next to her. Cindy was getting more excited. He saw her green eyes get glassy---and she was panting.

"I know you have a business meeting right after the match," Miles whispered in her ear. "But after that, you won't forget the more important appointment you have later on... I won't let you forget it." He slid his hand up her thigh and disappeared under her leather skirt. And he kept going. His fingers slipped into her personal flower, and Cindy tossed her head back and moaned, auburn hair fanning out.

"My warehouse is there for my own diversions," he said, remaining inside of her body. "I will have full domination over you later on this evening. I've checked the cuffs anchored in the ceiling to hold you up, and I'm using nipple clamps. You like them, don't you, hmmm. Aah... yes, I'll use all my tools, and don't arrive at my door without those extra braces I told you to order, or there'll be hell to pay."

He bent forward to seemingly adjust his sunglasses, but he was really camouflaging his retreat from under her skirt. Leaning back, he stretched. Cindy mouthed, *"Yes,"* and Miles looked away and crossed his arms. Anyone noticing the couple's affection had studiously overlooked it. What happens in Vegas stays in Vegas.

When the fight ended, Lazzo and Edgar quickly went to her suite, and as soon as they got there, they reclined in the lounge chairs to watch the crowd leave the stadium. The place had a small kitchen, a wet bar, and a bathroom. Whoever rented the place to watch the fight had left bottles scattered around and mauled-over appetizers in disarray across the table. Lazzo reached over had picked up a wilted cracker with crab salad on it. Edgar got up and made himself a Bloody Mary before sitting back down next to Lazzo.

"My intestines would knot up if I ate anything like that," Edgar said.

Lazzo grinned over at him and bit into a cracker, swiftly swallowing the whole thing. He snatched another one with dangerous abandon, according to Edgar.

The door to the suite slammed open, and they both got up and turned around. Cindy stood there, breathless and flushed.

"Enjoy the fight?" she asked. "I was surprised the Executioner lost, didn't see that coming." And then she frowned. "I must look like one of your worst nightmares! Your expressions are godawful...calm down and relax. I've more work for you, more money in your pockets."

"Hello, Boss," Lazzo said. "You look great."

The two hitmen stepped over to the bar while Cindy sat on the couch at the end of the room.

"Can I make you like a drink?" Edgar asked.

"Same as you, a Bloody Mary. It'll top off my evening nicely," and she nodded towards Lazzo. "Thank you. I love compliments."

Edgar tried to sound conversational as he poured her drink. "I didn't think he was going to lose either...ah well, nobody knows anything for sure."

Cindy nodded offhandedly, standing up again and forgetting about her drink. She had redirected her attention straight to business.

"I've had it with Samuel! I won't play any more games with that idiot. Now he owes me a quarter of a million dollars, so find him and tell him he owes me double that amount. Either he pays, or you shake it out of him. I'd rather have the money, so I will double your fee if you can get your hands on anything. If not, you know what to do."

"Are you in a hurry? Edgar asked.

"It doesn't matter whether you find him tomorrow or next month. What's important is finding him. Hunt at an easy pace. I've got a lot of things rolling out there in the big old world, but Eveland has certainly reached his limit. Time to straighten out his account one way or another."

Cindy went back to the couch, and she relaxed on the leather cushions with the fluidity of the erotic dancer she used to be. Her business with the boys was over, eyes half-closed, a languorous grin spread on her lips, a spider waiting for her prey to fall into her web.

New Orleans, Louisiana
5:56PM Tuesday, August 16, 2005

The maple trees shadowed the townhouses on Dalton Avenue, leaves rustling in a gentle afternoon zephyr. Dalton was a main thoroughfare in the city. Cars moved along the outer lanes with a trolley clattering down the middle.

Justin was enjoying the trolley ride on his way to the business conference. Sunlight warmed his face as shadows traveled along the floor in changing patterns.

Trying to buy tetrodotoxin without leaving clues had stumped him for weeks until an answer came to him on the Fourth of July weekend in the Hamptons. He was dipping a shrimp into cocktail sauce in the middle of a party when the memory of an old case in Connecticut came into his head.

Barry Rand, the plaintiff in the case, tried to sue a restaurant for his sickness, but Justin ate him alive in court. He knew Barry would not be in the mood to talk to him, but his older brother might. Morgan Rand might have the information he was hunting for. Barry had to have used shellfish toxin to poison himself, so where did he find it?

Justin returned to Cambridge on Tuesday. He went straight to his office to find Morgan Rand's telephone number, already trying to come up with an excuse to wheedle the information out of him--- assuming he had it. According to the file, he lived in North Grosvenor Dale on the Connecticut- Massachusetts border. Justin foresaw a two-hour car ride from Boston to the guy's doorstep. If he was right, if the guy had the info. Clattering along in the trolley, he remembered the following conversation he'd had with Morgan....

"Hello, Mr. Rand? This is Travis Stutz."

"Who the hell are you?"

"A few years ago, I did research on your brother's case in Connecticut. Right now, there's a similar case on the docket and I was hoping you might give us some light on a mystery confusing us in the old case. I'll compensate you for any information surrounding this ambiguity. A profitable trade, I think, Mr. Rand...hello?" Justin hung there. Maybe the man had fallen over and bumped his head. "Hello, Mr. Rand? Are you okay?"

"About time someone asked me about that jackass. I don't hang around with him anymore, not since last New Year's. We were partying, and he got tanked, telling me everything. What do you wanna know...' Travis'."

No love lost between these brothers, for sure...a possible blessing for Justin.

"We're curious about what was used. We just don't want to be stuck 'holding the bag' at some future point in the trial. If evidence surfaces and disproves our premise, we could be in bad shape. Do you have any idea where he might have found the toxin? Did he pay for it?"

"My uncle died last month, cause undetermined. No one can figure it out, but I know what happened. Since Barry knew he'd get a big chunk of change from his will, I'm sure he killed him for the money. I can tell you the real story if you want to meet me somewhere. That shit-heel was drunk on New Year's Eve. He told me the whole thing. Yup, and I *give you that info, but you have to pay for the down and dirty. Meet me at the Woodbridge, a mile out of town. You can't miss the sign on Route 131. Would tomorrow afternoon around 4:30 be okay? I'll wear a white and blue jacket, so you'll know it's me. We can hash out my reward when we get there, but it's gotta be a few thousand for sure."*

"The time and place are fine," Travis answered. "I will meet you there with more than enough cash to make you happy."

During the meeting, Morgan told Justin his drunken brother could not have come up with the story he'd told him on New Year's, so it had to be true. Over their second cup of very good coffee, Justin wrote out the pertinent info Morgan was telling him in a small notebook: travel to New Orleans, buy the Times-Picayune newspaper — find the ad for Organic Herbal Tonics at Veronica's Plantation in the classifieds. The address is fake; the phone number is real. Tell whoever picks up the phone that you are friends with Blue Beard, a code name to get you in the back door.

Justin gave Morgan two thousand dollars cash, driving out of Grosvenor Dale energized. Now, all he needed was an excuse to get to New Orleans. The final hurdle. A week went by, but he remained stumped.

And then Scott Weaver called him, a business acquaintance. He wanted his help to arrange some permits to transform an old textile factory into residential condominiums---in New Orleans. Weaver was surprised by Justin's energetic acceptance of this request. He sounded delighted.

Justin's memories faded. Back to the present, he looked out at the house numbers. 1225. He was close. He pulled the cable.

Meeting Weaver at his front door, the two men went to work on the documents in Justin's briefcase. They were done in a few hours. Weaver invited him out to dinner in the French Quarter, ending the evening with pecan pie and homemade whipped cream on top. Justin told his friend he was flying back to Boston in the morning, but that was a flagrant lie.

New Orleans, Louisiana
9:30AM Wednesday, August 17, 2005

Built in the 1800s, The Ambassador Hotel held its elegance after the full renovation in 2004. Stained glass skylights, and ivory columns rising above the marbled floor, Justin had picked it for location, not for its beauty. The French Quarter was two blocks away.

His room was on the seventh floor. Rolling out of bed, he stepped over to the windows. The older part of the city was easy to see. The Quarter. He smiled. Calling room service, he ordered coffee, eggs, and a copy of the Times-Picayune newspaper.

The waiter arrived and left the items he'd ordered behind. Justin snatched up the newspaper before the door even closed. The business name was already stuck in his memory. He sipped his coffee while he turned the pages. He found the ad and punched in the numbers. Hearing a faint ringing, it sounded like it was a thousand miles away, but it was finally answered.

"Bonjour, mon cher."

"Ah...hello. Can you understand me? I can't speak French, but I'm friends with Blue Beard. I need your help."

"Queen Tallu Boca will meet you tonight at 10:45 at her shop, the Magic Eye." There was a southern twang in her French accent, and she just went on like she'd said these words a hundred times before. "The shop is at the intersection of Royal and Dumaine streets in the Vieux Carre. Bring eight donations to her cause, and she'll honor your request. Au revoir."

She instantly hung up. Justin assumed the 'donations' meant thousands. She wanted eight thousand dollars to give him what he was asking for.

Justin decided to walk to the Magic Eye. He stopped at the front desk to get more precise directions before he stepped onto Baronne Street. It was a warm night. He took his jacket off and hung it over his shoulder. In under a minute, he walked into the French Quarter. It looked like a Hollywood sound stage for a romantic movie, vibrating with an aura linked to the past. The neighborhood surrounded him, a living cloak of smells and visions, and the thin threads of modernism were swept away.

Most buildings were made from wood or brick, usually painted in pastel colors. The second and third stories had balconies with elaborate iron rails and tall windows adorned with shutters done in iron filigree. The designs came from the Spaniards who had colonized Louisiana in the 1700s. Ornamental streetlights jutted out over the streets, mimicking the old gas ones flickering there a hundred years ago. Justin strolled down Dumaine Street, cobblestones under his feet, deepening the timelessness of the Quarter. Most businesses had closed, and the streetlights weren't very bright. Shadows slithered out of the blackened alleyways and pulled at his ankles.

Reaching the end of his directions, he stood between Royal and Dumaine streets. The bulb in the closest light was out, and the bar on the corner was closed. The darkness got darker. Justin didn't feel like he was in a modern city anymore. A light flickered at the end of the long alley on his right. He walked along the thin passage until he saw the entrance. 'MAGIC' was painted on a wood plank, and a neon eye hung below.

He opened the door to see incense burning in a brass holder on a counter at the end of the long room. The smell of patchouli made Justin curious. Candles of every kind, jars, and bottles with herbs, bones, and undecipherable curiosities, and books on voodoo and magic spells crowded the shelves.

The information Morgan had told him was five years old. Things might have changed. He was apprehensive, walking slowly up to the counter. Behind the register, more shelves rose to the ceiling. A five-gallon urn filled with bodies of rough-skinned newts floated in clear liquid. Those salamanders were loaded with Tetrodotoxin, the poison he was trying to get his hands on, but he didn't know that. Staring at those small creatures still made him uneasy anyway.

He rang the bell on the counter. A stout mahogany-skinned woman wearing a turban and a sequined scarf around her shoulders entered from a hidden door in the wall behind him. He turned around. Hot red lips beamed at him in a wide grin.

Justin bowed. "You must be Queen Tallu Boca? I guess you know why I'm here. Can you help me?"

"Je sais qui vous etes, ma cher, et vous etes dans un endroit dangereux. Pa Pa Legba n'est pas entendu votre message…"

He interrupted, "Wait a minute, wait! I don't speak French. Let's talk in English."

Her smile vanished, but she did switch to English. Of course, that didn't make much difference. "Spirit Vudu cannot help anyone tonight. We will change our course for the ultimate celebration of the renewed spirit…"

He interrupted her yet again. "You aren't interested in my donation, my queen?" He pointed at the satchel hanging off his shoulder.

"I can't be enticed into things the Bokor before me did." Waving her hands in the air. "He be a' cooking up a zombie brew with Datura selling dirty potions. No, no…you must go. Forget your quest and leave my shop." A taloned finger pointed towards the door, diaphanous fabric floating from the sleeve of her dress.

"Alright. Okay." Justin scowled at her. "Why did you waste our time in setting the whole thing up only to shoot it down when I actually got here? Why would you answer the damned phone, for God's sake? Come on…go ahead, explain it to me! Give it a try anyway!" He was angry. "I don't think there's a real reason behind this Hoodoo Voodoo crap. It's like an expensive joke that's not funny."

"Pourqoi je devraite? You snarl like a bete. I don't know anything about code names," but she whispered in his ear, "You really must go." As the queen pressed a piece of paper into his hand. Justin instantly read it:

"The Magic Eye is bugged. We will bribe the officials again. It will be safe here in two weeks. You can return then, and we can go ahead with the sale."

He shook his head. "Right…aha…as you command." He tossed the note to the floor and marched out of the shop, slamming the door behind him. Justin didn't know where he should go at that point, frustrated and bubbling with irritation. He stamped down Royal Street and turned on Bienville for no good reason. From there, he found himself on Bourbon Street. Jazz music came to him from a bar a block away, and he looked at his watch. 11:08. He decided to enter the establishment and order a shot… or maybe two. A limousine rolled up and stopped right next to him, and the passenger window lowered. The chauffeur, wearing the traditional cap and white gloves, leaned over.

"Aren't you friends with Blue Beard, sir?"

Justin was ready to accept anything thrown at him at that point, quickly answering his question. "Yes, I'm a friend of his."

"Please, get in the limo and relax. He really will take care of your problems."

"So…you're about to drive me where I need to go? Okay. Guess I can't ignore an invitation like that."

Caution tossed to the wind, Justin got in, and the driver rolled back into traffic. The streets sailed by. They turned onto Tulane Avenue, and hope returned to his heart.

"How long before we get there?" Justin knew he sounded like a child.

"Five or ten minutes. Depends on traffic and lights."

They'd left the French Quarter a few minutes ago, soon entering the parking lot of the Hudson Biomedical Research Institute on 413 Rocheblave Road. Two windowless rust-colored columns stood on either side of this large office building.

The chauffeur turned around and talked to Justin more directly. "Stay on the sidewalk until you reach the back entrance. Take that door. The person you want will be at the fourth office on the first floor---have a nice evening, sir."

"Thanks."

He got out and walked over to the ugly structure, windows all pitch-black. What happened to him at the Magic Eye had left him cynical. Meeting yet another stranger in an empty building in the middle of the night made him feel like he was in a Twilight Zone episode. He followed the sidewalk, and the door was open, stepping into a dark hallway. Light leaked under the bottom of the fourth door, and Justin stepped over and knocked.

"Hello! Come in."

He shrugged, opened the door...and ducked. A paper plane flew by exactly where his face had been a second ago. A middle-aged man was sitting behind a metal desk in a utilitarian-looking office, glass cabinets and fluorescent lights buzzing, hiding behind plastic ceiling tiles. Busily folding another paper plane, he looked a lot like Howard Stern. Justin stared at his large nose, afro, and a polyester suit, but the similarity vanished when he opened his mouth.

"I'm not remorseful over the obfuscation I have just put you through. You know we're both naughty boys---and one of us is a real practical joker. Don't worry about the Magic Eye. I was having fun at your expense. You aren't the only customer I pull this crap on."

Justin stepped over to his desk, and the man half-stood and shook his hand.

"My title is Professor, and my moniker is Byron Anderson. You can call me Ronnie. Relax---go ahead and sit down," as he gestured at a chair on the other side of his desk.

"I'm Travis Stutz. You screwed with my head, and that finale was cruel, professor... sorry, Ronnie, but I guess you have a good point. Buying items of this kind should give us fair warning. Expect the unacceptable and deal with the subsequent bruising." Justin shook his head. "The first connection I had with you was the talking to the woman on the phone. She hadn't been very clear about the payment."

Professor Anderson carefully pressed the last fold in his latest creation, before he put the latest paper plane down. He leaned back in his chair. "Eight thousand dollars, Travis. Your payment can be given to me as a donation to a wonderful charity. Everyone else will see that action of yours as honorable. Just write the check out to FACE, Founder's Alliance for Community Education."

"I didn't know you had cover that deep. I brought cash. Is that okay?"

"Certainly. I can handle the weight of hundred-dollar bills with aplomb."

He got up and stepped over to one of the cabinets, taking a small bottle off a shelf and leaving it on the desk in front of Travis. Most of the printing on the bottle was too small to read, but TETRODOTOXIN was unmistakable.

"How did you know I wanted that? Maybe I wanted cyanide or salmonella---or maybe paralytic shellfish toxin," Justin said. He sat down and dropped his satchel next to the chair.

"Most of my donations come from intelligent people. They want the fastest and easiest transmission. Certain snake venoms kill individuals faster, but tetrodotoxin is a universal soldier. It is predictable with stellar results."

Justin chuckled. "Alright, Ronnie, you picked the right answer."

"Would you like a syringe to go with that?" An extraordinary question, but the professor was simply being realistic and helpful. "The top of the bottle can be pricked by the needle of a syringe and filled without opening the vial. I can even give you a traveling case to hold the bottle and the syringe, protecting them from accidents...oh, by the way, you should not fly home."

"Why?"

"It's illegal to transport Tetrodotoxin in certain states. I'm not sure if security in the airport would notice it, but if they do, they'd confiscate it."

"Thanks. I'll get myself and my product home in one piece in a different way." Justin took packets of wrapped bills out of the bag and lined them on the desk.

The professor opened a desk drawer and took out the syringe and traveling case. There were perfectly pre-cut cavities in the grey foam padding inside the small box, and Ronnie nestled the bottle of poison and needle securely in their correct places.

"I realize the syringe and the case are almost indispensable," Justin said.

Ronnie closed the box with a snap, and he pressed the hidden catch to lock it. He opened it again and slid it across the desk to Travis. His customer needed to know how to lock and unlock the container himself. They went through the process together. Justin quickly understood out to use the subtle locking mechanism.

The deal was done. Justin put his box of tricks into his bag, a golden key. He would open heaven's door here on earth and send his problems to the grave.

New Bedford, Massachusetts
2:30PM Monday, August 22, 2005

A Bristlecone Pine tree rooted on the pinnacle of a mountain in California might be the oldest tree on Earth, chronicled to be living there for 4,845 years. In South America, a Patagonia Cypress was reported to be 3,622 years old. Baobab trees in Africa usually live for 2,000 years. At 1,622 years old, the Bald Cypress was the oldest tree in South Carolina, and in the Pacific Northwest, a Giant Sequoia's next birthday cake would have 3,267 candles on it.

There was a dispute over the Fortin gall Yew growing in a churchyard in Perthshire in the UK. Either it was there for two thousand years---or maybe three thousand instead.

Obsessed with the Yew, David Russel had read about all these contentions over how long a tree can live. He dove into yet another article.

In the fifth century, Christianity flourished in Europe as different countries adapted their pagan religions into the growing trend. Many Christian churches were built in areas the indigenous population considered magnetic. The yew trees captivated the villagers. Many of the older churches had yews on their property or in the adjoining cemeteries. The clergy told their flock they'd planted those trees to ward off cattle and sheep. Of course, that was not true. The ancient

180

Yews had been there way before they arrived. It didn't matter. The extended past gilded their lies into truth.

And David knew that too. He learned more and more at the library every day. He had just picked up a tidbit connected to Fairhaven itself.

European settlers landing on the east coast of North America in 1810, founded Fairhaven, bringing a Yew tree from their homeland with them. The colonists planted it near the place where they decided to build their church, believing the young tree could link them to their old spiritual foundations.

The transplanted Yew flourished for two hundred years, branching out with fruit every fall. The berry meat was free from any taxane, riddling the rest of the tree. Birds feasted on the fruit without peril, even though there was a concentration of poison inside the seeds within the fruit. The digestive juices in their avian bellies could dissolve the shells of the seeds. The birds evacuated them instead, possibly creating more Yews.

David knew the fruit on the tree in the cemetery behind the church in Fairhaven was not ripe. Too early to harvest anything.

Every morning, he drove his sports car to the New Bedford Library to sit on the second floor at one of their computers to continue his research. Two books sat on the table next to him. The History of the Yew Tree and a murder mystery by Agatha Christie named The Yew Tree. But he wouldn't take any books out of the library. They might incriminate him in a future act.

Leaving medical school, he never bought a personal computer. Going to the library was a prudent decision. If he bought one now, his wife could notice what he was doing and looking at, and it's good to get out of the house anyway.

Staring down at the glowing screen, the summer weather outside was not beckoning to him. He lived in this simple regimen every day. The library closes at five, so the usual craving tugged at him. He needed his cocktail. Concentration waning, his manicured hands trembled, mouth dry. He logged off and put the books back on the shelf. David skipped down the stairs and pushed through the front door, speed-walking to his car. Starting the engine, most wouldn't have the patience to allow the Triumph TR6 to warm up, but he liked his car, and his watering hole was minutes away. David handled those extra minutes before he wheeled out of the parking lot.

New Bedford, Massachusetts
3:00AM Tuesday, October 4, 2005

David silently left their bedroom and crept to the garage, knowing Holly was asleep. Earlier that day, he left a bucket in the corner of the garage holding his clothes, and he took off his PJs and got dressed. Mercedes was quieter than the Triumph. He'd use it on his trip to Fairhaven. Almost everything he needed was already in his shoulder bag, a heavy-duty flashlight, a stone bowl and pestle, and a pair of garden gloves.

He had already tossed a shovel into the trunk and a face shield in the back seat—knowing that Holly wouldn't go back to her car for the rest of the night. Plastic bags in his jacket pocket, he was ready to go. He got into the Mercedes, opened the garage doors, and drove onto the empty streets.

David did not speed when he entered Fairhaven, making sure he would not get any attention. Ignoring the main gates of the Church on Brewers Lane, he took the back entrance, parking between two high hedges near the office. The Mercedes was invisible from the street.

He took the garden gloves out of the bag and stuffed them in his jacket pocket. Grabbing the flashlight, he left everything else behind. He jogged other to the wooden arch bracketing the path that led into the cemetery. David knew where he was going. He'd Googled an image of Saint Mary's Church and the surrounding property on the library computer. Rushing along, he enjoyed the smell of cut grass still hanging in the air. He jogged around the next bend to see the silhouette of the oversized Yew Tree rising up in front of him.

The cemetery was dark and empty. David got nervous, but he calmed down fast. He knew he was alone. Turning the flashlight on, he angled it up at branches heavy with fruit. A giggle leaked out of him even as he perched the flashlight on the nearby hedge. He put his garden gloves on and grabbed a branch, picking off handfuls of berries. He tossed them into a plastic bag, quickly deciding he had enough zip-locking the bag. Snatched the flashlight off of the top of the hedge, he trotted back to the car.

He didn't put the headlights on until he turned on Gooseneck Road, a thin track petering out on empty acres behind the dump. David shifted into park, leaving the engine running because he needed those headlights. He'd used the satellite on the computer to pick this place for a reason. He didn't want anyone to see him set up his lethal weapon.

Taking the face shield off the back seat and the shovel out of the trunk, he hung the main bag off his shoulder. The lights allowed him to find a place with soft dirt. He dropped to his knees on crabgrass. Taking the bowl, the pestle, the gloves, and the yew berries out of the bag, he put the face shield on, a careful precaution. Pouring the berries into the marble bowl, he crushed them with the pestle...correctly, not to squish them *too* much. It had to look like cranberry sauce. Important to leave some lumps behind... no one would notice the extra dark specks left by pieces of the crushed seeds.

He returned to the car to get the spoon out of the console and the flashlight in his pocket. The headlights had been leaving deep shadows, so he angled the flashlight on a rock from the other direction to fix that. He kneeled down between those two light sources to spoon his crushed berries out of the bowl and into another bag...slowly and carefully, no toxic mush on the outside of the bag. Done, he doubled the bag and put the mixture into the shoulder bag. Taking the face shield off, he started digging. Nudging everything into the hole he created, he used the edge of the shovel to even push the spoon in as the last item left. He refilled the hole and stamped the area flat. Holding a flashlight, the shovel, the bag, and the face shield hanging off on his shoulder, he got back in the car. He put everything in the car and drove home.

The garage doors closed. It was 5:23 AM. More than enough time before Holly woke up. The Zen sand garden had been catching dust on a high shelf in the garage. He climbed the ladder to reach it and bring it down. The garden would help him again.

His breath came out as white mist. They wouldn't turn the heat on in the garage until December. At least the berries would remain fresh. No fermentation in his little bag of sweet delight. Pouring his surprise into the cranberry sauce at the party should not affect the flavor; it should taste like climbing a stairway to heaven.

He opened the sand garden and set it on the work table. Using the tiny rake, he pushed the sand around in the garden in a short meditation before raking a furrow down the center. Taking the bag of crushed yew berries out of the satchel, he flattened it into the depression, careful not to rip the plastic. Then, he used sand to cover the bag. No one could find it there.

Returning the garden back to the upper shelf, he put the shovel and the face shield away. David changed into his pajamas, leaving his clothes back in the bucket. His plucking, crushing, and shoveling were all done, and his devilry was out of sight. "That's all folks!" he whispered.

Back in bed, he drifted into a peaceful slumber, happy his wife had not noticed a thing. But he was wrong about that. Holly's eyes were open when he got back to the house, and she was mentally connected to a vision she'd had when he first left their bed hours earlier. Her curiosity grew over his odd disappearance, yet she had no concerns and stared at her snoring husband's back without calculation.

3:35PM Monday, November 21, 2005
Bass River, Massachusetts

After a romantic weekend with Peter, April returned to the estate on Sunday. Latham had stopped loving her years ago. She truly believed he would tie her to some railroad tracks and leave her there. He was going to Chicago for a week and, from there, a convention in Las Vegas. He hadn't said a thing about the house, their marriage, or his future in the company. This dearth of communication between them was an ongoing symptom of their specious relationship. April knew that questioning him would likely be pointless, turning her away with a cold shoulder---more likely a frozen one. And 'living' with him was the wrong term. Yes, physically with him in the same building was factual, but the real distance between them could span a galaxy or two.

April would soon extricate herself from her marriage with Peter's help, yet Latham's bizarre behavior lately left her rattled. She instructed her lawyer to draft a divorce decree without a date, not sure when the final hammer shall fall. April waited for Latham to put the estate on the market. She'd keep this sham up until then. So be it. In her mind, Latham would let the cat out of the bag during the Thanksgiving dinner. After he flies home from Las Vegas on Wednesday... or early Thursday morning, he'd tell her. He would sell the house and, dump her and leave for California the next day. This prophecy of April's was the ammunition she wanted, returning his nasty salvo with Olympic speed. But what if he doesn't do it? *What if he doesn't do anything?*

She couldn't put the estate up for sale on her own, and her current standings in any divorce proceedings would be weak, so he had to start this. He'd give her a decree and the card of a realtor after the rest of the family had gone home. Again, this was not carved in stone and her confidence was crumbling, apprehension growing like a weed in her mind.

She slumped in a chair at the edge of the koi pond, shadows stretching across the floor. Gazing at nothing, she began to worry if Latham would actually show up at the reunion at all. Adrenaline jolted into her. She got up and ran to the library... she had to call him, cajole him into this commitment!

Entering the room, April poured herself a glass of wine and sat on the couch, holding the house phone in her hand. She could gaze through those large windows to see a peaceful scene, a visual shield against his endless cruelty. Closing her eyes, she took a deep breath and hit the numbers.

Latham's meeting with the board members in Chicago had been seamless. After the four-hour flight to Las Vegas, he rested in his hotel room, dreaming about Russia---his bright escape. Attison had helped him install his entire estate, including the estate, into the Heinem Corporation's holdings. The last conversation he'd had with his wife had been fun, and he stretched out onto the bed and smiled. He would vanish Friday morning, and the divorce decree would arrive by messenger later on that day. He'd tell her the rest of the good news on the phone. No more money for her or the children to fight over in probate court. Latham wanted to leave her destitute, a good prediction that lifted his equanimity even higher. Irony and contempt were energizing him. He imagined living his last hours on American soil, acting as if he was a jovial family man. The phone rang.

"Hello."

"Hello, dear. The Thanksgiving dinner is set up, and everyone is committed. You'll be there, right? Mirabelle has responsibilities with her family this year, but she and Vince will arrange things for us." April's words came out of her in a rush. "We can serve ourselves. Cozier that way."

"That sounds fine, dear." Latham wanted to laugh at her, but he stopped himself. "I can't believe we're having another reunion. It will work out fine." Then, his voice dripped with concern. "I'm worried about Robert. Do you know if he's making it this year?"

"I'll call and check…when are *you* arriving?" His sudden worry over his son unnerved her, but she tried to sound okay. April stared out at the velvety green grass and tranquil brook for support. It didn't work. She swallowed the rest of the wine in her glass in a gulp.

"I'm flying back Wednesday; I told you that," Latham said. "I'll be there that night or early Thursday morning. Don't worry, honey! I'm not going to California until Friday. Oh, I should let you know. I might find a break in my schedule and hop on a jet, get back to you, and say hello in the next couple of months. Doesn't that sound great!"

"You're freaking me out, Latham!"

Her distress delighted him to the nth degree.

"I'm sorry, April. I'm... ah...jazzed up over the California project, that's all. I've gotten frustrated for a long time. No challenges here for me, and this is a real turning point."

"I didn't realize the West Coast was such a big deal. I hope the move does work out for you... and the upcoming conference in Las Vegas will go well, too."

After her latest surgeries, April's eyebrows trembled in one position. At least her mouth could pucker. "I'm looking forwards to seeing you for sure on Thursday!"

"No problem, no worries. Hey, what would you like for Thanksgiving? Las Vegas is a shopping mall, and I can get you anything. A pendant, earrings, or a paperweight...what would you like?"

April got queasy, stuttering, "Huh...ah...oh...," She didn't get full control, "I don't know...perhaps a watch with dia... dia... diamonds on it."

Latham loved her stumbling answer. "Okay then. You're younger and more beautiful every time I see you. We'll ring in the next holiday together." After sending out his out-of-character compliment, he hung up.

April tossed the phone to the far corner of the couch as a cancerous lump, nesting between two cushions, staring back at her, buzzing like an oversized insect. She got up and refilled her glass.

Her purse was on the coffee table. April scrabbled into the depths of it to find the right pill bottle, quickly popping three tranquilizers down her gullet. She wanted to muffle her paranoia. Minutes crawled along her skin like ugly slugs, fingernails digging into the couch leather. Latham's words sliced into her... he'd never shut up!

Until the tranquilizers kicked in. Latham had asked her about her son. It might be important to call Robert and confirm his plans for Thanksgiving as well.

North Dartmouth, Massachusetts
4:03PM Monday, November 21, 2005

The ground was usually covered with snow, and the roads slick at that point, but so far, this section of the county has gotten nothing. A dusting a week ago swept away in the wind. The winter queen is holding her breath.

Robert parked his motorcycle near the front door of his yellow cottage, a rental on Bryant Street. The bike sparkled in the brittle air while the truck sagged in the driveway. Weeds sagged in the flower boxes under the windows, and brown grass graced the yard. He had no shame in the desolation of his landscaping, yet the inside of his cottage was immaculate.

The window blinds were closed tight. Robert went inside and sat at a glass table in the center of the living room. The only light came from a bathroom off the hallway with the door open. Bridge of Sighs, one of Trower's songs, blanketed the air. He had lines of cocaine set up on a large mirror right in front of him. But he didn't snort them up, instead escaping on his inner island, a creation he'd built a few months ago. A wonderful respite. He'd go to this imaginary world to toss balls on a grassy field with faceless beings…or he'd just walk around.

When he was first released out of rehab, he was healing. However, listening to his father's drunken tirade at the family reunion had been too much to handle that morning. He stopped working at Home Depot. From that point on, all his income came from dealing---and his bankroll got fat while he got thinner. He was wasting away in his own looking-glass world.

His phone rang, loud enough to break through the music and into his head. He picked it up, but he wouldn't say anything.

"Hello…hello? Robert? It's Mom, I'm just confirming. I need to know if you're coming on Thursday." She'd gotten tipsy. The pills mixed with the wine. "I hope you're coming. You know we love you, Bertie, you know that."

"Hi, Mom."

"Robert, is that you? Can you hear me?"

"Yes. I'm here. I'll be there. When would you like...I mean, what, I mean, when do you want me to..."

"Robert? Hello?"

"I can hear you, Mom. Everything's fine. You want me to come to the party, right?"

"Yes, of course. Come over early on Wednesday. A day early, if you want...or Thursday is okay too. Bertie, are you still there?"

"Okay. I'll show up on Wednesday. It's gonna be alright."

Robert felt funny about the next reunion, but he would certainly be there. No plans to do anything else—no plans at all. *Yet.* It was very important for him to be there this year. He flipped his phone into speaker mode, leaving it on the table. Robert snorted up a line, and it threw him through the ceiling, the attic, and then the shingled roof, floating in the cold night air above the cottage. It was harder to hear his mother's voice now, but he really wanted to know what his father's travel plans were. A wanting powerful enough to get the next question out of him.

"What's Dad going to do? I thought he was leaving?"

"He's going to California right after the reunion. We won't be able to see him for a very...very long time. He's driving to the airport on Friday morning. So, it's important to bring the whole family together for

Thanksgiving. Don't you think? You're going to be there? You'll make it, right?"

"Don't worry, Mom. I'll be there for sure!"

Part III

Ventura Casino, Las Vegas
11:00 PM Wednesday, November 23, 2005

Samuel Eveland huddled over his gin and tonic at the Minerva Cove Lounge, and he left his sunglasses on. One side of the establishment was open to the main floor of the casino. Every few minutes, Sam looked over his shoulder. He'd heard Cindy's thugs were hunting for him, but he wasn't as concerned as he should have been over that gossip. He stayed in town.

Still believing he would win big and pay off his debt. Gambling was responsible for his current woes, and gambling would soon get rid of them...but he wasn't that stupid. He wore a disguise---sunglasses, a Panama hat, a shaggy red wig, and a gaudy Hawaiian shirt with pink flamingos flying over a safety-orange lagoon. He believed this flamboyance would camouflage him. As he sipped his drink, a mantra ran in his head: nothing bad will happen to me.

He watched a guy wearing a white linen suit stuffing tokens into the dollar machine across the aisle. He seemed familiar, as if he personally knew him--- or something. Samuel squinted his eyes and stared straight at his face lit up by the screen in front of him, and he was suddenly shocked. His face, height, and posture echoed his own. If *he* put that snazzy suit on, no one could tell who was who!

Two goons sauntered over to the white-suited man. Samuel grabbed the newspaper on the bar and raised it in front of his face---but he kept on peeking over the top.

The management of Ventura knew who those men were. Their own security men generally ignored what they did in an ongoing agreement with Cindy. Edgar leaned against the nearest slot machine, off-handedly cleaning his fingernails with a pocketknife while his partner turned Latham away from his game. He held him in place with oversized hands clamped around his shoulders.

"Hello, Sammy," Edgar said. "You must have won big to pay for a suit like that one...and a Rolex watch on your wrist too. Wow! I guess those winnings have gone straight to your head---whatadaya think, you schmuck? She ain't looking for you? You must be dumber than a rock."

"My name isn't Sam." Latham glowered at them or tried to under Lazzo's painful grip. "You have the wrong man! Let me go right now, or I'll put you both in jail for assault."

Edgar put his pocket knife away. "You're the wrong guy? I guess you're right. We'll just walk away. Oh, sorry. There's a problem. Whoever you've decided you are now still has to pay her back with interest."

And Lazzo then shook Latham like a bottle of dressing. His eyes rolled up, and the chain around his neck holding his keycard snapped and fell to the floor. Edgar and Lazzo grabbed his elbows and speedily dragged him to the elevators. Latham had gotten dizzy. He couldn't get away or even call out, but he got a little more stable when they were almost inside the car. Seeing one of his employees leaving the other elevator, he needed to remember his name fast! *Was it Bella? Bender?* And then it clicked. *Benson.*

"Benson...hey, BENSON! Tell them who I am. Tell them to let me go!"

Leland Benson looked over. His boss was being kidnapped by two dangerous-looking men. Seeing him in that position was perfect, but fake concern lit up on his face. *Ah, sweet revenge. It seemed the king was no longer in control.*

Benson's belly swelled out enough to cover his belt, and his comb-over was godawful. None of that mattered. He'd been ordered to tell these henchmen to free his boss. He must comply.

"He's Latham Donnelly, the CEO of Heinem Corporation. Let him go, or I'll call security!"

"No! NO!" Latham screamed back at him. "Don't call security, call Attison Korybante. Tell him what's happening. He can take care of this problem and--"

The elevator doors closed.

Latham didn't want security or police to be involved. They'd screw up his plans and slow everything down. He really thought Benson was already punching Attison's number into his phone, but he was wrong. This employee of his was angry at him. Benson's friend, Harrison Griffin, was supposed to take Latham's place when he left, but that's not happening. Benson heard that one of Latham Donnelly's lackeys was already set up for the job.

Yeah, yeah, I'll call Korybant right away. His number is on my cell phone in my room. He shrugged--*But what could a few extra minutes matter? I'll play a game or two before I go up there and call the damned lawyer.*

Samuel dropped the newspaper and left a fiver under his glass. Lazzo and Edgar had dragged his lookalike away. Sam went where Latham had been playing and searched the carpeting around the machine. It didn't take him long. He picked up the plastic key and slipped it into his pocket, almost jogging to the nearest restroom. Entering a stall, he took the keycard out of his pocket and turned it slowly in his hands---nothing was on it but a black-and-white symbol. Samuel needed to know what room it was connected to, and he believed a little luck could wheedle the information out of someone at the desk.

He left the stall and stopped at the counter in the lavatory to see himself in the mirror. Time to toss his glasses and wig in the garbage. He couldn't remember the exact length of his doppelganger's hair seeing him across on the main floor, but he rubbed his fingers across his scalp to fluff up his flattened hair. Taking his comb out of his back pocket, he tried to civilize himself even more. And he had to replace the Hawaiian shirt. Almost broke, he went out there and bought himself an olive-green polo shirt for thirty-five dollars at the sports shop. It was the lowest price he could find. That purchase dropped him to the bottom of the barrel, but Samuel prayed the T-shirt would turn his burlap to gold…and he had actually nothing to lose since his life was on the line.

Back to the bathroom, he tossed the Hawaii shirt in the trash. He took the new shirt out of the bag and, shook out the fold-lines and put it on. Crossing his fingers, he went to the main desk. Leaving his fingers crossed in his pockets, he thought the superstition would increase his chances.

Remaining a few feet away from the counter, he hoped anyone working there might notice him before he said anything. Samuel watched other customers walk up, credit card receipts sliding back and forth across the sleek marble surface. Crossing his fingers that long was affecting his circulation. The ends were getting numb.

Finally, an Asian woman beckoned towards him. She smelled like wildflowers and vanilla.

"Mr. Donnelly! Good afternoon. Can I help you?"

Samuel read the tag on her shirt. "Hello...Kara. Has anyone left a message for me? I haven't gone back to my room yet, and I left my cell phone there. Can you check that for me?" *Luck was holding.* He took his hands out of his pockets and shook them.

"We'll know in a second, sir," Kara pushed some buttons on the keyboard in front of her. "No. Nothing, sorry. Is there anything else I can do for you?"

"I'm expecting a package this afternoon. Can you send it up to my room...358, or is it 385? I'm having a brain freeze on the number."

She smiled in commiseration. "Your room number is 2453, Mr. Donnelly. Hey, you got two of the numbers anyway. Oh, and it's on the fourteenth floor. I'll send your package up the suite as soon as it arrives." She glanced over at a different screen. "You're set up to check out today. Would you like to stay with us a bit longer? There's a show tomorrow at the Stadium. I know you'd enjoy it." Kara smiled.

Samuel wanted to stay at the Ventura forever, but her invitation was shattered by the danger he was in.

"If I could, I'd stay, Kara, but my commitments are rock solid. I must decline."

"Alright, sir. We look forward to seeing you again soon. I'll send the package to your room as soon as it arrives."

He got on the elevator and took the key card with the broken chain out of his pocket. Guests came in and out of the car on his trip to the highest floor of the building. Samuel ended up alone when he got out. Moving down the hall to the suite, he attempted to look sedate. Using the purloined key, he stepped into luxury. The place reminded him of the days when he'd had it all.

It was midday, and he didn't know how much time he had to steal someone else's life... and get out of town. He shifted into high gear, walking into the bedroom and opening the closet. A suitcase and computer bag were on the upper shelf. Samuel grabbed at the larger bag, and they both fell off the shelf. The suitcase missed his head by an inch, bouncing a few feet away. He put both bags on the bed, and he started to pack---and he couldn't leave anything behind. Stuffing files and papers off the desk and into the computer bag, the minutes were ticking by. His anxiety rose. Donnelly's computer had fallen off the shelf. He hoped the cushioning in the expensive bag had supported it well enough.

Samual looked over at the desk. There was a plane ticket left on the complimentary stationery. He picked it up and smiled and put the ticket in a zippered pocket on the side of the computer bag. The flight was going to be his free escape out of there.

A suit was hanging in a dry-cleaning bag in the closet. It was clear that Donnely had intended to wear it on his trip home. Samuel was about to change his plans. Finding clean briefs, socks, and a cotton undershirt in one of the bureau drawers, he peeled all his clothes off and put these items on. A shirt was folded on a shelf in the closet. Perfect; he shook it out for another layer. He was a duplicitous snake shedding his skin. The suit was tailored to his body. These new scales felt comfortable and extravagant. He left a dirty sock and his underpants on the side of the bed, leaving the rest of his rumpled clothes on the carpet in a haphazard mess.

Knotting a tie around his neck, he combed his hair and looked in the mirror. His reflection confused him for a second, but the deep fear of losing his life got him back on track faster than a rabbit diving into its burrow to get away from a hungry wolf. Everything Latham had in that suite was now packed in the bags. Samuel was ready to go. Taking his wallet out of the back pocket of the pants he'd left on the floor. He took most of the cash and put it into Latham's wallet, even though there was a credit card or two and some cash already there. Sticking his old wallet back in his pants, he'd left thirty dollars behind. If they actually make it to this suite, his own license should help cloud the water for Cindy's retrievers.

Latham's phone sat on the desk, and he slid it into the breast pocket of the suit. He had watched those thugs kidnap Latham just a few feet away from his perch at the bar. Lady Luck had to have been there to hold his hand---one more time. He tossed the room key on the desk and hung the computer bag strap over his shoulder, the suitcase handle in his hand. Samuel glanced at his reflection in the tall mirror near the door. It was clear that Samuel was gone, and Latham Donnelly had taken his place. Inhaling deeply, he straightened his shoulders and opened the door. He walked toward the elevators as a rich and free man, not a single care left to bother him.

Samuel whistled up a taxi when he left the casino. Donnelly's flight was leaving at 8:00 PM. He'd use the extra time at the airport to dig up more information about Latham on his own computer. Breezing through the concourse towards the exit, a disheveled and drunken man stumbled towards him, waving. Samuel did not stop. The man kept on moving toward him anyway.

It was Benson. He'd eventually gone back to his room and called Attison. All he got was an answering machine, so he left a message about what had happened, that Latham needed his help. After that, he went back to the main floor to keep on gambling and drinking.

"I called Attison, but I got his machine...but, but you're free. You looked a lot worse when I saw you before with those awful-looking men. Do you know who they are?"

"I'm fine. It was a disagreement that is now straightened out. You don't need to call anyone else...and it would be wise to forget the entire thing, okay?" Samuel tried to inflate his voice with power, hoping the man wouldn't start any rumors that might come back on him.

Benson leaned up close to whisper in his ear, "No problem, sir. It's our secret." He put his finger to his lips. "Now you can tell me what really happened to you a few hours ago, 'cause you sure...sure looked...screwed up."

"I'm sorry. I have no more time to talk. I have a plane to catch. Take care of yourself."

Samuel briskly walked out of the casino and onto the street, moving way too fast for Benson to keep up.

Las Vegas, Nevada
3:30PM Wednesday, November 23, 2005

Lazzo and Edgar had blindfolded, gagged, and tied Latham to a chair in a storage room, telling him he must give them the money he owed them or else. They vanished and left him there.

The paid assassins returned to the main concourse and entered Rose's Petals, a cocktail lounge.

A live tribute band played Rod Stewart's music, and Lazzo loved his songs.

"Their vocalist isn't bad, Edgar, not bad at all. He sounds a lot like him, don't you think?" Lazzo sipped at his Long Island Iced Tea.

Edgar shook his head, not answering at first. "Maybe we shouldn't have left him down there alone. I mean, we could probably get the job done faster if we just pushed him. Cindy would be happier when that idiot spilled the beans—oh, you're right, Lazzo. His singing ain't bad, but I think we gotta go back."

Ed dropped a fifty-dollar bill on the bar, and Lazzo followed his partner out of the lounge. Passing the elevators, they ducked into a service entrance, clattering down metal stairs to reach a delivery elevator that dropped them yet another level. Getting out, they walked the dingy hallway to the storage room they used to jail Samuel.

Latham could hear them on the other side of the doors. He pressed his body against the back of the chair, hands roped up tight to the armrests. He scrabbled against the leather cushions while Edgar unlocked the door.

"Hello, Samuel. Give us what we want, okay?" Edgar untied Latham's blindfold and gag. "It is time to pay your debt to Cindy, and we're running out of patience. Come on, Sam, just tell us where the money is…or something bad will happen to you. Come on, let's end this problem right now!"

Latham had no saliva, so he could only croak at them. Edgar sniggered.

"We need to give him some water," Lazzo said.

"I guess you're right."

Lazzo stepped over to the utility sink to fill a paper cup to hold it to Latham's mouth. Drinking, he started to cough, still unable to talk. "I've...told you....I'm not who you think I am and." He fell into another coughing fit. He tried again. "I can prove it. I can prove---"

Lazzo lifted the cup of water to his mouth yet again. Latham's voice finally came back.

"I've been staying in the presidential suite on the thirty-seventh floor in room 3752." He looked down at his chest. The key was gone.

"I had a key, but it must have snapped off. Just call the desk." Latham's voice was weak---but at least it was there. "Call the desk. They'll tell you who I am. Latham Donnelly in 3752. Just get me to the room. I can give you whatever you say you need. Hell, I can even give you more, and everyone will be happy, and we can go our separate ways. Please! Let's go to my suite. Then you'll know the truth!"

Lazzo and Edgar stared at him. Lazzo broke the holding silence.

"Whadaya think, Ed? Check his story out? Maybe he's living two lives at once, and we've found him out? Weird things like that happen in this town. A lot of people change their names when they get to Vegas."

"Good point, Laz."

Edgar leaned over to look into Latham's eyes. "Of course, the entire thing could be a dead issue."

"We have nothing to lose," Lazzo said. "Let's give him a chance to pay."

"Yeah...okay. I'll get the master from Tommy and meet you there. Give me a five-minute head start."

Sunlight beamed inside the acres of glass on the high-rises marching along the main strip, but the corridor on the thirty-seventh floor of the Ventura had no windows. It was cool and shadowy, and a chandelier glittered in front of the elevators. Every thirty feet, royal blue curtains bracketed beautiful pictures of mountains and country roads.

Lazzo herded Latham out of the elevator to reach his presidential suite. When they got there, they had to wait. Latham knew salvation waited for him on the other side of that door, but it was still an uncomfortable moment. He would be free from Samuel's life---any minute, but he remained nervous. Edgar trotted up to them.

"Here you go, Sam." He gave Latham the key. "I can't wait to see the gold you have for us on the other side of this door!"

Latham frowned as he pushed the door across the thick carpeting with a soft whoosh. He looked over his shoulder. "You should have taken me here in the first place to avoid this confusion." The first thing he saw was the desk drawer left open, and his cufflinks weren't there. Neither were his receipts, his gold pen, or his wallet. He felt a chill as he raced into the bedroom. Filthy clothes were tossed around the bed, and the medicine cabinet in the bathroom was empty. Lazzo and Edgar watched him.

"This can't be...it can't! It isn't right," Latham howled. "Someone has stolen my things, damn it." Lazzo grabbed him and shoved him down on the seat cushion of a chair in the corner of the main room. "Noooo! Let me go! This is wrong. Give me the phone. I'll--"

Lazzo slapped him with the back of his hand. That shut him right up. Edgar walked into the bedroom and picked Samuel's pants off the floor to check the pockets. He took the wallet out—a small amount of cash was in the billfold. He looked at the driver's license and tossed the wallet on Latham's lap. The earlier blush of excitement in his prisoner's cheeks had drained into the ashen color of dread.

Edgar reveled in his sudden anguish. "You don't look good, Sam. Isn't it nice to get your wallet back? So, tell us where your footlocker, brimming with gold, is? Under the bed? Should we check there, hmmm?"

Latham tried to put his brain back in his head after Lazzo's slap. "I'll call.... I'll call my bank in Massachusetts. They can wire whatever you want right now! You've got to believe me! I can get you the money. My name is Latham Donnelly. I'm the CEO of the Heinem Corporation." Latham looked up at Edward and went on...

"Ever used a pain pill? My company makes them and almost everything else your doctor prescribed."

He waved Samuel's wallet in the air. "That bastard stole my stuff. For God's sake! You have to believe me! Wouldn't it make more sense to get money from me instead of leaving a dead body behind? I can even give you more than what you're asking for!" Latham had gotten jittery, breathing in huffs.

"I guess you're out of touch, my boy," Edgar said. "Tomorrow is Thanksgiving. The banks are closed, and they'll stay closed until Friday." He was speaking slowly, mocking Latham's nervous speed.

"Shit! You're right; blast it. Listen…listen to me. I know what to do! Get me to Bass River in Massachusetts. I have lots of cash in my safe. It's unmarked and undyed, and I won't miss it." Latham had put emphasis on those words. "Seriously. You can't avoid an offer like that, and you'll win big time. I won't do anything to get it back---please!!"

Latham had painted an inviting possibility, and it began to grow in their minds. Besides his ragged breathing, it was quiet in the large room---until Lazzo broke the silence.

"What if we do haul his ass to Massachusetts? What would happen? If this is all a lie, we can just dig a hole and close his account. Cindy might go for this. The irritating problem vanishes out of Nevada, and there's still a very good chance we will get a lot of cash in the effort."

Edgar stared over at him. "I guess there's a chance. When I was in the office, I looked up his latest name online. He does seem to have a big company…okay. I'll call and see what she says. I know she'd rather have the money, and this is a lot of moolah!"

Cindy instantly picked up. Edgar explained the situation to her as Latham cowered on the chair. He only heard Edgar's wordless grunts from her response to his summary. At least the call was short. He slid the mobile phone back into his pocket and frowned, even though he was basking in Latham's apprehension.

And then Lazzo interrupted his fun. "What did she say, Edgar! Come on, I gotta know."

"Okay, okay." He glared over at him. "Cindy said to fly to Massachusetts, depending on what we can find on standby. We should make it by early morning tomorrow." He wrenched Latham out of the chair. "Let's make sure Sammy here has his wallet with him so we can get him on the plane."

Latham was relieved. He was almost positive the trip would save him and get him out of this mess. He'd make it to Russia on Friday, after all!

Somewhere over the East Coast
3:00AM Thursday, November 24, 2005

Soaring over the Canadian border and into the United States, the biting cold up there didn't bother Slethim. It used the jet stream to increase its speed. A rebirth was coming to Bass River, and Slethim needed to be a witness. Another hour passed, moonlight reflecting off its wings. Flying over Gloucester, he was reaching the end of his journey, beginning to drop in altitude.

Las Vegas, Nevada
7:30PM Wednesday, November 23, 2005

Samuel sat in the coffee shop at the airport, hunting on Latham's computer. If he was going to enter Donnelly's house and take his place, he needed more information about him. He needed to know about his life. Slogging through digital rubbish, he saw the word *'confidential'* at the top of the screen. He hit the popup, and it opened the site. The oldest entry was a year old, and the most current was inserted just a few days ago. The file was a treasure trove!

Latham was about to double-cross his entire family financially and then move to Russia on the twenty-fifth. No one knew about this devious plan but 'Attison.' Samuel had no idea who this man was in Latham's life.

Everyone in the family thought Latham was going to California. His wife didn't know a divorce decree would land on her lap hours after he left the country.

Samuel found a wrapped gift in the items in the hotel room. The attached card was addressed to Latham's wife. He had intended to give it to her before he went to Russia as another painful jab at her. Reading more of the file, Samuel realized his doppelganger was a real piece of work. He was not a very nice man.

Latham's kidnapping may still end his life. Things might be simpler for Cindy if her goons do kill him. Samuel intended to drain one of his accounts and wire the money to a new account in Canada. Then, he'd change his name and transfer the cash to a secret account in the Bahamas and fill his pockets with plunder completely off the grid.

Latham gambling twenty feet away from him still stunned him. A fortuitous connection. He was going to get rich. Samuel saw no flaws in his upcoming plan, believing his demeanor, diction, and speaking voice would be close enough to Latham's. The entire family will instantly accept him.

Attison had heard Benson's message even while he was recording it, but he did not pick up the phone. Still, in LA, he changed his clothes and called his helicopter pilot to fly him over to Harry Reid Airport in Las Vegas. Jumping out of the craft, he took a limo to the main terminal. There had been real urgency in Benson's message, but Attison wasn't there to extricate Latham out of the position he was in. He had more important things to do.

Entering the main concourse, Attison moved at a swift pace. And then he stopped to search the large area with the eyes of a hawk. He found what he was looking for in a coffee shop across the way.

Samuel looked up from Latham's computer to see Attison sitting across from him at the table. Sam fell into Attison's eyes for a few seconds, but he got his bearings.

"Leave my table!" And Samuel then stood up.

"Hello, Samuel." Attison didn't move. "We don't need a long conversation. All you need is a simple adjustment---I advise you to sit down and relax. I'm here to help you."

Samuel looked around. Someone should help him oust this strange intruder, but anyone watching had turned away. Attison remained comfortable in his seat, sleek with those magnetic eyes. Samuel got more confused and sat down.

"What do you want?"

"I only want your attention. That should be agreeable enough."

In reality, Attison really didn't need an acceptance or any agreement from Samuel. He leaned forward and pressed his hand on Samuel's forehead and he did not move away from his touch. A couple, a few tables away, watched their odd interaction, riveted. Sam was motionless as if he was in a deep trance. Bluish light radiated out of Attison's fingertips, and the light spread across Samuel's forehead, vanishing under his hairline. It looked like that blue glow was alive. The couple got uneasy. They paid their bill and hastily left.

Attison stopped touching Samuel's forehead and leaned back in his chair.

"You won't have any problems communicating to anyone at your next stop, Samuel. They will know exactly who you are."

Samuel stared at the stranger, apparently still oblivious to the physical and mental connection Attison had just come through with him.

"What did you want?" Sam asked. "This whole thing isn't making any sense. You need to stop bothering me."

Since Attison's task was over, he did what Samuel had just advised him to do. He walked out of the coffee shop and disappeared into the crowd.

His server came over to Sam's table. "Do you need anything else?"

"Yes. Another burger." He'd use the extra time to learn more about Latham on his computer---and he was actually still hungry. And Samuel wanted to give his waiter a compliment.

"You've done your job well. Not interrupting me, just checking to see if I needed anything. Your name is Steve, right?"

"Yeah. Thanks." But Steve frowned. "I'm not supposed to talk to anyone on a personal level, but I'm too surprised by the change. How did you find a way to affect your voice and mannerisms that much since the last time I talked to you twenty minutes ago? You sound like a different man. Do you use that wild ability on stage?"

Samuel was baffled. "I'm talking the same way I did when I first got here, and I haven't changed a thing. Maybe you ate something hallucinatory in the kitchen a few minutes ago." And then he chuckled.

"Okay, sir — if you say so. I'll bring out your next burger. Do you want it to be cooked the same as the last one?"

"Yup. That will be fine."

Steve walked over to the small window to drop off the new order, and he was shaking his head. The guy had to be flat-out nuts, not accepting his transformation…or he was playing head games with him. Either way, the whole thing was weird.

Samuel walked out of Logan Airport in Boston at 2:15 AM Eastern Time, busily reading the parking stub he'd found in Latham's wallet. "D-45".

Section D was in the far-left section in the acres of cars, parked in tight. When he got there, he pushed a button on the keys. A coffee-colored Mercedes beeped to him three lanes away. Samuel walked over and stowed the luggage in the trunk. With the help of a GPS to guide him, the next and last part of his trip started.

He drove over Bass River Bridge at four in the morning. The tide was going out, so the current in the river was carrying the water out to sea. The car's tracker blinked, letting him know. He was close. Still anxious over his new role, he felt better after learning quite a lot about Donnelly. There was a powerful disconnection throughout the entire family. If he put on a cowboy hat and line danced across the living room, they'd likely clap and support his show. Imagining dancing in front of them, he smiled, and the vision calmed him even more as he drove through the last twisting curves in the road.

The mansion blazed up in the headlights. Samuel didn't know how to open one door in the six-car garage. He parked next to a motorcycle. Taking the bags out of the trunk, he rolled them over to the front door. The secondary key on the ring got him into the entrance hall. Looking up at the two staircases rising to the second floor, Samuel moved towards a large entrance into the living room. He hit some switches on a nearby control panel. A chandelier in the middle of the room lit up, and he saw a couch in front of a fireplace in the distance. With the computer on his shoulder, he dragged the suitcase behind him. Reaching the couch, he tossed a throw pillow under his head and lay down. Then he reached out and flicked a switch and turned the overhead lights out.

Bass River, Massachusetts
10:00AM Thursday, November 24, 2005

"Good morning, Mrs. Donnelly," the chef said, delighted to see her enter the kitchen.

"Good morning, Vince."

"No worries about the meal. The sides are set up." And he tapped his finger on his palm: "Wild rice, yams in syrup, fresh petite peas, chestnuts, homemade cranberry sauce, and, of course, the oyster stuffing." He smiled. "The turkey is roasted in a slow oven. Someone has to bast it every hour after I leave. That should begin at three, okay? It's important. I glazed the ham with orange brandy and triple sec, with pineapple rings from Belize on top. Please relay my compliments to Justin on the ham. It's a superior brand. I've never heard of the company before, but the brine used to cure it was unique."

"I'll let him know," April said. "The air in this kitchen smells divine. Every year, you make our Thanksgiving dinners even better." Picking a spoon off

217

the counter, she stirred the gravy simmering on the stove. "We'll have dinner at six. Mirabelle won't be with us this year either, but we can handle it with your directions."

"I know you can. Mirabelle is stacking the sides in the cooler for now, arranging them in the steam table before she leaves. They'll reach the right temperature by six."

Mirabelle sailed out of the walk-in cooler and waved over at April.

Vince went on, "The ham and turkey will be ready on time as well. Take the turkey out at five thirty and let it rest for half an hour before carving. There's nothing else to worry about. Remember to use gloves when you move the turkey in and out of the oven since a work towel isn't foolproof. When I get back, I don't want to see any burned skin on anyone in this house!"

Vince put his overcoat on, patting a pocket to hear his car keys jingle. "I'm sorry I can't stay, but my in-laws are coming this year, and my wife's orders can't be denied."

Mirabelle's voice floated towards them from the corner of the room, "And my sister got sick. I have no choice. I have to drive everyone everywhere tonight, but I'll be back in the morning to clean everything up."

"Both of you relax. No worries! Everything is fine. It'll be more intimate for us---and you've both done a great job." April pointed at the door. "Thank you, Vince. Go ahead and run."

"Have a wonderful Thanksgiving, Mrs. Donnelly. Give my best wishes to the rest of the family. Mirabelle, I pray you and yours will have a great holiday too!"

"Happy Thanksgiving, Vince!" Mirabelle called out.

He waved goodbye and left. The service door at the end of the hall closed with a thud.

Mirabelle helped April set up the appetizer cart, and she saw apprehension in her gaze. Make-up and expensive clothes didn't hide it. Done with the simple task, Mirabelle watched her leave the room way too fast like she was suddenly running away from some hungry monster. With a shiver, Mirabelle returned to her work, trying not to think about Mrs. Donnelly.

Leaving the kitchen, April trotted through the living room. She glanced through an oversized window to see Latham's Mercedes parked out there. Her head tilted…why hadn't he put his car in the garage? And then she saw his suitcase near the fireplace. She tiptoed closer. He lay on the couch asleep. Why wasn't he in his bed? April turned back to the kitchen to ask Mirabelle, but her husband's voice stopped her in her tracks.

"Hello, April." He rubbed his eyelids to get the sticky sleep goo off. "How are you?"

"Fine, Latham, but you look terrible." She trembled slightly with nervousness. "Why didn't you go upstairs last night or…even this morning? Wouldn't you feel better in your bed?"

"You're full of curiosity, aren't you. Okay, I'll tell you. I was too tired last night to go any farther, but I agree with you." Samuel reached over to his suitcase. "I'm going upstairs to get more sleep. When's dinner?"

"About six...what...what are you doing?"

Samuel was unzipping the suitcase to find her present.

"Here, honey. I bought this for you in Las Vegas because we're not going to spend a lot of time together over the next few months. I thought you'd like to open it before everyone else gets here."

"Thank you, Latham."

April took the gift out of his hand and tore the wrapping paper off. Her belly began to hurt. Monaco's was printed on a snazzy box, and when she lifted the top, she saw the wristwatch. Diamonds indicated hours, and a larger stone shone in the center. An expensive trinket. Beautiful enough to be called art. A tear ran down her cheek.

"You like it! I can see that in your expression."

Rezipping the suitcase, he stood up. Samuel put the computer bag over his shoulder, and then he pecked April's cheek and walked towards the staircases.

"Thank you, Latham. It's quite..."

He would be too far away to hear the rest of her sentence stuck in an emotional knot in her throat, and it wouldn't matter anyway. She crumbled on the couch to breathe out the word beautiful.

Samuel did not know where the elevator was, so he climbed the stairs. Two hallways led off from the landing, and he picked the one on the right. He moved to the end of the corridor to begin his search. He knocked on the first door. Silence invited him into a suite painted blue with a touch of perfume in the air. It was clearly not the answer. The next door opened into a closet with cleaning supplies, and he was relieved when he opened the third door, dropping the bags and closing the drapes against the morning light. Samuel took the suit off, tossing his fifty-nine-year-old body on Latham Donnelly's California king bed. He pulled the covers up to his chin. The memory foam of the mattress hugged his body as if he'd been sleeping there for years.

Boston, Massachusetts
3:00PM Thursday, November 24, 2005

Lazzo, Edgar, and their prisoner waited at the McCarran Airport. Three seats opened on flight 749 departing at 6:00 AM on Thanksgiving Day. Cindy's ruffians were able to bring their handguns on the flight using three different kinds of permits. They landed in Boston at three that afternoon, considering the three-hour change from PST to EST.

Cindy had a contract with Apache Car Rentals, and Edgar had already called the office in Boston to set up a car for them when they got there. Landing on time, they took the escalator to the first floor to reach the line-up of car rental companies near the exit. The kidnappers weren't watching their hostage as diligently as they had before. Crossing the terminal, Latham might have had a chance to get away. He

221

didn't even try. Exhausted, he was twenty years older than his captors, and he wasn't sure how painful that escape could have been. He just wanted to get home. In his dazed mind, the easiest answer would be to pay off these lowbrow lackeys. Standing in front of the Apache Rentals counter, Latham's possible escape was now gone, no matter how he felt.

Edgar took his wallet out. "We talked on the phone a few hours ago. There should be transportation set up for the Phalanx Group from Las Vegas." He raised his eyebrows.

"Hello, sir." The clerk smiled, punching his name into the computer. "Yes---it's all ready." He took the contract out and gave the document to Edgar to sign in four different places.

"Someone will be bringing it around for you right now."

They went outside, and in a minute or so, a black Lincoln Town Car wheeled around the corner. The driver got out and dropped the keys into Edgar's hand. Lazzo gave him a tip.

Holiday traffic was sluggish as they left the airport. Edgar drove, and Latham stretched out on the back seat. The soft upholstery began to sing a lullaby to him, but it was not quite enough to break through the fear his captors had installed within him. Maybe talking to them about something completely off the point of their trip could calm his nerves...

"Hey, Lazzo, we've got time to waste. Can I ask you a personal question? Would that be alright?"

Both killers twisted their heads to stare at him. Edgar turned his attention back to the road, but Lazzo put his phone back in his pocket. Hard for him to play games since his fingers were too big to hit the numbers on the screen every time. Samuel's question might be a fine distraction.

"Sure. What do you want to know?" Lazzo asked.

Latham leaned forwards. "You don't seem very religious. Why do you have three crosses around your neck? Is there a reason for that?" He sat back, clasping his hands behind his head.

"I hedge my bets." Lazzo laughed.

"Is that a joke? I hate to say it, but it sounds lame."

"It's no joke. My family is Greek Orthodox. We'd go to church every Sunday."

"And God sits on a throne in heaven?"

"Yeah... of course."

Latham was surprised by his response. "Is there a religion that excuses the murder of people who are late on their bills? How could your own family's religion let you into heaven? A cross around your neck, or even a collection of them, should not be enough to open the pearly gates."

"You think you know what I do, but you don't have the real story, Sammy, not at all!" Lazzo was irritated. "I do what I'm told. I get rid of bad people, people who ignore their responsibilities...like you. Lazy, greedy dumdums. I'm cleaning the world up right now."

Spinning an absurd rationalization out of thin air, he was happy. He felt righteous. Staring out at the

223

highway, Edgar was smiling too—for a completely different reason.

Latham kept on going, "What about the Ten Commandments? You're not supposed to kill? Isn't that a big one? You break that law a lot."

"'An eye for an eye' is another law in the bible too…and…ah, there's the other commandment saying you can't steal. God works in mysterious ways. He put me here to stop you from stealing. How's that! Oh…and you were curious about my crosses. It's the Trinity…the Father, the Son, and the Holy Ghost. Each one should have its own cross."

Latham almost started laughing, but he restrained himself. He didn't want to upset the ungentle giant.

Edgar piped up, "All these years, and I haven't had a clue why you had those extra crosses on. I didn't want to ask you, afraid you'd get mad." He glanced over his shoulder again and nodded at Latham. "Thanks, Sam! Mystery solved."

"You're welcome."

Latham unlocked his hands and dropped them like dead meat on his thighs. Staring out at the passing countryside, the strange conversation he'd had with Lazzo didn't make him feel better. Under the thrall of these two killers, paying them all the money they wanted still might not save him. He really should have run for it at the airport.

Bass River, Massachusetts
3:06PM Thursday, November 24, 2005

Mirabelle drove over the bridge that spanned Bass River while David and Holly, in their Mercedes, passed her at the same time, squeezing by nice and tight on the thin span. They both honked and waved.

Wearing his custom-tailored suit, David looked magnificent, a squire ready to present his lady to court. Holly was just as remarkable, with a tight dress and her dark hair curled into long ringlets. Hanging between her collarbones, blue fire burned in the form of a large sapphire on a platinum chain.

The couple had not spoken since they'd left the house as the music from the album *The Twelve Dreams of Dr. Sardonicus* from the band Spirit filled the silence.

An hour before they left, David Russell returned to the garage. He retrieved the secret bag he'd hidden in the Sand Garden and slipped it into the inner pocket of his suit jacket. Besides erasing his duplicitous wife, David would also exterminate the rest of the family. A secondary blessing since it would give him the monetary power he yearned for.

As the miles rolled by, Holly was mulling over her plans. It was extremely important to talk to David one more time before they got to the estate. It was serious. She had a powerful intuition that something deadly would take place at the reunion… and she wanted to save him---maybe give him a way out, maybe give them both an escape.

225

Holly turned the stereo down. "Did you ever want to buy a boat?"

David looked over at her and grinned. "I wanted to own a thirty-five-foot yacht in some marina off Pope's Island and vacation on it with you... but things have changed. I don't believe in much anymore." David was careful. He didn't want her to get a hint about the bag in his pocket.

We should buy one! Since you're blowing in the wind, and I'm bored, we should get out of here. My upcoming promotion heralds nothing but headaches. I need a break, and I pray you feel the same way, sweetheart. Let's sail away!"

Holly had startled him badly. David had not foreseen an invitation like that one coming out of her. And he had no time to ponder over the new possibilities.

David drove through some hard turns in the road, while Holly dug into her bag to get her lipstick. The ongoing instability in the car didn't affect her precision in applying the makeup. David was shaken and stirred and too busy driving to notice yet another impossibility in her actions. Her lips were perfect, and her lipstick went back into the bag.

He looked over at her as long as he could. His wife seemed to have become a different person. Living into a money hole, he thought he'd gotten there by her lies and his father-in-law's scorn, and asking for a crust of bread monetarily, he'd been left high and dry.

So, what was she offering him now? Were there romantic overtones in this offer? Would she renew their relationship in bed? That sexual utopia bloomed in his mind, and he was about to change his plans. Holly's erotic flower was about to find purchase in his heart... but at the last moment, it wilted, drifting out of the car window like an invisible mist. David's emotional corruption trumped his love, foreseeing his future ride into the Atlantic in the new boat as an easy way for Holly to avoid a court battle in divorce proceedings. She'd push him overboard like shark bait. The entire problem will end soon---he'd just play along for now.

"Don't you have a fleet of yachts in some cove off the coast of Rhode Island, honey?"

"I didn't know you knew about them, as well as the cruise ship anchored in the Mediterranean named Aspersion's Foil? Seriously, can you answer me, David? Are we going to get away or not? Should l put some feelers out for that boat and write out a resignation to the hospital?"

"It will be a dream come true---but I'm surprised you're breaking your work addiction. Anyway, I agree our current situation is untenable. I love your fairytale. We can make it happen and sail into the valentine heart you've painted around a rising sun." He laughed, and she frowned.

"We both need a break," Holly said. "If you mean what you say, I'll start looking."

But she already knew the real answer. Her offer had been rejected. The love she had for him had not been enough. Her premonition about the family dinner got heavier and pulled at her like a thick iron chain.

David parked next to Robert's Harley, surprised that Latham's Mercedes was not in the garage. As they walked to the front door, Holly hooked her arm around his, and he rang the bell.

"In only a few weeks, we could be motoring away somewhere," Holly said, yet a faint line dug into her forehead.

Latham's smarmy conversation with April on the phone had unsettled her. She needed to believe her predictions were true. The bad wolf shall announce his evil intentions, and she'll deflect and parry. Arranging a curl in her hair, she didn't notice that a tear was running down her cheek. Unlike imaginary monsters under our beds, the creatures besetting her were born from real problems. More kernels of fear germinated in her mind. There was no real life without luxury in her reality, and those kernels grew into tall stalks of folly.

Her new diamond watch sparkled on her wrist. It was three o'clock. Time to baste the turkey! April tied a yellow scarf around her neck and took the elevator to the kitchen. Apron and mitts on, she opened the oven door and lifted the oversized turkey out, setting it down on the center island. Having spooned the pan drippings over the bird, she put the turkey back in the oven, but this time, her arm muscles shook. From now on, she'd transfer future basting responsibilities to Justin or David.

Returning to the living room, she looked at her reflection in the mirrored wall. A long-sleeved white satin shirt tucked into a skirt with spots of green, orange, yellow, and blue splattered across the white fabric. She'd added a gold belt and matching gold shoes. A yellow scarf — the final touch. The occasional tear left no track on her waterproof foundation.

The doorbell rang. The children had arrived! April almost ran there. She opened the door and hugged her daughter.

"Happy Thanksgiving! It's wonderful to see you!"

"Happy Thanksgiving, Mom." Holly squeezed those words out against a hug that was more like a clamp.

David leaned over and pecked his mother-in-law on the cheek, "Happy Thanksgiving!"

He started to take his jacket off, but April turned around and redirected him. "No, no. Don't take your coats off! You have to see my new hedge sculpture." April quickly took her coat out of the closet. Holly and David looked at each other. "I know, I know. You probably think it's a jockey on a horse or a chess piece, but it's not. It's a surprise!"

She led them through the library door. They tramped into the maze, and the sculpture was just around the first turn. April pointed up. A twenty-mile-an-hour wind was tossing the leaf dolphins around as if they were almost alive.

"It's delightful!" Holly said. She was holding her cape tight to her body. "I've never seen anything like it before. What made you think of the idea?"

David chimed in, "It's surprising! Where did you come up with the concept?"

April couldn't tell them the truth. She'd been in bed with her plastic surgeon, staring at pictures in an article about the Gulf of Mexico. She had to come up with a different explanation, lickety-split.

"Have you ever heard of Charlene's? It's a salon in Boston."

"I know the place," Holly said. "They won't give me the time of day, but I heard they're worth the money if you can get in." She didn't want to take her mother's glory away, but in reality, the owners pampered her. After her last cut, they'd ask her if they could put a picture of her in the window.

April went on, "Well, I was waiting for my appointment, and flipping through a magazine, oh, they have a good organic fruit concoction to drink while you wait. Anyway, I saw a picture of dolphins, and I couldn't get it out of my head. I called Gregory and Paul. Remember the arches near the fountain and the Q-tips near the boat dock? They did those installations. I told them what I wanted, and presto, there it was!" Her hair was going wild.

"I think it's getting too gusty out here," Holly said. "We've seen the flying dolphins, but maybe we should go back to the house?"

April told Robert his father intended to drive to the airport on Friday, and that knowledge burrowed into his head. Robert had arrived a day early. During the first night there, he tossed and turned, unable to sleep in his old room. At 5:30 in the morning, he popped his head into the hallway. It was silent as a tomb out there; everybody had to be asleep. Leaving the door ajar, he put his clothes on, grabbed his leather jacket and took the main stairs to the entry hall. Walking into the living room, he saw his father sleeping on the couch. His spirits lifted---things might still work out!

Returning to the entry hall, he carefully opened the front door. Robert didn't know why his car wasn't in the garage, but that didn't matter. He can take care of things either way. It ain't brain surgery. The reading light in his pocket would be enough. He walked over to his bike and unlocked the seat to get his pliers. An oversized paperclip was also nestled in his pocket. He opened the driver's door of the Mercedes and leaned in to flip a lever under the dash to open the hood. Robert's previous experience as a car mechanic for a few months had given him all the knowledge he needed to set this up. Leaving the small light on the washer fluid container, he could see the seven-by-five-inch master brake cylinder...and the black cap in the center of the container. He took it off and put it in his pocket. Then he bent the paperclip into the shape he needed before he squeezed his fingers into that small opening to find the floater. Hooking the now curved end of the paper clip around the metal arm of the floater at the bottom of the brake fluid held in the cylinder, he carefully wriggled the rest of the paperclip into a side ridge where the cap sat. Robert screwed the cap back down hard, making sure the connection to the floater was secure even with the paperclip passing through it. This iffy contraption should stay in place even if the car hits a pothole.

The floater was wired to a display on the dashboard, alerting the driver if the brake fluid dropped too low. After Robert's jury-rigging, those safety protocols, like stopping the engine, were off-line. The floater was stuck in place, even if all the brake fluid drained out. And anyone backing out of this parking space on Friday morning would not notice the puddles on the pavement. He closed the hood and wriggled under the car, using his pliers to open a tiny hole in one of the brake lines near the engine. The fluid would leak out slowly in the next twelve hours.

His job was done. He went back to bed, imagining his father driving those last miles of twisty road. Robert sniggered. Patricide was a culmination for him, ending Latham's life, a wonderful climax. This inner wanting of his could not be stopped or fine-tuned. His latest action was far from ingenious, clearly leaving clues behind. Nevertheless, those future potholes didn't bother him.

Bass River, Massachusetts
3:32PM Thursday, November 24, 2005

Justin removed the case he'd bought in New Orleans out of the glove compartment and slipped it into an inner pocket of his coat. The trees at the edge of the parking field were bending in the wind, and he flipped his collar up before getting out of the car.

No answer at the front door. Justin assumed they'd all go outside. He walked around the house and then into the hedge maze before putting two fingers in his mouth to create an ear-splitting whistle, followed by a loud shout, "HELLO! Anybody out here?"

"Take the main path...we're right here." It was David's voice. Justin stepped around the corner to enjoy welcoming hugs and hellos, even as he complimented April's hedge sculpture.

"Certainly unusual. I think it's great. Where's Robert and Dad?"

"Dad got home very late last night. He's probably still sleeping," April said. "He'll meet us later. Robert's resting." She looked up. Clouds were racing north fast. "It's too windy and cold out here. We were already on our way back inside to enjoy the holiday."

Robert took the elevators to the kitchen to get coffee. Vince and Mirabelle were busy setting everything up, and they just nodded towards him. Holding his cup, he snagged a pastry left on a plate on the center island and returned to his bedroom. Putting the cup of hot coffee and donut on the end table, he lay back on the bed and fell asleep.

A fanged beast prowled through his dreams and frightened him. He woke up rattled and sweaty. Rolling out of bed, Robert took the cocaine out of his backpack to set lines up on the mirrored surface of the small table. He inhaled them to blow away the heebie-jeebies and give him full control again---the master of all. The cushioned seat in the garden window was his throne, and King Robert overlooked the driveway. A Mercedes rolled in and parked next to his Harley. His sister and brother-in-law got out.

The lower lid of his eye started twitching. He rubbed at it. He guzzled brandy from a flask he had in the back pocket of his jeans. That should calm the spasm. It did not. The pesky tic kept jiggling under his skin like a microscopic bed bug. Robert had another idea to end the problem, and it was left under the seat of his bike.

He jogged out to his Harley and lifted the seat to reach the box holding the few tools and paperwork. He ripped off the duct tape he'd attached to the side of that container. His salvation was wrapped in silver foil, and he stuffed the silver egg in his front pocket. He closed the cushioned seat and returned to his room. Robert stuffed a chunk of hash in the bowl of a brass pipe, lit it up, and inhaled. He did this three more times until the nerve under his eye relaxed.

He peeled off his sweaty turtleneck. On the bottom of his backpack was a long-sleeved black cotton shirt, a suede vest, and matching pants. It was the best he could do to be formal. He zipped up the pants and buttoned the vest, and Robert went downstairs to have Thanksgiving with his family.

Samuel stretched and looked at the clock. 3:45 PM. Time to impersonate Donnelly yet again with a touch of his own personal aur. He had to feel comfortable in a challenging position. Stepping over to the closet, he began to pick through his suits. Seeking one in white linen that reminded him of the one he'd put on in Las Vegas, he ended his search. It would be fine for the upcoming affair. He'd gotten used to it.

In the crazy escape mode in Las Vegas, Samuel had packed everything Latham had in the hotel room as fast as he could. He had also tossed the two packs of cards and wrapped-up chips the management had left in the room into the luggage as well. Another idea came to him. He could use the cards and chips as tools to introduce himself to the family as an improved version of their father. He chuckled.

Dropping cards and chips into his pockets, he strolled out to enjoy Thanksgiving—with a family he did not know. And why not? Lady Luck was still holding his hand---wasn't she?

Bass River, Massachusetts
3:50PM Thursday, November 24, 2005

April slipped out of her coat and tossed it on the nearest chair. "You know where the library is, right? I have to get the appetizers." And she darted through the door had bumped into Robert.

"Oh! Robbie...I didn't see you...are you okay?"

"Relax, Mom. Slow down, it's a holiday." He grinned and hugged her.

"You're right. I have to stop and relax! Oh, you look very nice."

April resumed her trip more sedately---for a few steps anyway, before her inner tension winded her right back up again. She powerwalked into the cooler to grab the trays: shrimp puffs, cucumber sandwiches, and black caviar on water crackers. Putting them on a cart, she rolled them out of the kitchen and into the library. April set the finger food on the coffee table, and then she looked at the jeweled watch on her wrist.

"I basted the turkey at three. Vince insists we must baste the bird once an hour…and it's almost four. One of you needs to take that chore off my back. Would you mind doing that, Justin?"

His mouth filled with caviar and cracker, and only a gurgle came out. He tried to answer. Crumbs popped out. "Noprrobblemm!"

Everyone laughed as he stood up and began his journey to the kitchen. After his trip into the hedge maze, he'd left his coat in the hallway closet. He stopped to retrieve the case and stepped into the nearby bathroom. Opening the case, Justin left it on the toilet tank and removed the bottle and the syringe from their foam inserts, imagining these actions a thousand times in his head. He opened the bottle and punctured the foil with the needle to fill the syringe with poison. Taking the needle out, Justin wrapped the point in toilet paper to avoid run-off. Then he arranged the loaded syringe in a nest of more toilet paper in his pocket and put the bottle back in the case. He dropped the box in his other pocket and flushed the toilet.

The aroma in the kitchen made his mouth water, usually triggering the idea of eating dinner. However, in Justin's case, something else would take its place. Done basting the turkey, he left the brush on a plate near the sink. Time to set up his deadly trap. He peeked into the hall. Nothing but faint conversation coming down the hall from the library. All clear---no one was coming. He took the syringe out of his pocket and tossed the tissue in the garbage, inserting the needle into the bird's breast. He pushed the plunger down, but only halfway, taking the syringe out to reinsert the last of the tetrodotoxin into the stuffing. Done, he removed the empty weapon, rinsing it off in the sink before replacing it back in the case. Oven mitts on his hands, Justin slid the turkey back into the oven. He briskly left the kitchen, dropping the box back in his coat on his trip back to the library.

He started to foresee what was going to happen in the middle of dinner. When they all felt the effects, he'd call for help. No one would be able to watch him run outside to throw the case into the creek before law enforcement and a medical team arrived. He shouldn't count his eggs before they were hatched, but Justin had forgotten the old adage. He sauntered into the library with satisfaction on his face.

"Was there a problem? You were gone for quite a while," April said.

"I just had a pit stop is all. And the turkey smells great!" He grabbed a new glass off the rack above the bar, grinning and flipping it in the air before pouring himself a victory drink. Triple sec, cranberry juice, orange juice, and Grey Goose vodka. He leaned against the bar...but only for a minute. Dad wasn't there. Justin got worried until Samuel stepped into the library. The charlatan instantly showered everyone with an inclusive greeting.

"Happy Thanksgiving! Sorry, I'm late. My meeting in Vegas had been a drag, and it hadn't been easy getting home."

Samuel draped his arm around April's waist and kissed her on the cheek. His sudden affection for her mystified everyone else in the room. April started to unravel, her well-crafted face collapsing into a rictus. Holly stepped over and redirected Samuel's attention. She hugged him, and he returned her embrace with enthusiasm. That worked. Holly had peeled Samuel away from Latham's wife, not even knowing for sure that was the case.

"I'm impressed by your stamina after all those miles under your belt," Holly said. "Can I make you a drink?"

April had lurched over to the couch, sitting next to Robert, while Samuel followed Holly to the bar.

"What would you like...Dad?" Holly inserted faint suspicion in that familial greeting.

"Gin and tonic." But Samuel's brows lowered having heard that hint of doubt in her voice.

Holly looked around. No one was looking over at the bar. She was almost positive the man standing at the bar was not Latham Donnley, and she decided to play with his head with one of her exceptional talents. The sapphire at her throat sparkled while she mixed his drink, but Samuel had never seen anyone in his life move that fast. It was unnatural. He got uneasy and a bit pale as Holly slid his well-mixed drink across the bar. It stopped right in front of him. Tongue-tied, Samuel just sipped at his drink, Holly smirking at him like a teenager. He had to untie his bafflement and say something right then and there…

"Ah…it…it tastes great, my dear. Your technique is out of this world, faster than a…I don't even know what!" His voice cracked with nervousness, but he needed to keep on talking, "Did you go to bartending school?" He looked over his shoulder and threw a question out there. "Did anyone else see what she just did?" No one heard him.

"Now, now, *Dad*, you know what I've been doing, and it wasn't tending bar."

"Of course, I know that. I'm just giving you a compliment. You were born with a knack, is all. I can't move like that, so you must have taken after Mom."

He smiled widened as if he had no problems at all, while his uneasiness grew. Samuel looked up at Latham Donnelly's portrait on the wall…and he remembered. He was his twin. No one noticed any difference in their voices, still not realizing what Attison had done to him in the airport coffee shop. His apprehension faded. Samuel turned away from Holly's weirdness and raised his voice to get everyone's attention.

"When I was in Vegas, they gave me some gifts." He raised the cards and chips out of his pockets and lifted them up. "Let's play some cards. One chip would be a hundred dollars. It'd be a hoot and no harm done…well, maybe a little harm if you keep losing."

It was suddenly silent. No answer, not even a nod. Samuel got nervous. "So, what do you think?" He had no idea why his invitation remained floating out there like a transmission from outer space…

Until Justin chimed in, "Sounds great. What game do you have in mind?"

"Poker. A five-card draw, gents and ladies. Tried and true, a classic with nothing wild." Samuel winked, and another smile bloomed across his face, larger than before---almost cartoonish. "Nothing will be wild, at least in the beginning. Everyone okay with a hundred-dollar chip idea?"

A general agreement, except Robert, who stared into his large glass of brandy. He retreated to an unlighted corner of the room to sulk. Justin and David cleared off the main table and rearranged some of the furniture. Samuel sat down in the armchair and shuffled the cards. Justin had dragged another chair over and sat down next to him. April stayed on the couch, and Holly took Robert's place next to her. David perched on the edge of the divan. Arranging themselves around the coffee table comfortably enough. Samuel moved the shuffled deck over to Justin for a cut, and they started to play.

They agreed that the dealer would change every five games in a clockwise direction. April said she wasn't up to deal, so they skipped her. The game went on, but it seemed something was badly wrong. Samuel won almost all the time. Holly decided to fix the unlikely odds. When she got the deal, she whispered into Samuel's ear, advising him to accept what was about to happen. Whether it was his own experience or he just had good luck, Holly put a mojo on him by lowering the magnetism around him. His winning streak quickly lowered to a normal percentage. Justin and April won the next two hands.

"Please deal me out for a couple of hands, okay?" David said. "I'll be back in a flash, but I want to check on the temperatures to make sure everything is cooking correctly."

Walking away, he gazed over his shoulder to see his family playing cards. There was an expression of stone-cold detachment, and his eyes gleamed.

Entering the dining room, he lifted the covers of the steel pans heating on the steam table. Yams, petite fresh peas, gravy…and homemade cranberry sauce. He left that cover off. Debonair in his three-piece suit, David slipped into the silk-lined inner pocket of his jacket to take the bag of berries and the gloves out. Putting the gloves on, he opened the bag and squeezed the yew mush into the cranberry sauce. The color of the wild invaders mixed in perfectly as David blended them together with the ladle. Dastardly deed done, he covered the container.

Then he saw a real problem. He was holding the empty plastic bag in his gloved hand. He couldn't flush the bag or the gloves down the toilet. It might clog the system. There has to be a way to dispose of them instantly and right away!

Adrenaline rushed him into a plan. Opening the hallway door, he made sure no one was out there. He jogged past the koi pond to the fireplace. Toxic fumes might come out of that small amount on the gloves and bag, but at this juncture, he had no other options. He took the gloves off, stuffed them in the bag, and threw the plastic ball into the middle of the fire. Stuffing the lump even deeper into the flames with the poker, he watched it twist and curl and shrivel to black. He dropped the poker on the hearthstones with a loud bang as if it was too hot to handle. David raced away, not knowing if anything was really coming out of it or not. When he reached the library door, he had to wait for his breathing to settle down. It wouldn't be right to walk in panting like a Retriever. Deciding he had returned to normal, he entered and sauntered over to the bar to pick up his drink.

"Deal me back in, okay?"

Samuel nodded, including him in the next deal. "You really do want to play, don't you son. It looks like you ran full tilt, leaving you panting for more!"

Bass River, Massachusetts
4:56PM Thursday, November 24, 2005

"It's five o'clock!" April said, staring at her diamond-riddled wristwatch. "One of you must baste the turkey." Then she sipped her drink.

Samuel found Latham's illegal Cuban cigars in a humidor on the desk. Lighting one, a plume of smoke floated towards the ceiling. Latham himself would have done the same thing. April would say, 'Not when we have guests!' But this time, she was distracted.

"Time for an intermission," Holly announced. "Justin or David will baste the bird, and Mom and I will relax. We'll play a few more games in fifteen minutes or so---right before dinner. Sound okay?"

After they all agreed, Holly and Samuel sat at the bar. She looked through one of the large windows. Leaves tumbled across the yard. The powerful wind rushed over the roof, and, for a few seconds, a susurrus overpowered the soft music in the library.

Robert had gone upstairs to refresh himself, and Justin and David had both gone to the kitchen with April in tow. David leaned against the counter while Justin took the turkey out of the oven. His mother-in-law fluttered around the kitchen like a moth, opening cupboards and peering into drawers, bumping into him on her second trip into the cooler.

"What are you looking for, April? Maybe I can help you."

"Where did Vince put my parmesan cheese? He usually leaves it in a drawer in the cooler or on the counter before dinner. It's always in one of those places. I can't eat dinner without parmesan cheese!" David stayed out of her way, and her question was actually self-directed.

"Calm down, April. Cheese on your food is like putting salt on it." David raised his voice, "Mom!" He wanted her to enjoy her dinner. After all, what was the point of everything he'd been working for if the end result failed?

She wasn't listening, focused on her hunt for Parmesan. April ran into the hall to get her cell phone out of her pocketbook and called Vince...and then Mirabelle. No one answered. She was running out of options. Otto's Delicatessen was seven miles away. She wondered if they had parmesan or even if they were still open. Nothing to lose, she called them too. A girl picked up and told her they had parmesan cheese. They'd be open for another twenty-five minutes. April snatched her purse and ran to the entry hall. Samuel had left Latham's keys on the table near the front door. The Mercedes was in the driveway. Since her own car was in the garage, she thought it might shave off a minute if she took Latham's car. She picked those keys up and opened the front door with the strength of the damned.

Bass River, Massachusetts
5:05PM Thursday, November 24, 2005

Justin basted the turkey for the last time; time to leave the bird on the counter to rest. In his mind, Latham will soon be carving up more than turkey meat, death hiding in the slices he'd cut off with the electric knife.

April ran off---David's attempts to dissuade her had not worked.

"She's flipped out! Have you ever seen her go that crazy before?" David said.

"Not really, but I think there's something else going on in her head besides the cheese. Hey, don't worry about it. All women are nuts, and the two at the reunion clearly underline the truth. Mom will be back in twenty, holding her sacred parmesan, fine as she can be. Looking forwards to playing a few more games of poker. Are you into it?"

"Sure."

Walking to the library together, David glanced at his brother-in-law and narrowed his eyes. "Should I be worried about the food tonight, bro? Last I heard, you didn't even want to show up. Yet, lo and behold, here you are. Is there something more powerful than love bringing you here?" And then he sniggered.

"I seriously considered sending you all to your graves, but work used up all the time I had to set it up." Justin shrugged. "Maybe next year...wait a minute, should I be concerned? You're free and clear for more than enough time to set up anything you wanted to end us all."

"I just get soused, play golf at the club, and eat fattening food, so don't worry about it." Then David sounded more somber. "What was behind our conversation in Boston, anyway? I was downing in flames in court, signaling a depressing part of my life, and I think we were just blowing off steam, dreaming up stuff that only happens in the movies. I've gotten a lot better. Holly and I are about to buy a boat, and she wants to start things up between us again."

Justin burst into laughter. "Are you really talking about the devil in a blue dress in the library with Dad right now? The same one you married? Nope, I don't think you have that story right. I think you've lost it. She's hypnotized you into a brain-dead acolyte."

David raised his hands, a barrier against Justin's barbs. "Being a house husband is less stressful than cutting people up. I'd used to look over my shoulder at the defibrillator while I clamped off an artery, hoping I'd get the job done fast enough to allow the patient to stay alive. A life on a boat with Holly looks more appealing every day."

He followed Justin's laughter with a cackle of his own, and his brother-in-law didn't notice the odd texture in his uneven chortle. Even if he did, it wouldn't matter. He believed David would never touch a hair on anyone's head, and David himself believed the same thing about Justin. As the men relaxed at the bar, they felt regretful over what was about to happen. However, neither of them concerned about slaughtering the other or the extended mass murder of their entire family. Robert stepped up to the bar to fill his glass with Jim Beam before retreating to the back corner of the room.

"Where's April?" Samuel's question was thrown out to anyone in the room to answer, and he sat in the large chair at the table. "I thought she wanted to play cards a little longer."

"She'll be back in twenty," Justin said. "She drove to Otto's to buy parmesan cheese. I can't believe the deli was still open!"

"She took her car, right?" Robert's words wavered out from the shadows... "She took the Fiat?"

"The deli was about to close, so Mom took the Mercedes. It was already parked outside. I guess she thought it would speed her up."

Justin tried to make his brother out, crouching back there. Robert suddenly stood up and streaked out of the double door, ignoring them all as he dug into his pockets for his motorcycle keys and his cell phone. It was probably way too late to save her, but he had to try — maybe there was a last-ditch chance. Bursting out of the house, Robert didn't have his leather jacket on. The north wind's cold touch seared into his skin, but the certainty that he'd likely killed his mother overwhelmed that chilling pain and everything else as well. He got on his bike, stopping long enough to hit speed dial on his phone. Just voice mail from her, and he shoved the thing back in his pocket. He backed the Harley up. Robert started to wheeze, and his leg muscles shook.

He started the engine and toed the engine into first gear. Twisting the throttle, he shifted into second gear… and then third. Robert sped along the driveway. He shouldn't have used the fourth gear, but he kicked it in anyway. Flying on cocaine *and* alcohol, the sudden wrenching horror of his mother's death pulled him even deeper into madness. He reached forty-five miles an hour. Leaning into the turn on Bass River Road was a joke. He lost traction, and the bike began to slide, tires skipping across the pavement. He hit the curb on the other side of the road, and one thousand pounds of metal between his legs jumped into flight until an oversized oak tree stopped the Harley's trip, turning it into a pretzel. Robert was thrown back onto the road, landing on his back. He looked abysmal, and the wounds on his scalp were bleeding like rivers of red at first. They were surface abrasions, soon drying up. In reality, he was just stunned. Nothing of real concern had damaged him.

His eyes opened, and he slowly stood up. While the wind revved up around him, he swallowed his accountability for his mother's death like a capsule of strychnine. He stared up at the mansion glowing on the hill as the last of his sanity seemed to dribble out with the blood leaking out of his head wounds. In his mind, he envisioned his father's body in an open grave, and this vision changed into a clarion call. Now driven like the north wind, he would bring Latham to his demise.

Tree branches had become fingers scratching at the car, but April had not noticed that, instead distracted by the heavy leaves swirling under the wheels. She'd been driving way too fast, trying to get to the Deli before they closed. She stopped using any gas at all as she touched the brakes. And then she did hit the brakes three more times. After that, she pressed the brake pedal to the floor…even while the Mercedes sped up. So did her heartbeat.

Her dream of dancing the nights away on a tropical island with Peter was replaced with panic. As if someone else's hands were frozen on the wheel, she barely held on the road. Her speed increased — yet she needed to believe she'd make it to the bridge. Tight turns kept coming like a carnival ride. She glanced at the deadly truth on the speedometer: 66…67…67…68, but April fought the horrible truth away, self-preservation painting a happier ending.

She'd make it over the bridge. Bass River Road straightens out after that, allowing her to ride the speed out to a slow stop.

Slethim was circling the Donnellys' property in a repeating pattern, but the entity suddenly flew to the river. Maneuvering through wind gusts, it landed on a large branch at the top of a black pine. That tree overlooked the bridge. It seemed that Slethim had picked front-row seats to watch or perhaps even interact in the upcoming finale'.

The Mercedes stayed on the far edge of the pavement. A branch was swept a few inches farther out by the force of a gust of wind. The limb smashed into the driver's window. Still attached to the tree, the branch wrenched out, and the airbags had not been triggered. The errant bough's half-a-second journey into the car had managed to slap April, sending her straight into shock and ending her ability to drive. Time for her slowed to a crawl, staring down at the dots on her skirt. April didn't remember red dots in the design before, but her sudden confusion over that faded. Life memories shuffled in like Polaroid pictures, even if she wasn't interested in looking at them.

The tree branch that had concussed her also guided the car around the last turn and onto the bridge — badly angled. The car was pushing seventy-five, breaking through the guardrail as if it wasn't there. Airbags inflated at that point, swaddling April in place, and the Mercedes sailed over sixty feet before slamming into the river.

April's phone played Forever Young by Rod Stewart as a ringtone, but she couldn't answer it. The irritating memory pictures soon stopped with an image of her daughter. And then Holly's face dissolved. Nothing was left. No pain. No fear. She surrendered. She welcomed the end — but it wasn't quite over yet. An intruding force beckoned April in this twilight. A huge eye popped into being, eyelid closed, and then another one appeared. Those closed eyes blinked open, revealing eldritch-like colors in the pupils like oil on water. April had seen those eyes before…years ago, nine months before Holly's birth.

Slethim's spirit traveled into the river, then through the steel roof of the car and the airbags to reach April. Life was flickering out of her like a candle in the salty water, and this being embraced the drowning woman's soul in order to speak to her.

"Thank you, April. We will remember you and appreciate your gift."

And then April was gone. Slethim's dropped its head in a rolling motion and hunched its shoulders to drop off the branch. Its wings opened to circle above the estate.

Bass River, Massachusetts
5:43 pm Thursday, November 24, 2005

Miraculously, Robert walked away from the crash and returned to the house. He paused in the entry hall, momentarily unable to remember what he was about to do. Then it all flooded back, and he lurched up the main stairs to his old room. Setting lines of coke on the table like a tiny platoon waiting for orders, he snorted them...all of them. The drug hadn't been stepped on much, so he'd pushed himself to the edge of a fatal overdose. Robert could have had a heart attack, but he had a seizure instead. After a few minutes of hell, the event ended, and he remained alive against all odds yet again, still cohesive enough to continue with his mission.

Robert scrubbed the blood off his face and neck, not wanting anyone to notice him. He put his motorcycle jacket on this time and returned to the library.

251

Still playing poker, the family didn't realize he was even there — and that was exactly what he wanted. After grabbing a bottle of Jim Beam behind the bar, Robert intended to leave the building through the back door of the library, but he left his hand on the knob for a second. He glared over at Samuel Eveland with the loathing he had for his father, eyes momentarily transformed into white-hot fury. Then he opened the door and went outside.

Still high as a kite, he walked across the patio, raising the bottle to his lips, believing the alcohol could get him even higher. Walking farther into the backyard, he noticed a filigreed iron bench that faced the woodshed twenty-five feet away. He planted himself on the unlighted bench. Clothes black, he was an invisible and turbulent shadow, a whiskey bottle hanging loosely in his hand. Robert tried to calm down a notch, stretching his legs out and digging his booted heels into the sod.

With oxygenated air and the enhanced pink bulbs in the ceiling lights, everyone in the library looked heartier. Samuel relished his stolen cigar, while Holly's unusual senses gave her even more information. She knew he was not Latham Donnelly, remaining curious over who he really was. Either way, she was enjoying his charade. Holly would not stop it.

Justin stood up. "It's almost six o'clock, and I'm getting hungry. Mom isn't back yet, but by the time we carve up the turkey, she'll certainly be here." Putting his hands on his lower back, he leaned back and stretched.

"You can carve the ham you sent, and I'll operate on the bird," David said. He looked over at Samuel. "Unless you'd rather take care of the turkey, Latham?"

"No, no. You two can do the work."

"When we're done, we'll bring them to the table."

Justin and David left, and Samuel was alone with Holly again.

"I didn't realize you were dexterous with cards before this afternoon, Dad. What happened to you in Las Vegas? I thought it was a business meeting for Heinem, not a gambling tutorial." Holly grinned. Samuel looked calm enough, but he was cringing inside. Pouring herself a dollop of Bailey's in a short glass, she patiently waited for his answer.

"Um, well…I use the cards to meditate and control my nerves when I'm on the phone or waiting for a business deal to go through. I just shuffle or play solitaire. Guess I got good at it. The more you do something, the better you get."

Samuel had no idea what Latham would have really said, not realizing there was a divide between Holly and her father. Holly would never ask Latham that question, and if she did, he would have stared back at her in silence. But she knew she wasn't talking to Latham, so…

Samuel went on, "Wish it had been a gambling event. That would have been more fun." He glanced over at her. It seemed his play-acting wasn't working that well, and he was getting apprehensive. Noticing the fireplace in the library had no wood looked like an

253

excuse to get distance between himself and Holly. At least for a few minutes, anyway.

"The cold wind is still howling out there, and I think we should start a fire, but there's no more wood. I'll go out and grab some at the woodshed — enough for the rest of the evening. Right after dinner, we might come back here, and it will be warm and friendly."

"That's a good idea," Holly said. "Don't stay out there too long since you don't have the right clothes on for the trip."

Sam remembered the woodshed and where it was when the sun was up. It wasn't very far from the house, so he didn't need a coat to get there and back. Swallowing the last of his drink, he left the glass on the bar. The short escape would cool down his worries over Holly's suspicions of him.

Bass River, Massachusetts
5:47PM Thursday, November 24, 2005

Edgar was a good driver. He moved fast and safely. The rental barreled over Bass River Bridge evenly enough, besides the bump Latham felt that hadn't been there before. He looked through the back window. Part of the guardrail was gone, but he didn't trust his eyesight after Lazzo's pummeling. The Lincoln swung into the tight corner after the bridge before Edgar guided the car through the uphill turns on that tough grade. He left the speed constant — until they reached Donnelly's driveway. Edgar slowed to stop.

"What kind of holiday is your family having, Samuel?" Lazzo said as he powered his window down and pointed. "There's a motorcycle crashed into those trees. It's twisted into a knot."

Chrome reflected their headlights. Edgar smirked, smiling. "You weren't doing very well in Vegas, and it looks like you weren't having a great time here either. Those skid marks come out of your driveway."

Saddled by their heavy curiosity, Latham had no choice. He needed to placate these hooligans with an explanation...even if it was going to be a truculent one. "My son's problems are not a subject you should be concerned over. Most of the time, he's never here, and you can see why."

Latham knew that Robert might be out there bleeding to death, but he couldn't care less. All he wanted to do was get out of town and cut the remaining contacts he had with his aimless, greedy family.

Edgar shook his head and hit the gas, driving into the parking lot. He parked in the way of two other cars and near the front entrance of the house. Everyone in the Lincoln got out. Latham faced his kidnappers with resolve. He needed to figure out what was going on in there.

"Look, we don't have to frighten them yet," Latham said. "Let me go inside alone to get the cash and bring it out to you. My safe is on the second floor, so I need enough time to get there and back. Please! Just wait right here."

"Why should I believe you, Sam?" Edgar said. "You could close the front door and drag your family into a panic room and then call the cops."

"I won't do that! I told you — I have to fly to Russia tomorrow. Calling the cops would screw everything up for me and sink my own plans. If you want the money, just let me go and get it...just wait thirty minutes. If I don't come through that front door after the time we agreed on, come inside and go on a rampage. I have no panic room, and besides, the cops can't get here that fast anyway. Look around! We're forty miles from the station."

Lazzo spoke to his partner, "Maybe we should give him those thirty minutes? He's right about how far out we seem to be." He shrugged. "Maybe see what happens?"

Edgar looked over at Latham. "There really is no one around besides your neighbors, that's for sure...okay. Let's see what happens. I'll watch the time. If you're not back by six-thirty, we'll come in and find you." There was a devilish smile on his face. "Hope you like your family well enough to get back on time." And he waved toward the door. "Go ahead. We'll wait for the money."

Latham checked his watch. The front door was unlocked, and he disappeared inside. He had enough time to reach the safe and return and extra time to see if Samuel was actually there. If the doppelganger was there, his connection to these lowlifes would dissolve.

The moment the front door closed behind Latham, Edgar gave Lazzo more orders, "I have no idea what he's really going to do. Jog around the house and watch the backyard. We can't let him disappear into those woods back there — and we don't even know if he really owns this place. Oh, there's a flashlight in the bag on the front seat. You'll need it…go on!"

Lazzo trotted to the car to grab the flashlight. He powerwalked around the corner of the house. The north wind slammed into him like a linebacker, but he would not slow down. A storm-front himself at two hundred and fifty pounds. Avoiding the yard lights, Lazzo climbed the berm that followed the edge of the property and stayed on the eight-foot rise until he saw the woodshed just three hundred feet away from the back of the house. It looked like the perfect place to keep his eye on the prize.

But Lazzo didn't catch his breath when Samuel stepped out onto the patio. He took his gun out and screwed the silencer on. Better safe than sorry.

Samuel strolled over to the woodshed. Lazzo stood a few feet above him, and he watched the gambler pick through the wood. Lazzo guessed he was searching for a hidden panel…maybe the safe was out here. Maybe they could steal all the cash in there and fly off, and no one would have a clue who they were! Samuel would never tell.

Robert took another gulp of whiskey, leaving a trail of fire on its way to his belly. He watched his father come out of the library exit. It was easy to see him in his ivory suit as he walked over to the woodshed. He started to pick up wood from the pile. Robert rested the liquor bottle on the grass and stood up, silently creeping closer to Samuel. A long-handled splitting maul leaned against the shed door. Robert slowly picked it up. Quietly. *Perhaps his father would appreciate his help to re-split some of those pieces?*

Lazzo had not seen Robert's measured approach, remaining intrigued over where the safe might be. When Samuel quickly turned back to the house holding an armful of wood, Lazzo was perplexed. And then stunned. Robert exploded out of the shadows, charging towards Samuel at breakneck speed. Lazzo's confusion got worse. Robert Donnelly's face had convulsed into an alien mask of savagery. He was a monster in black materializing out of thin air, holding an axe in the air, inches above Samuel's head. Then he swung the sharp blade straight down.

"NOOOOOOO!" Lazzo's frustrated scream flew off in the wind, even though he'd already raised his gun against this upcoming attack. Robert planted the axe strike into Samuel's head. It opened like a ripe melon. Blood splattered on Samuel's back and Robert's front. A few drops landed on a piece of firewood and Lazzo's shoe. Robert really thought he'd split his father's head wide open while Samuel's body crumpled to the grass with the wood he'd held in his arms scattered around him.

Lazzo stared at Robert with indignation. He had no idea who this interloper was, but he'd likely taken away his fortune! He was already aiming his gun at Robert to stop the attack...half-a-second too late, but his finger was still on the trigger. Too late to save the day, Lazzo decided to end things anyway. He held back long enough for Robert to look up and see him standing above him on the berm.

"Goodbye, asshole," Lazzo said, sending a bullet into his forehead with a whisper from the silencer. No one in the house heard a thing.

Edgar had been leaning against the rental car, arms crossed against his chest, waiting for something to happen. Hearing an echo of Lazzo's scream on a gust of wind, he jogged around the house using a penlight for navigation. He'd taken the berm as well, panting when he reached Lazzo's side. His partner looked down at the scene in front of the woodshed, and Edgar followed his gaze. The question he had for Lazzo died on his lips. Samuel Eveland lay flat on his belly with an axe handle poking straight up, the blade deeply anchored into his head — and there was another body a few feet away, tossed on his back by Lazzo's bullet. The ghostly smile on the stranger's dead face did not help Edgar's mood.

"What the hell happened, Laz?"

"I don't know… I really don't. I guess Sammy was out here getting firewood, and this guy came out of nowhere and killed him." He groaned. "I tried to stop him, but it was very dark, and I didn't see him coming. I really thought Samuel was out here getting the money. I'm sorry. Hey, I evened out the score anyway."

Edgar's mind skipped to escape mode, curiosity taking second place to *get the hell out of here.*

So far, the family hadn't noticed a thing. So far, no one knew they were out there staring a dead bodies bleeding into their grass. So far....

"I can't explain this to Cindy. We need to send her a picture." Edgar said, stumbled down the side of the berm, Lazzo following him. "After that, we'll haul them to the creek and throw them in and get out of here as fast as possible. Let's hope the family stays where they are. They don't have to come out here looking for them."

Taking his phone out of his jacket, Edgar told Lazzo to stand behind him to shield the flash. It worked well enough. Anyone looking out didn't see a thing. He snapped two pictures and put the phone back in his pocket. Time to move the bodies. He threw a curt nod at Lazzo.

Samuel's body was a lot heavier than Robert's. Lazzo picked up his heels, and Edgar was relegated to the scrawnier corpse. Shoulder to shoulder, the hit men dragged the dead to the water's edge. The gentle slope helped the process. The axe remained in Samuel's head for at least part of the trip. The long handle swayed with Lazzo's measured steps. Then Sam's chin bounced off a deep furrow left by a lawnmower wheel, dislodging the axe. It fell out with a squishy plop. Lazzo and Edgar turned around. The tool lay flat on the ground, invisible to anyone until the sun rose — and they'd be gone by then. They left it there and kept on going until they reached the water's edge.

"We'll swing them out as far out as we can... without getting our feet wet," Edgar loudly pronounced. "There's an undercurrent out there. It should pick them up and drag them along the creek. They should be under the water for a while, and we will be in Las Vegas when and if they rise to the surface."

Lazzo stared at Edgar. How did he know anything about that creek — well, it didn't matter. It was the best they could do under the unforeseen circumstances. "I guess so. It sounds okay. Let's go for it."

Lazzo grabbed Robert's ankles — Edgar his wrists. They swung him back and forth, counting together, "One...two......**three**!" At the highest point in the third arc, they both let go at the same time. The body landed over ten feet out there, instantly sinking below the surface. They went through the exact same process with Samuel, but it was more difficult with a heavier body. They just doubled the count to reach the same height. Walking away from the second splash, they felt relieved. Edgar and Lazzo marched towards their rental with the wind pounding at their backs.

Bass River, Massachusetts
6:05PM Thursday, November 24, 2005

Latham shivered in the entry hall, exhausted. Samuel wouldn't be able to use his masquerade anymore, and he was about to use the last of his physical energy to find him. Walking through the great room and into the long hallway, he stumbled twice. He intended to throw the doppelganger into the jaws of the jackals waiting in the driveway. Latham walked into the kitchen, and David and Justin were aghast when they saw him. David dropped the carving knife while Justin stepped over to his father with concern.

"Are you okay, Dad? What happened? Did you fall on the stairs outside?"

Then Dave rushed over as well, trying to hold his father-in-law's elbow and guide him to a stool in the corner of the kitchen. "Tell me where it hurts. I'll get you some water and..."

Latham tossed his hand off and stared into his son-in-law's eyes. "Where was the last place you saw me?"

"In the library with Holly ten minutes ago...if you can't remember these simple things, it's obvious you're not yourself. Do you know where you are right now? You had to have fallen and landed on your head."

Latham had gotten the information he needed, and he trotted out of the kitchen, fueled by the final end of his problems. His fatigue was fading in excitement.

David and Justin watched the door close behind him.

"He was not acting like himself, was he?" David said.

"Yeah, I agree. It was almost as if Latham was someone else, and he seemed extremely upset. He seemed fine when we left him in the library a few minutes ago. Something must have happened to him... I mean, you saw his suit. It was like he slept in it for days."

"Maybe my wife talked to him for too long — or he had an arm-wrestling match with her."

They laughed as David went back to carving the turkey, setting the pieces of meat on the platter. Neither of them was actually concerned over Latham's condition, but they wanted him at the holiday table healthy enough to swallow down his dinner!

Latham walked into the library. No one was there. Bone-deep weariness started to creep back, making him stupid. Paranoia took control. He could see Samuel opening his safe and stealing his cash, and the impossibility of it became real. He ran toward the elevator, driven with adrenalin, passing Justin and David, who were taking the ham and turkey into the dining room.

"You okay, Dad?" Justin said. "Where are you going? Can we help you? Dad..."

"I can check your vitals," David chimed in. "It'd only take a second."

Latham ignored them, and ran through the swinging doors and got on the elevator. Reaching the second floor, he strode the corridor to his suite, still picturing Samuel on the floor of his closet. *He'd corral him!*

A minute later, he stepped into his oversized closet and pushed his suits out of the way. No one was there. Kicking a smudge on a molding, a section of the sheetrock rose. His safe was still welded to a steel pillar. He used the combination, and the safe door swung open. The old air inside puffed into his face.

The cash was there...why wouldn't it be? He'd flipped out for a few minutes until sanity finally found purchase in his head yet again. He realized the time limit Edgar had given him had certainly elapsed, but he didn't hear them crashing around downstairs. The ruckus they'd forecast did not happen. Something else must have gone wrong. It didn't matter. Their true target is right here. He relocked the safe to find Samuel and put things back to normal!

Still pumped on adrenaline, Latham returned to the library. Justin, David, and Holly were at the bar, waiting for the rest of the family to arrive. Lazzo and Edgar weren't in the house yet. Maybe they'd found him? Latham was getting unsteady again. It was important to stop the confusion before he lost it all and just passed out on the floor.

"Holly, when you talked to me a few minutes ago, where did I go? I know it sounds ridiculous, but tell me that information anyway."

She wasn't bothered by his dishevelment or the odd request. "You took the back door outside to get firewood from the shed."

David and Justin had lost their interest in his ongoing absurdities, and they ignored Latham's power, walking through the back door and onto the patio. The wind slammed the glass door closed behind him with a nasty slam. The men remained at the bar, even more irritated, thinking the same thing: 'Why can't they all stay in one place and eat their damned dinner!'

Latham walked around on the lawn, wondering if Sam had actually crossed the brook to disappear into the wild acres on the other side? Or was he hiding somewhere else on the estate? He peered under the nearest evergreen bush, but he quickly stood up. The situation was a surreal joke at this point — until he gazed toward the tributary in the distance to see Lazzo and Edgar walking towards the house.

Bass River, Massachusetts
6:31PM Thursday, November 24, 2005

Trudging up the rise, Lazzo shook a cigarette out of his case. He used his jacket as a windbreak to light it up. Edgar waited for him as he looked at the mansion… to see the impossible. He nudged Lazzo, waving and pointing and whispering in his ear.

"Look, damn it, look! Samuel's ghost is haunting this place. It's near the house." Edgar was truly afraid this sinister spirit could hear him. *"Oh…look! It's drifting to the wood pile… Laz! Can you see it?"*

Lazzo ignored his nervous punches and most of what he was whispering. This was the end of a disappointing job, and smoking a cigarette might be the only paltry reward for all the exertion he'd gone through. Inhaling as much smoke as he could, he followed Edgar's finger up the slope. Lazzo's mouth opened in surprise, and the cigarette fell to the ground.

"I see him! But it's not a ghost. It has to be Donnelly or Samuel."

Whoever it was drifted back and forth in the distance until they saw Lazzo and Edgar and yelled out to them, "You saw him, didn't you? You must believe me now. I'm not Samuel. I'm Latham, Latham Donnelly!"

Reaching the assassins quickly enough, Lazzo unhappily answered Latham.

"How could we have known? I feel bad about the mix-up." He actually did feel bad about pounding on him in Las Vegas. "I'm sorry, Mr. Donnelly. You know what happened, right? He tricked us all. He does look a lot like you."

Lazzo towered over Latham, and he didn't that to interfere with his apologies, so he spread his feet to lower his height. And Edgar's face had pinched into a knot. All his jobs are supposed to be controlled — not running off the rails like this.

"What happened to Samuel?" Latham said. "Where is he? I thought you wanted to get money out of him?"

They didn't have any time to come up with a feasible lie, and Edgar faltered out of the gate... badly. "Ah...well, we saw him run out of the house, and we followed him. He dove into the creek and swam to the other side. We didn't want to get wet. We decided to drive around and flush him out."

Latham smiled and seemed to accept this fairytale equably enough. His problems with them were gone.

Lazzo and Edgar were certainly villainous, paid to snuff people out for a living, and they enjoyed their job with elation. Nevertheless, attacking innocents held real hazards for themselves and the business in Las Vegas. They really wanted to placate Latham, hoping he would forget what had happened…and never tell the authorities about them.

They all walked back to the house, icy wind pushing at them. The group stopped at the patio. Latham looked through the window. Holly, David, and Justin were still at the bar, but he was not quite ready to go inside. He wanted to tell his family the convoluted story as they rang the holiday in, but it would be a lot easier to fill the tale out if Lazzo and Edgar were also at the table. They would support the unbelievable truth. Latham waved the two men closer, and they huddled behind a stone bench to avoid some of those gusts.

"Listen, boys, I know this may seem odd, but I have an invitation for you. You have a very long trip in front of you, with or without Samuel under your guard, and I have a Thanksgiving dinner ready to be eaten right now. Can we allow sleeping dogs to stay asleep? Samuel has duped my entire family, and I'm here to replace my replacement. If you stay, you can help me explain the situation, and you'll have more energy to get him out of those woods and back to Las Vegas with your bellies full." Latham chuckled. "I won't call anybody about anything you've done." He narrowed his eyes. "Or anything else you might have done without my knowledge. Anyway, I invite you to slow down and have dinner with us. Break bread and bury the hatchet."

Lazzo recoiled. Edgar sneered, but they were puzzled by the invitation. Latham saw their confusion, and he quickly tried to alleviate it.

267

"My kids are soused. Don't worry. They won't call anyone or do anything either. Especially if I tell them not to." Latham swayed in the wind since the bench wasn't much of a barrier. He really wanted them to stay.

"So, you are inviting us to your table for dinner...really? Well..." Edgar calculated the depth of the creek against how hungry they'd both become. How much time did they have before everything they'd done was found out? "Yeah, okay. That's generous of you. I guess we'll walk around to the front door after you explain things to them first."

"Nope. The reunion has already run off the rails. You can walk in with me from this porch right now. My son and my son-in-law are lit, and my so-called daughter never gets upset about anything. We need to get this chilly storm out of our bones and eat some hot food! Come on, follow me. We'll deal with introductions at the table."

Latham opened the door and stepped in, announcing, "Thanksgiving dinner is served. I don't care where April and Robert are. My new acquaintances and I will convene with you at the table. Besides eating this wonderful food, we can explain a few things that have gone badly wrong."

The assassins trailed behind Latham through the library. David and Justin got up and followed them to the dining room. Holly remained at the bar for a few more minutes as the strange parade went by. She was amused, and she too took her place at the dinner table

to enjoy the holiday with what was left of her family —
and the mysterious visitors.

Putting turkey and stuffing on his plate, David
didn't know if his mother-in-law or Robert would
arrive or not, so their personal roles in his financial
future remained murky. Either way, these tough-
looking men would support his innocence in the
upcoming investigation. Their arrival and following
deaths would be another mystery to muddy up the
waters. Robert's survival wouldn't make much of a
difference; however, April's current existence might
shrink his winnings. Ah, well...Holly had money of
her own, and he was the only beneficiary in her will. If
Robert and April don't partake in this delicious meal,
he'll still get rich from his deception. Who knows — he
might make a bundle writing a book about the
traumatic murder as the only survivor of the toxic
meal.

Justin piled ham on his plate with peas, yams, and
homemade cranberry sauce, looking forward to
hearing his father's story before the poison took
hold...and these enigmatic visitors will support his
innocence. They had the aura of a casino in Las Vegas,
and the feeling of ominousness and danger circling
around them made him feel even better.

Mom hadn't shown up, but he wasn't worried. If
she made it through his trap, he would guide her
through the deposition of the will. But she was running
so late Justin thought she'd had an accident.
Depending on the severity of her crash, his plans might
remain the same. Robert's inheritance was already tied

up in a trust he had control over. He was optimistic. Either way, there would be no more hiding his sexuality, and he'd also retain his inheritance!

Latham sat at one end of the table with Holly facing him on the other side. Justin was on his father's right, and David to his left. Lazzo and Edgar sat on either side of Holly. In the center of the table, candles surrounded a bouquet of pine branches, hydrangea blooms, and orange mums. Pleasing enough, it did not match the magnetism of the horn-of-plenty the year before.

After filling their plates, everyone sat at the table. David and Justin stared at everyone's food. No one was shy with stuffing or homemade jelly, and the bad forecast they had created looked good!

As the family enjoyed drunken conviviality, the poisoners locked eyes across the table: a brief psychic connection enhanced by their own nihilism swirling through the atmosphere in the dining room. *Happiness at any cost.* They both sang that short ditty in their minds at exactly the same time, neither realizing that wonderful silent link highlighted their own personal demise.

Lazzo's religiosity took control. It wasn't right to consume the food on Thanksgiving Day without a blessing. He politely asked if he could give out a prayer.

"Look, I don't know how you all see the world, but my family used to say grace before every meal. Since this is a holiday to remember the blessings of the year, maybe you guys would let me recite a short prayer."

Latham looked over at Lazzo with a half-smile. Edgar snickered again.

But Holly interrupted the following silence. "No reason why not. What's your name, sir?"

"Tony Milazzo." He reached over and shook her hand, and she shook back *gently*. She did not want to frighten him.

"There's no reason Mr. Milazzo can't give us a prayer. Perhaps it can bring Mom and Robert to the dinner table." Holly's shoulders rose and dropped in this simple gesture. Having seen everyone's halfhearted acceptance, she answered Lazzo, "Go ahead, sir. Please give us a prayer."

Lazzo's leather jacket expanded his bulk as he stood up. He seemed to darken the whole room.

"Merciful God and Father, let us pray." His voice broadened and got deeper. "Let our hearts not be weighted by the cares of this life, nor be attached to earthly perishable things. We shall be nourished by the everlasting life coming from the eternal food of your word. Bless the meal we shall share together today. We invite you into our hearts and your love in our lives. Amen."

Everyone was silent but Holly, who echoed the Amen. Lazzo exhaled and sat down. Justin and David began pestering Latham with questions. The sound of conversation, classical music, and silverware clattering melded into a merry song of holiday cheer.

Lazzo and Edgar remained straight-faced when Latham told the story of his abduction in Las Vegas. Everyone was completely enthralled. After half an hour, there was a short break. Holly remarked about the cranberry sauce.

"The chef must have used turmeric. It's sweet, with a touch of tanginess, a new dimension in those cranberries this evening."

David looked over at his wife, concerned. "You like it, don't you? I think it's the best we've ever had." A large dollop of cranberry sauce still sat on his own plate near the turkey and stuffing he'd already eaten. Oddly, he had not touched his cranberry sauce yet.

"Of course, David. It's fine. You shouldn't be upset about anything."

Slathering more cranberry sauce on his own piece of roasted ham, Justin swallowed it down—with no intention of eating turkey or stuffing. "It goes with everything! I can't wait until…"

Suddenly, he stopped talking, and David watched a transformation in the muscles of his face. Justin's eyes swelled, and his mouth opened as if he was about to scream. But nothing came out. He hopped away from the table, beginning to shiver before twisting to the left—as if an invisible rope had wrenched him toward the hallway. Lazzo stood up to help him, intending to pick him up and put him on the couch. That wasn't going to happen. He fell headfirst onto the table in front of Holly.

Dinner was over. There would be no dessert.

Bass River, Massachusetts
6:07AM Friday, November 25, 2005

A white shirt tucked into her black skirt, Mirabelle stuffed her stockinged feet into clunky work shoes. She was ready to go. Cleaning up after the reunion this year would be harder for her after chauffeuring her family around the day before. She was exhausted, but she had to get to work on time. Stopping at the deli near her house, she grabbed a twenty-ounce cup of coffee, even pouring a container of 'Stok' into the cup. Forty milligrams of caffeine on top of what was already there. Twenty minutes later, Mirabelle's eyes had widened, and her hands shook on the wheel, wired up by the legal speed she'd swallowed. It was still dark outside when she drove over Bass River Bridge. She gazed over at the ocean. The wind had died. The river water looked like molten glass, and the trees on the shoreline looked like stage props.

A section of the guardrail on the bridge was missing. Mirabelle tried not to think about that as she drove through the dips and turns of the road. She got queasy, chalking that up to the coffee now burning in her belly. Robert's motorcycle was wrecked near the entrance to the driveway. That didn't bother her. Looked like yet another of his antics. He was probably sleeping his bender off somewhere in the house. She parked near the kitchen door and got out. And then she paused. Mirabelle looked over her shoulder to see the cars still parked in the lot. *That's not right*—and there was even another vehicle she'd never seen before left in the center of the courtyard. That wasn't right either. No one had even tried to back out. The one night she wasn't around, things had gone crackers?

The sun was rising. This natural light should have revitalized Mirabelle. It had not worked. The things around her were tomblike; squirrels weren't scurrying, and the birds weren't chirping. Her mind was getting rattled. Opening the service door, she hung her coat in the work closet. She'd start with the library, taking the glasses and food trays back to the kitchen. Hearing music playing in the dining room, the housekeeper frowned. She stepped over to the console and switched the audio off. Why had they left it on before when they went to bed?

Passing through the dining room, she took the left side of the table leading to the hallway into the library. Latham was resting, head on the back of the couch. Mirabelle assumed Mr. Donnelly was asleep, believing he'd feel better in his bed. She nudged his shoulder to wake him up, but there was no response. Mirabelle pushed a bit harder.

Seeing the pallor of his neck filtered into her eyes and then into her mind. She looked across the room. Edgar was impaled through the glass panel of the backdoor, an arm hanging on a shard of glass pointing straight up from the shattered pane. The side of his torso also skewered on another red icicle. His head dropped over the lower panel, out of Mirabelle's line of sight.

Her hand loosely resting on her boss's shoulder cramped...hard as an eagle's talon. Her attention remained on the door. There was a heavy stain of Edgar's blood absorbed in the carpet around the bottom of the door. After hours of exposure to oxygen, the red changed to black, and the contrast against the light color of the rug made the stain dramatic.

The world, as Mirabelle had known it, was fading. The fact that she was clutching a corpse slammed into her, fingers straightening out and let go as if Latham's body was on fire. She lurched backward with a high-pitched gasp, turning back into the hallway faster than she'd ever moved in her life. Her feverish escape was interrupted when she reached the right side of the dining table, having not seen the bodies tangled near the wall during her first trip. Still sprinting full tilt, she hooked one of her feet on Lazzo's leg, and momentum gave her wings. She soared seven feet into the wall. The collision knocked her out.

David and Lazzo died intertwined under the table. When Mirabelle woke up a few minutes later, she was staring into Lazzo's eyes, just an inch away from her nose. David's head rested on the other man's arm, mouth frozen in a silent scream. One of his own eyes had popped out...or something. It wasn't there anymore.

Mirabelle was lucky. None of her bones had broken when she hit the wall. What she was looking at, smelling, and even touching wrenched her on her feet like jet fuel. Racing through the kitchen, she reached the work closet and snagged her coat off the hook, car keys in the coat pocket. She barreled out of the service door, ran across the parking area, and got in her car. She started the engine and pushed the accelerator to the floor, back wheels spinning on the asphalt. Blue smoke rose to the roof of the mansion. Grabbing traction, she left skid marks behind, unintentionally underlining her torment.

She did not know what was responsible for the cataclysmic end of Latham's dream castle. Mirabelle wanted to hold on to her sanity, so she had no interest in figuring it out. Her phone was in her purse, lying on the back seat. She could not reach it… yet. Driving the road too fast, she did make it to the bridge, nonetheless. Mirabelle's motivation to escape remained with her. The road straightened out on the other side of the river, but she kept on hurtling onwards. However, she finally realized she needed help. One hand off the wheel, she reached back and got her purse. Mirabelle shook it upside down on the passenger seat and found her phone. She hit 911.

Mirabelle had not seen Justin's body in the narrow hallway near the elevator, nor did she see Holly face down on the marble floor next to the koi pond, one hand floating in the pond water. The fish were gently kissing the ends of her cold fingers. No. The housekeeper had not seen those things, and that was an incidental blessing.

Cedarville, Massachusetts
9:12AM Friday, November 25, 2005

The property sat just five miles south of the New Hampshire state line, and most of the shingles were blown off the roof of the farmhouse, and there wasn't much green paint left on the walls. It was disintegrating in the middle of a forty-acre apple orchard, trees worm-riddled and wilted. Locked in foreclosure for three years, the owners had simply left the state, and the resolution was stalled in court.

The sky was blue that morning with a warm breeze. Anyone standing on the sagging porch of the farmhouse might look out at the orchard and believe the shriveled buds on the apple trees would flower. But even shrunken apples could not grow there now. Winter was about to bite back at sunset like a white wolf with an appetite.

Ryan Poretta parked his white station wagon next to the farmhouse. He buttoned up his trench coat, got out, and stamped over to the steel doors leading into the basement. He'd driven a long way, and his toes were numb, hopping up and down to get his feet warm again. At fifty-three, grey overpowered his blonde hair. Almost six feet, Poretta was thirty-five pounds overweight, but he looked solid enough. Ancestors from northern Italy were responsible for his light complexion and grey-blue eyes. Lifting one of the two steel doors, he climbed the concrete steps into the cellar.

The body of an eight-year-old girl was tied in a sitting position to a pillar in the center of the basement. Poretta walked over and kneeled in front of her, up close to her face, but worried about grinding dirt into the knees of his pants. The small corpse wore a baby blue dress with a white ruffled apron. The apron was unwrinkled and still virgin white, perfectly arranged around her on the filthy floor.

Taking latex gloves out of the deep pocket of his trench coat, Poretta put them on to examine her hands. He gently squeezed her fingers before rocking back on his heels. He looked at the toolbox only a foot away. Opening the orange cover to see pliers, a power drill, and a chisel on the upper shelf, Poretta seemed stuck in that uncomfortable position as he looked at the tools and thought things over.

Poretta's deep meditation was over when Detective Cassidy pounded down the stairs from the first floor, almost yelling for his attention. He looked up at Cassidy's howling and closed the toolbox.

"Inspector...Inspector Poretta, there's a helicopter coming! Andes will take this case off your hands because of the red ball blowing up on Cape Cod. The chief wants you there ASAP."

A red ball? The concept lit up in Porretta's mind. Public scrutiny is drawn to certain cases, divvied out to detectives who can handle that kind of pressure. He stood up, slapping dirt off his knees and peeling his gloves off.

"Okay, okay, Cassidy...calm down. Why couldn't Ferguson take the case? He just closed the Daisy Chain last week — and I know he's free. Right now, I'm about to figure this one out."

"I don't know, sir. The chief won't budge. It's you and no one else. There are six bodies at the Donnelly estate, and the CEO of Hienem Pharmaceutical Corporation is one of the victims. I think Chief Coleman thinks it's too much for Ferguson. I hate to say it, but I agree."

The men climbed the stairs, and the old boards under their feet groaned. On their way to the front door, they avoided the parts of the floor so rotten they'd fall through. Then, the helicopter noise shook the walls of the ancient farmhouse, and Poretta couldn't hear what Cassidy was telling him. A deputy stood near the front door and waved to him. The copter had landed outside, and Poretta got in and closed the hatch. The pilot remembered what the captain's orders were: "Land the thing long enough to pick him up. Don't even turn the engine off. Just get him over there!"

And the pilot did as he was told. In forty minutes, they flew over Bass River, and Ryan Poretta looked down. The number of official cars parked around the farmhouse in Cedarville didn't match the number of vehicles lined up on the driveway leading to the Donnelly mansion. Cruisers barricaded the main road and parked nose-to-nose just five hundred feet in front of the Bass River Bridge. Officers would only let residents through. Scuba divers came out of the river water, and a tow truck had parked on the bridge, lifting a car out of the river.

Poretta whistled through his teeth. There was even a medical support vehicle, emergency lights pulsing like a Christmas tree on the driveway, plus nine police cars, six ambulances, and more ATVs. There was a seventy-five-foot-long tent erected behind the house, a hub for evidence collection.

The helicopter landed in front of the house. Poretta got out and stayed low at first to avoid the blades. Straightening up, he trotted into the open front door. The entry hall was deserted, but that changed when he stepped into the great room. Officers and medical teams were busy tagging and labeling evidence. Inspector Poretta offhandedly wove through the hubbub on his way to the tent outside. An officer stepped over to give him a two-way radio.

"Hello," Poretta said, and he smiled. "I assume Detective Franken is overseeing things?"

"Yes, sir."

Getting Franken on the radio, Poretta asked him to meet him at the tent. The detective sprinted around the corner of the house holding a clipboard and a flashlight, without a single hair on his head out of place.

"Good morning, Inspector...well, I don't know if good is the right word for it, but it's good to see you for sure."

Poretta gave him a distracted nod, too busy lining things up in his head. "I saw something floating in the small tributary at the back of the property when I flew in."

"Sounds suspicious, sir," Franken said. He gave Poretta the clipboard.

"I can see everyone beating bushes and checking flowerbeds to find the victim connected to the axe we found," Poretta said, even as he read the information on the papers Franken had just given him. "But I think we should check that waterway right behind the house. Divert two of the divers from the river up to the creek near the boathouse."

Franken nodded and got on the phone to set it up. Poretta went back into the house to examine the bodies. He also talked to the officers at the motorcycle crash on the radio for a few minutes. Spending over an hour inside the house, he walked down to the creek. The divers were dragging out two bodies to the edge of the creek, waiting for the Medical Examiner or the evidence team to take over.

Samuel Eveland and Robert Donelly's clothes were badly ripped, their skin dead white. Sam's face and skull were almost cleaved into two.

Clues were piling up in a contradictory mix, and that might make most investigators uneasy, yet Poretta thrived on disorder, deciphering minutiae like a human android.

If national attention swells to saturation over the case, the Inspector's frosty demeanor would just get colder. In some of his past cases, famous interviewers would hunt him down. Poretta would embrace them with calculation and panache.

The State Police took Mirabelle out of her car six miles passed the bridge. There were no other witnesses at the crime scene, and she was all they had, but they had a problem. She was traumatized, and she'd built a barrier against those memories. Detective Franken installed Mirabelle into the medical vehicle, and a medic plied her with hot soup and diazepam. Franken didn't want her to leave the property or even go to the hospital. He hoped she would soon go back inside the house to describe her experience to himself and Poretta.

Mirabelle would not go back inside that mansion for hell or high water, but he did not realize that yet. Franken kept calling the medic to ask him how she was doing...whether she could talk to them yet or not?

Their other options were falling flat. The chef had been with his family in Providence. He had nothing of interest to give them, and their nearest neighbor was seven acres away, swimming in their indoor pool. All *they* could remember was who had brought out the fresh lime to the outside bar.

Poretta was poking through contents he'd tossed out of a wastebasket onto one of the worktables outside under the tent. He was thinking over what he did know when a young lab assistant jogged out of the house and moved toward him, talking fast.

"Inspector! Joel told me he saw a hand move... and...dead bodies don't move. He got one of the medics to come over, and they found a pulse! They put the victim into an ambulance to get them over to the hospital fast."

Poretta was incredulous, yet he heard the siren start up and fade away down the driveway. *But every victim in that house was dead!* He had walked through the house three times, close to all the bodies, and they were all far gone by any measure. The family and their guests had been murdered — to death.

"Who survived? What were they saying?" Poretta's eyebrows had furrowed deeply.

"I'm not sure, sir. Joel didn't tell me that. I'll...I'll go ask him, hold on." He ran towards the house, but Poretta raised his voice.

"Stop... it's okay, son. I can sort this whole thing out. Thanks a lot for the heads-up!"

The assistant said, "You're welcome, sir." And he returned to the house.

Franken jogged over and tossed Poretta his own mobile phone.

"The medic in the ambulance wants to speak to you, sir."

"Hello, it's Poretta — tell me about your new passenger."

"We have no time, sir. We've stabilized her for the trip to the hospital, but she's still in coma. We don't know if she'll come out this in thirty minutes or thirty days... or never waiting up at all."

"Thirty minutes or thirty days, or an endless sleep. Okay, thanks. Did you know that Holly Donnelly was pronounced dead a few hours ago? It seems that things have really perked up for her, crossing the heavy line from death to heartbeat. Most of us don't have that ability."

He frowned and tossed Franken's phone back to him. "Right now, I can't ask her anything. The guys in the ambulance tell me she's in a coma with no forecast on when it'll end. Nothing has really changed…she's come back to life—sort of."

Poretta went back to sifting through the garbage, but his cheeks had flushed. There was no way to know if she would tell them anything or not.

"I'm going to the hospital to ask the doctors about Holly's impossible trip over River Styx. They'd know more about what's going on with her than the medics."

To take his mind off a fact that should not exist, he changed his attention to the men from Nevada. What had drawn them there? Landing in Logan Airport, they'd rented a Town Car, arriving a few hours before they were murdered. Las Vegas addresses on their licenses, they had legally brought handguns. One had used the digital camera on his phone, and Poretta was looking forwards to seeing those pictures.

Latham Donnelly's wallet had been in the pants pocket of one of the bodies the divers had retrieved from the creek. The damage to the head made visual identification useless, and floating in salty water for twenty hours made the entire thing even worse. They believed the other body, an emaciated young man, was Robert Donnelly. He had a bullet wound in his forehead; it looked like a professional hit.

Poretta dried out Latham's license with the help of a light bulb. Walking into the library, he held it in his hands and stared at the face of the body on the couch. The identification in the pocket of that corpse indicated he was Samuel Eveland from Las Vegas, the same place the gun-wielding men came from. The tall, lean body found in the creek and the one on the couch wore almost identical suits. The inspector had noticed the similarities in the photos on their licenses. He began to piece a story together and it was a twisted one.

The officers at the bridge called him on his own phone. Winching a Mercedes out of the river, they found another driver's license in a wallet left in an evening bag on the floor. The woman inside the car was Mrs. Donnelly.

Ryan Poretta sighed. Responsible for unearthing the facts behind the extinction of an entire family, a lingerer seemed to be hanging on — perhaps the story wasn't over yet.

Finalhaven, Maine
2:32PM Saturday, November 26, 2005

Attison Korybante was at his mahogany desk in his own great room larger than the Donnelly's. Flames crackled in a marble fireplace in a wide chimney rising to the ceiling. A gifted sculptor had used realism for the chimney. He echoed the Hellenistic period in Greek history. Naked bodies of men and women were carved in different kinds of marble, and they intertwined throughout the structure. The diverse shades of stone generated a wave of light rolling along the length of the chimney, fireplace to ceiling. The illusion created an erotic current moving through the forms forever.

285

Attison was not enjoying the beauty of his fireplace, chimney, or the panoramic view of the Atlantic Ocean sparkling through the glass wall in front of his desk. He was busy rearranging the Hienem wide-reaching network, and drafting up legalizations to warrant the new ownership of the company.

Many of Attison's personal possessions had been shipped to a palatial rental in Yarmouth, and heat and power had been turned on in the sprawling place. The dwelling was close to the Donnelly estate. That's why he picked it.

Having not watched any news channels, Attison knew what had happened at the estate. He also knew the name of the detective in charge of the investigation. He was about to call him up, and Attison knew that as well. Leaning back in his chair, he relaxed his neck muscles and closed his eyes. Lining up the importance of his responsibilities, he speculated on whether his own interference to control the direction of the upcoming case would be necessary or not.

Sitting up, he moved his computer to the side of the desk. He opened the small refrigerator behind him and took out a lemon and a bottle of seltzer. Setting up a tumbler from the wheeled bar behind him, he poured the seltzer into the glass and then squeezed the lemon flat with just one hand above the glass. He wanted fresh juice in his drink. Off-handedly, crushing the lemon flat was a tip-off to his exceptional strength.

The phone rang. He let it ring, throwing the rind into the fireplace thirty feet away. Attison dried his hands with a linen cloth as he listened to Inspector Poretta record a message for him.

"It's extremely important you contact me at once. My personal cell phone number is 856 55...."

Attison picked up. "Good afternoon, Inspector. It's Mr. Korybante, the family attorney and the executor of Latham's will."

"Hello, Mr. Korybante. It's important to get connected with you."

"I'm devastated. Do you know who's behind this? You mentioned someone was hanging on?"

"You're up to par, aren't you. I don't have to tell you the gravity of this crime. Holly Donnelly is currently the sole survivor. She was transported to the New Bedford Hospital yesterday. Considering her condition, they'll airlift her to Boston in a few hours."

"I have medical guardianship over her, so I plan to meet the doctors involved in her case as soon as possible. I'll fly to Boston on Monday to be at your disposal and answer any questions you might have." He sipped at his lemon seltzer, eyes tranquil and dangerously deep.

"Thank you, Mr. Korybante. The current inquiry can't be discussed on the phone. We should meet at the Boston University Medical Center on Monday."

"Does 2:30 sound feasible?"

"Fine. I'll wait at the nurse's station on the sixth floor."

"It's a date, Inspector."

The moment he got off the phone, Attison called his pilot. He directed him to pick him up on the roof of his house at nine-thirty that night, intending to arrive at the hospital earlier than Poretta.

University Medical Center Boston
1:45PM Monday, November 28, 2005

At forty-three, Doctor Thomas Berman was pudgy and content at his job—before the survivor arrived. Still alive on the sixth floor unnerved him. After lunch in the cafeteria, he returned to his office and peeled off antacid tablets from a roll in the drawer of his desk. He popped them in his mouth, worried his wavy auburn hair was beginning to turn white...and then fall out. She'd been admitted on Saturday. His belly had begun to churn after he read the report the coroner had sent him. Her health makes no sense. No explanation for any of it. Rereading the latest lab reports left him stumped.

She had been at a holiday party. Everyone there had swallowed enough poison to kill a herd of moose. Yet, Holly Donnelly lay in the hospital with a stable pulse. Doctor Berman was an esteemed toxicologist but ducked questions surrounding the case. When he did get cornered, he would describe similar histories that didn't exist. He'd use double-talk and jargon. As public curiosity grew, his position became more difficult. He believed it was his responsibility to explain her current condition—which was an incomprehensible mystery.

He returned to his computer one more time, hunting for the explanation, even if Doctor Berman already knew it was pointless. It allowed him an escape, and he stared at his screen saver, swimming with a school of tropical fish in the digital sea to forget everything.

Until someone knocked on his office door, a reality hook snagging him back to the surface. He saw the badge on the man's belt through the glass panel of the door. Berman invited him into his office. More pointless questions were coming. He stood up and shook Poretta's hand, off-handedly tossing yet another tablet between his teeth. *Maybe this time, he'll stop acting and just tell him the truth.*

"Good afternoon, Doctor. I'm Inspector Poretta in charge of the Donnelly case. I'm sure you could give me more information...how's our survivor doing? Can I talk to her?"

"Hello, Inspector. I'm sorry. Ms. Donnelly is still comatose, and oddly enough, I can't help you any more than she can right now." Doctor Berman waved to the other chair. "Please, sit down. At least I can tell you about her condition. Her liver is busy cleaning poisons out of her body. She'll be free from all of it in ten more hours. Impossible as that may be, it's happening, nonetheless. I don't know if the contaminants injured her nervous system permanently or not. Only time can answer that...oh, by the way, you thought she was dead for a while, didn't you? That should have denigrated her entire body, but I guess that didn't happen."

Poretta tilted his head. "If the poisons killed everyone else, what saved Holly Donnelly? Did she have an antidote right before dinner, or does she have an extra chromosome or a weird blood type to fight it all off?" The Inspector already knew the answers to his own questions, but he wanted to dig into Berman's wider knowledge anyway, just in case.

"I'd feel a lot better if any of those options were possible, but there are no antidotes for taxane or tetrodotoxin, and I won't waste your time with statistics. Those poisons are virulent. Tricking people into eating a lethal poison was difficult enough. Why the murderer would use two agents when one would have been sufficient is another mystery. Another twist, I guess. Ah…the world of socio-psychosis. We can't explain their inexplicable actions. In this case, it broke a new barrier. Besides the complexities in certain individuals who'd been frozen to death and warmed back to life, I used to believe there was a real difference between a dead body and a live one."

The doctor's face wilted, dropping his hands into his lap. He decided to tell the Inspector what had been bothering him from the beginning. Holly Donnelly's increasingly stable physicality scared him. He could not deal with this preposterousness alone anymore. Poretta had no medical degree. That reassured him. Berman thought it would be easier for him to handle the puzzle if he was outside the box…

"No blood type could forestall cell denigration from these toxins. Right now, I'm in a conundrum." Berman's cheeks shone with a thin sheen of nervous sweat. "From her respiratory system to renal functions, Holly was returning to normal. I can't explain her longevity, considering what her body had just gone through. Besides her unusually long brain waves, the rest of her tests match the levels of an Olympic athlete. And that isn't right either."

Rebounding from death itself, Supergirl was picking at Berman's educated mind like poison ivy. Poretta could clearly see his distress, and he decided to support him by using the power of awe to find his anchor through his associates.

"Thank you, Doctor, thank you very much." Poretta pressed his fingers together and looked at him across the desk. "I know where you are in your head. It ain't easy to deal with incidents like this. They've confounded me too, over the years—well, maybe not quite as far out as this one, but when I couldn't find an answer to a riddle, I would turn to one of my colleagues. That action saved my sanity and my soul. They'd give angles I hadn't seen or maybe a different plausible theory. Even if nothing they told me worked, their camaraderie was enough of a salve. We'd stand together and look into that yawning black hole, and our personal connection fought off a gravity pulling at us from the cold and unknown."

Berman straightened up. "You're right, sir, you're right! I've got to let go and relax. I'll call Carter and explain the entire thing to him. I'm not responsible for what happened in that mansion. You helped me to acknowledge that. After I tell him the story, he'll be in the same boat with me." He started laughing. "I can't wait to see how he personally feels about it...who knows, maybe he could come up with an explanation!"

Berman breathed in deep and slowly let his tension drift away in the exhale, imagining commiseration with a comrade in toxicology. No longer forcing himself to handle the problem alone, Poretta's advice had deflated his own self-isolation.

"One last question, Doctor. I realized it hadn't been too difficult to get to the taxane, but I don't know how he got the tetrodotoxin. I know it isn't in shellfish. Do you know where he might have found it?" Donnelly hoped Berman might give him a hint.

"I'm surprised you haven't looked it up, sir. It's in a small lizard, a tropical fish, and a few other creatures. How that monster found the amount he needed is beyond my ken. I can't come up with an easy way to procure poisons to slaughter my family and those around me... I'm sorry."

Donnelly chuckled. "Of course not, Doctor Berman. I appreciate the information you've given me so far. And if you don't mind, I'll return if I have any more questions."

Bass River, Massachusetts
4:00 PM Thursday, November 24, 2005

Holly was dying as she stumbled out of the dining room and into the great room. She was looking for a way out of the lethal poison uncoiling within. Agony slammed in. She cramped and fell forwards with her forearm dropping into the Koi Pond. Lying paralyzed on her belly, Holly was unable to go any farther, still attempting to find a bridge to escape the unescapable. Born with unusual abilities, she also had ingenuity. In those last moments, she drew on everything she had to win a battle she'd apparently lost.

Digging into her core, she took control of her life force and transferred most of it into a Koi Fish swimming inches away from her motionless fingers. She left an infinitesimal bit of herself in her poisoned physical form. It was a fragile link, but it was enough to secure her a way back to a body that very soon would appear dead. Holly went through this confusing and dramatic transformation. It included a few hours of spiritual white noise while she settled into the fish's brain until she was snugly nestled in its skull. During the process, there was no machine or physical calculation out there to notice or reach the hidden pilot light she'd left behind. The coroner wrote out Holly Donnelly's death certificate, positive she had died.

After accepting her new physical parameters, she calmed down. Her lifelong interaction with oxygen had now been changed as water flushed over her gills. Living on the immunity she had in the Koi fish, she kept on using her telekinesis to support the few healthy blood cells she'd hidden away in her left lung. Soon, she began to speed them all up — they'd expand like cellular weeds while she removed all the poisons in her body. The process was fast. A dark liquid stream came out of her bladder from the flattened dead cells as healthy blood gained in volume. She knew her consciousness had to remain in the Koi. Her human body was coming back from the edge of death, but her mind was stuck in coma. The entirety of Holly remained too far away. She still needed outside support to actually come back.

The rough edge of a plant leaf rubbed against her scaled flank, and Holly swam closer to the plastic wall. Nothing could bother her there, but she was tired and hungry. She watched other fish swim around her. A large white Koi sporting an orange spot over one eye wobbled over and kissed her.

No real eyelids of her own. She had a problem. It looked like endless boredom floating there for days in this claustrophobic tank...but Holly came up with a way out of that. She imaged a country field with a thin cover of snow, and then she made the vision surround her. It would be a temporary escape from this hideaway. Holly found herself walking along the frozen crunchy field on her way to the illusionary ocean in the distance. She halted near the water's edge and watched the waves break. Her self-generated fantasy soothed her, fins gently fluttering to stabilize her position in the man-made pond.

Boston, Massachusetts
2:15PM Monday, November 28, 2005

Attison Korybante sat in the uncomfortable plastic chair right next to Holly's hospital bed. Normally pale, she now looked like sculpted alabaster. He'd heard the doctor's predictions surrounding Ms. Donnelly's future, and Attison tried to look worried, but he knew they were wrong. His own forecasts were usually spot on.

It was 2:27 PM. He stood up, straightened out the papers he'd been working on, and put them back in his briefcase. Attison left his leather coat and his briefcase on the chair; no one had ever touched any of his possessions when he wasn't around. The reasons behind that ongoing immunity were another mystery. He entered the hallway to see Poretta waiting for him at the nurse's station, gold shield and gun concealed under his jacket.

"Greetings Inspector Poretta. I'm Attison Korybante."

Poretta shook his hand and looked into the taller man's eyes, "Hello, Mr. Korybante."

"Perhaps we should adjourn to the cafeteria," Attison said. "I need coffee and something to eat. What do you think?"

"Fine idea, but it's important for me to actually see Ms. Donnelly first."

"You know she's unconscious, right? The doctors don't think she'll ever wake up." But he paused. "Of course... we'll stop at her room." Soft and melodic, his voice was mesmerizing. "You can observe her for as long as you wish."

Poretta nodded to Attison. "I didn't know you had control over Ms. Donnelly's rights over her interaction with law enforcement agents working on this murder investigation, even including observing her unconscious on a hospital bed."

"I didn't mean to suggest you wouldn't be able to question Ms. Donnelly when and if she wakes up. I'm just extremely careful at this juncture to avoid anything to trigger more problems."

"Yeah...okay," Poretta said. They had been walking down the hallway to her room, and when he opened the door of her room, he was startled. Berman had described her organs flawlessly, never mentioning anything else. Her beauty was a double rainbow at the end of a storm. Her physical grace might even be connected to her cryptic survival. Either way, Holly captivated the lawman's curiosity, yet he can't ignore his responsibility. He must solve the murders. His sudden interest in Holly would stay on the back burner for now. Living through two poisons that had killed everyone else had to be dealt with at another time and place as well.

"She's a beautiful woman," Poretta said, "But I don't think giving her a compliment will open her eyes."

Attison looked over at him. "I don't think so. Not right now. She's a sphinx this afternoon. However, I have a good feeling she'll come out of this."

The men left her room and took the elevator to the first floor. During that interlude in the elevator, Attison had read the Inspector's mind, wanting to make sure Poretta would stay within the boundaries of the investigation and not tarnish Holly's reputation. As the sole survivor, she could easily be a scapegoat. After

Attison's fast look-see inside his consciousness, he had no worries. Poretta's intelligence would lead him to the truth. He'd untangle most of the knot, knowing the murders had nothing to do with Holly.

Inspector Poretta also wanted to look inside Attison's head—but he did not have that gift. He'd already looked him up on his computer the day before. The only option he had. It hadn't given him much. After an exemplary education, he'd built a worldwide reputation in commercial law. Then, Poretta found gaps in his profile. He dug through another database, reaching a wider horizon. Still, nothing more to find. Then, he dropped into a government site used by the FBI. Wherever he went, he could not find very much. Facts about Korybante's life and social connections before he went to college were unavailable. Attison had hidden his life away from the technological eye of Mordor, a feat almost as remarkable as Holly's escape from two poisons that had held her tighter than Lucifer's girdle. So what he had found on Attison Korybant was wafer-thin, and even the secretive, on-the-edge illegal locations he'd used hadn't given up a thing. Attison was invisible on the web.

With the small intelligence he did have, Attison was supposed to be fifty years old. Poretta stood next to him in the elevator, and he felt vibrancy radiating out of him. It seemed to undercut one of the few facts he thought he had. The entire case was becoming more confounded by the minute.

Coffee and sandwiches on their trays, they sat in the corner booth.

"How much do you know about the dynamics within the Donnelly family, Mr. Korybante? Are there rivalries or lifelong hatreds?" Poretta bit into his BLT, waiting for his answer.

"I've given them privacy over the years, so I can't help you with their dirty laundry. I can tell you about Latham's business contacts, and you're cordially invited to call me and ask me anything in that regard. Besides that, I can help you in other areas...as a kind of sounding board. I'm staying in Falmouth, and you're invited to stop by anytime."

Inspector Poretta nodded. "Thank you, Mr. Korybante, I may take you up on that. Right now, I'm turning every rock I can find to put the whole thing together. You've been working with Mr. Donnelly for years. You had gotten closer to him and the family. I ask you a second time to reconsider my question. Anything you know about them, even if it seems inconsequential, could be significant in a way you might not realize."

"Alright, Inspector, I'll think over my recollections and let you know if I can come up with anything." A half-smile darted across Attison's face.

"Do you know what the last business meeting Mr. Donnelly attended in Las Vegas was about? Two of the victims hailed from Las Vegas. It's possible the conference is connected to the murders."

"Latham was spearheading a project in Russia for Hienem. Hienem wants to expand into the pharmaceutical market over there, attempting to even get control over it. He was about to start the process. In his last meeting in Las Vegas, he introduced the section chiefs and the rest of management to the man taking his place in America since he's leaving the country."

"Is it possible someone wanted his old job, and they felt overlooked enough for deadly revenge?"

"Unlikely. No one in the company knew about his transfer until a few weeks ago. And no one knew who would replace him besides myself, Jeremy Berlin, and Latham himself. Even if there had been a leak, the deviousness and the planning behind the murders undermine your theory. It couldn't have happened without setting things up."

Attison was right, and Poretta knew it. Pushing his sandwich plate away, he sighed. "I guess it had to have been you behind the whole thing!" Poretta waved at him in an overblown gesture.

Attison grinned to reveal movie-perfect white teeth. They talked for another fifteen minutes. At the end of their meeting, the lawyer repeated his invitation to call him or stop by anytime. Reaching the main entrance, Attison walked back to the elevators, and Ryan Poretta left the hospital.

He called the department a few minutes ago and asked for a deputy to pick him up. Waiting for the expected ride, Attison seemed stuck in his head. He'd never met anyone like him before. The Inspector remained stoic. The touch of cold wind whistling along the streets must have crept under his jacket. That would explain the chill racing down his back.

Boston, Massachusetts
3:14 AM Wednesday, November 30, 2005

Attison sat in Doctor Berman's office on Tuesday afternoon, and Berman explained to him that Donnelly's blood had returned to normal. Yet he was pessimistic about a full recovery for her. He didn't believe she would ever wake up. Attison looked grim over his forecasts, and then he politely thanked him and left the office. Returning to Holly's room, his expression changed, and he started to whistle.

Back in her room, he sat back on the uncomfortable plastic chair to begin to meditate. Attison remained by her side until the afternoon became evening. He only left the room for a sandwich. At 2:15AM on Wednesday morning, Attison arrived at the nurse's station to have a conversation with the young man on duty.

"Good morning, Mark."

"Is there something I can help you with? Is Holly okay?"

Attison eyes were pulsing before changing into a deep blue. Mark's attention fell deep into his fascinating pools: The young nurse would now follow Attison's next orders with diligence and clarity.

"Holly Donnelly needs privacy in her room for one hour beginning at 3:00 AM this morning. Remember. She's in room 29. I need your vigilance to maintain the isolation during that time. No one can enter Donnelly's room—no hospital employees, or doctors or nurses. Not even the janitor. Do you understand?"

Mark beamed at him. "Certainly, Mr. Korybante. I can take care of that!" He was calm and relaxed, but he was talking to thin air. Attison had already turned on his heel and walked away. He had already seared that order into the nurse's mind like a brand. He'd do as he was told with anything he had in hand. The adaptable lawyer had also inserted something more inside the nurse. Mark could now use a certain vibration in his voice to stop possible visitors in their tracks and then turn them away if he had to. After the designated hour was over, the nurse would not remember any of this, and the grafted power would fade away along with the memories.

Back in Holly's room again, Attison pushed her hair away from her forehead. Her pallor had lifted, color blooming in her cheeks. He gently removed the IVs out of her veins and the electrodes from the EEG off her scalp. He then untied her green hospital robe. Holly needed to be naked for the upcoming transition. Arranging her on the blankets, he sat down and joined his own life force to Holly's. Then, he left his material shape in an astral body free from physical restrictions to start his hunt.

Leaving Earth's atmosphere, he navigated through the solar system in half a second. Attison knew about the ancient mysteries surrounding Iapetus, the second moon circling Saturn, and he swept there... looking for something in particular hiding there. He broke the thin crust made up of primarily ice on the outer surface of the moon. In an astral form, he could burrow through eight hundred and ninety-two miles of ice and space rock to reach the core of Iapetus. It was the heart of the moon. Attison stopped. Even in his astral form, he could make solid matter around him vibrate in a certain way to radiate light. He had to see that he was floating in a cave of gold, uneven walls glittering in claustrophobic beauty. A cosmic fire a millennium ago had produced this mineral deposit, but something else had happened as well. Two twisted bands of force, five feet in length, mimicked the human strands of DNA found in human chromosomes. The bands had been dancing together in the center of this golden geode for centuries. Attison tapped into the shimmering power between the strange dancers even as he tightened the hold he had over Holly's spirit. He had opened a gate, inviting her into a level most cannot handle or comprehend.

The ceiling lights in the hospital room started to flicker out has Holly began to glow with cosmic frost on her skin. A blue flame, three inches high, burned just above the frost, and she was enveloped in that freezing fire. She rose above the bed, rising to the ceiling. Holly hung there while glowing spheres materialized around her. These globes swarmed around her like bugs, weaving an iridescent cocoon around her body. Now, Holly was filled with stellar magnetism. Attison had used them to infuse her earthly body with astral force. The entire process took about ten minutes. When it was over, the cocoon surrounding her vanished, and the ceiling lights trembled on. Attison had returned to his material body as Holly lowered back to the bed.

Checking his watch, Attison put the hospital robe back on her body. She was no longer in a coma, sleeping naturally again. He reinserted her IV and replaced the electrodes. His final task was to arrange her blankets.

Attison had orchestrated Holly's re-birth flawlessly, yet he had no vanity on the point. It had been a miracle to him as well, and his love for her was profound.

Mesmerized by the rhythm of the surf breaking on the beach, Holly gazed out at her ocean. She kneeled on the frozen ground, oblivious to the cold. Time did not exist. Thunderheads swelled on the horizon, and cumulous clouds raced above her. Wind ruffled her hair, but Holly's concentration was locked on a spot in the distance, and she was hypnotized. The daylight faded. The entire scene melted to nothing. Holly stared out at nothing.

Then two eyes, big as pie plates, popped into existence, hovering close. She heard female voices blended into one to speak to her.

"Hello, Holly. Can you see? Can you feel? There are more abilities inside you now, and we will guide you home. It's time."

Holly surrendered. The eyes vanished, directions silence. There was nothing but a faint sound of air bubbles inside the Koi Pond in her parent's house. She didn't have to exist in a fish anymore. Holly returned home. She could be comfortable in her own body again.

Opening her eyes, the first thing she saw was an IV bag hanging off a metal pole. And then she saw an onyx stone in a twenty-four-karat gold ring on the finger of a hand holding her own. Her eyes widened. She knew exactly who it was.

"Good morning, Holly."

Bass River, Massachusetts
10:56 AM Friday, December 16, 2005

Attison sat at Latham's desk on the second floor of Holly's palatial home. A passing snowstorm had made the grass white. In his mind, the heiress could transcribe her own legacy across those sparkling acres with aplomb.

A week ago, Inspector Poretta had stopped at Attison's rental property in Yarmouth, updating him about the resolution of the case. Attison was pleased. Poretta had deduced that Samuel and Latham looked identical, a coincidence joining them together forever. Justin or David, or possibly both of them, were responsible for poisoning the holiday meal. David had died from tetrodotoxin, and Justin's sayonara was triggered by *taxane*.

The Inspector was not positive if their avoidance of the other poison was serendipitous or not. That part of the case remains unsolved. Attison kept rooting for

Ryan Poretta, hoping he'd figure the entire thing out. It would not affect Holly's standing.

During the one interview Poretta had with Holly, she'd been gracious, and she gave him no answers. She told him her work schedule at the hospital had left her blind to the pressures in her family. The intrepid officer had not accepted her excuse at first, but Attison explained she'd been blameless throughout, installing a touch in Poretta's head to make sure he'd remain compliant on this simple point. Holly needed solitude to heal from the tragedy, and the family lawyer's legal dominion over her was unbreakable. Poretta could not get close to her again.

During their last meeting in Yarmouth, Poretta asked Attison how Ms. Donnelly was doing since he had not seen her since their interview at the hospital. Still attracted to her survival, the enigma stayed locked in his mind. Attison saw his captivation, but he was not concerned. His interest would soon become secondary after certain events explode planetwide. Soon enough, Poretta will be collaborating with a small team, including Holly and two more members, to stop the end of the world.

Latham's holdings had reverted to Hienem at his death. He had known that Attison owned just over fifty percent of the company, camouflaging that truth in a lineup of bogus corporations that owned percentages of Hienem. Currently, Attison Korybant owned the entire company — but not for long. He had transferred his ownership of Hienem Pharmaceutical Corporation to Holly Donnelly, so ipso facto, the previously unconscious woman on the hospital bed became filthy rich after her father died. Soon enough, Attison stabilized her position in this new heritage, holding a bevy of documents on a small table next to her bed. He asked her to keep on signing until the parade of documents ended. If Mr. Donnelly had known that his last legal act before his death would, circuitously, give the daughter he despised all of his holdings, he would be twirling in his grave like a dervish. In retrospect, his ghost would have been even more upset by being murdered by his own sons.

Attison had been on the phone with the president of Goddard Bank in Toronto that morning to build an economic foundation to allow Holly full control over the company in the next few months. He would only advise her about business opportunities or counsel her on projects.

Holly lived at the estate, but her recovery was taking too long. This upset Attison. He left the office at twelve to find his fledgling. Whether her grief over the loss of her family was responsible or not, he did know she was puzzled over her position between death and rebirth. She had to expand her cerebral muscles like a baby learning to walk. It was time to give her a pep talk and an inspirational display. She needed to see what she could do by displaying some of his own manipulation and skill...and as much as he truly didn't want to do it, he had to tell her what she instinctually knew. Doomsday was coming.

Holly's old house in New Bedford was on the market. The estate at Bass River was now her home.

She didn't stay in either of her parents' suites, instead sleeping in one of the guest quarters. Waking up that morning, she rushed downstairs. Vince would cook eggs benedict for her. The chef had been devastated by the murders, but after a short hiatus, he came back to work for Holly.

Mirabelle stayed in therapy until she found peace. Attison was touched by the housekeeper's wretchedness, and he set up a ten-million-dollar trust fund for her. Twelve thousand dollars would be deposited into her bank account every month, and it would continue for the rest of her life. Her old job was filled by Ms. Cecilia McLain.

Opening the swinging doors with her hip, Cecilia entered the dining room, holding Holly's breakfast.

"Good morning, sweetheart!" She said, green eyes shining with life. With salt n' pepper hair and a muscular body, she appeared to be turning out to be a comfortable replacement.

After breakfast, Holly wandered into the great room, lackadaisical. She curled up on the couch with her PC and began working on one of her projects — but she felt restless. She didn't want to be in one place.

Don Cooper had landscaped for the Donnelly's for years. After the tragedy, Attison's assistant called him to see if he would still continue working on the estate, and he sweetened the deal with a bonus. Cooper stayed on.

Snow had fallen the night before, and Don arrived at the estate before the sun rose. He plowed the driveway, the auto park, and the walking paths around the house, even the garden maze and the sitting area around the central fountain.

Cecilia did not touch Holly's possessions. The mistress had left her winter cloak crumpled on the armchair near the fire. It stayed that way. Holly closed her computer and decided to go outside for a walk. She grabbed her cloak, and the inner lining flashed in a burst of purple while she swirled it around her shoulders. She left through the repaired library door, following the plowed path into the maze. Attison watched her through the office window on the second floor, a figure in black on a field of white as she disappeared in the snow-covered hedges.

Snow crackled under her boots. She heard it precisely. Holly's senses had increased after her death experience—and the rest of her abilities had followed suit. She stopped at the fountain in the middle of the maze, closed her eyes, and centered her thoughts. Inhaling cold air into her lungs, she raised her arms and opened her hands towards the sky in supplication, red fingernails bright against the blue above.

Silently, Attison stopped three feet behind her. Apparently, the snow does not crunch beneath his own boots.

"Hello, Holly."

Surprised, she lowered her arms and turned around. "Hello, Attison."

"I've finalized the last of your holdings this morning. Your empire is solid as a rock."

"Thank you, that's wonderful." After she came out of the coma, the link between them got stronger every day. It was as if they were family.

"The world is at your fingertips," Attison said. He scooped up some snow. "The Western world has lost cohesion, and we can slip through anything. No one will be surprised by what we can do because they won't see it."

Wearing leather gloves, he created a snowball as hard as a rock. He threw it past the fountain and into the trunk of a silver birch one hundred and fifty feet away. The snowball exploded with an audible snap when it hit the trunk. Attison made another one even as he spoke.

"You're not using all of your power. You can sculpt the environment around you if you realize you are free from constraints."

"Of course, you're right. I'll get myself into more training this afternoon."

"I'm very sorry about our next subject, but there's no way out. I know you know what's coming. What is coming is a mystery right now, but we must work together with a psychic and a detective to get control over it."

"I was reading an article about Keith Fischer a few weeks ago, knowing I'll meet him soon."

Holly dropped her head, hoping Attison hadn't seen the tear on her cheek. *Yes, she remembers the chilling predictions in her dreams. She can't avoid them anymore.*

"As much as you don't want to accept this, it is what it is, but I heartily agree with your stance. We shall enjoy what we can when we can."

Attison's eyes suddenly flickered into ultramarine blue as he effortlessly tossed his second snowball straight up. The ball hung motionless in the air, twinkling before transforming into a dove. The bird circled the fountain and landed on the highest tier. Attison's show kept on going. The dove fragmented into mist, drifting to the ground while water burst out of the highest basin of the fountain. Steam roiled off the water, running to the lower basins, an entrancing creation soon fading away. Attison's eyes returned to their deep brown. He put his hand protectively on her shoulder and whispered in her ear,

"Wake up, Holly, wake up and fly!"

Epilogue

Portsmouth, Rhode Island
11:35PM Sunday, November 27, 2005

Mary-Louise, a commercial dragger, docked in Portsmouth. Her radar screen didn't work. The owner had called Keith to get over there and fix it. A gifted repairman, he worked at night if he could — fewer people around. After only three hours, he had gotten the radar functioning perfectly. He left the wheelhouse, toolbox in hand, crossing the foredeck and hopping onto the dock. Getting home by four that morning, he slept like the dead.

Keith woke up at noon. He sat on the edge of his bed, not caring what time it was. He'd go to the local deli to get some fresh coffee and the day's paper. Putting on a winter shirt, leather pants, and boots, he left his bedroom and grabbed his motorcycle jacket and a down vest out of the hall closet. This time of year, he usually took the work van, but the roads were clear, and there was no wind. He'd go for it. Sitting on his 750 Yamaha, he put his helmet on and started the engine, hitting the switch to pull the garage door up. It clattered over his head, and he rode out on Shannon Road. It was an empty stretch of highway, and he twisted the throttle back for a happy jaunt to Exeter.

Parking in front of Owl's Roost, he hung his helmet off a mirror and brushed his fingers through his hair, trying to undo what the helmet had done. Ignoring a feeling that something Godawful was coming, he wanted the sensation to pass away, inhaling crisp air to give him positive energy. The tiny bell attached to the entrance door jingled as Keith stepped briskly into the deli. The smell of freshly baked donuts and brewed coffee made him smile. The newspapers were displayed on a rack across the room.

THANKSGIVING DAY MASSACRE
Nine Bodies Found at Bass River

Those headlines punched into him. Before he even got close enough to read anything, he knew those murders were connected to Holly Donnelly, the woman he'd seen in his dreams, and his premonition over some kind of doomsday grew until a certainty.

Hands trembling, he picked the Morning Bugler up in his hands. Future plans he had in his mind were shattered, and he put the paper under his arm. Keith filled his thermos with coffee, grabbed blueberry muffins out of the wicker basket on the counter, and paid for his items at the register. Riding home, every pebble and groove on the pavement seemed to add more invisible weight to his mind. Entering the kitchen, he tossed his backpack on the table. He looked through the large picture window and up at the blue sky. He shook his head. *A sea change was coming*. Clumsily taking the items out of the bag, he sat at the table like an arthritic old man. He opened the paper to page A32, leaving it flat on the table. It displayed photographs of the Donnelly's estate and portraits of the victims. Keith Fischer stared out the window again. His peaceful career fixing fishing boats was fading like a sunset. He was not happy about a prediction in which he'd be fighting off an adversary with powers that could easily eclipse his own.

But he was born a warrior. Now healed and rested after his injuries, he had thickened his internal armor. But he remained afraid...was there really a way to overwhelm what was coming?

South County Road bordered his land. The Veterans Memorial Cemetery spread out on the other side of the road. Leaning back in his chair, he rested his boots on the table and crossed his arms behind his head. The monuments and gravestones marched away in the distance. It usually helped him find peace. This time, he saw something alien squirming around in front of one of the headstones. He straightened up and grabbed his binoculars. It vanished as quickly as it had appeared...just a trick of the light, raising his hackles for no good reason. He bit into one of the muffins and tried to calm down.

To Be Continued!

Coming Soon: Toxic Tinsel

Thank you for Reading Toxic Turkey
Please post a review on Amazon.com.

About the Author

Gage was born in NYC. A descendant of Martin Beck, a sculptor and painter from Littitz, Pennsylvania, she is also the niece of the late Jane Peterson, a notable impressionist painter. Gage's mother was a descendant of Henry DuPont and a great-niece of Washington Irving. The literary giant had built his home on the banks of the Hudson River, and he named it Sunnyside. Gage's mother spent her childhood there. Years later, New York State purchased the magnificent estate from her grandfather, and now tours are conducted through the historical site. Living in Hastings on the Hudson until '67, the family purchased a house in Southampton on Long Island.

Gage earned her BA from Goddard College in Plainview, Vermont, in 1976, and in the following years, she worked in a variety of different trades. Whether she was working at a ski resort or enjoying her long stint as a commercial clammer on the East End of Long Island, Gage Irving spent as much of her life outside in the natural world as she could. In the mid-80s, she won first prize for two years in a row, garnering second place on the third and final year of her submissions to the Westhampton Poetry Competition. Nevertheless, she couldn't find the ultimate path to 'find herself.'

In 1988, she was badly injured in a car accident. In a coma for over three weeks, the almost fatal brain injury left her epileptic for over two years. A life-changing event, it was a clarion call for the forces inside and out to forcefully pull her out of her shell. She started a rock and roll band. Gage fell head over heels in love with the lead guitar player, marrying him in 2000. With her best friend and life partner at her side, she opened up every level of her creativity. Gage began to paint, and she worked part-time as an art teacher in the nearby town and soon after that, she turned her hand to writing fiction. Previously, she lived with her husband in a log home they had built on the North Fork of Long Island. After he passed away in 2017, she moved to Vero Beach, Florida.